CHF

Salvation of Jack V., won the Commonwealth Book Prize, Africa. He lives in London with his partner and works as a freelance writer.

JACQUES STRAUSS

The Curator

VINTAGE

1 3 5 7 9 10 8 6 4 2

Vintage
20 Vauxhall Bridge Road,
London SW1V 2SA

Vintage is part of the Penguin Random House group of companies
whose addresses can be found at global.penguinrandomhouse.com

First published in Vintage in 2016
First published in hardback by Jonathan Cape in 2015

www.vintage-books.co.uk

A CIP catalogue record for this book is available
from the British Library

ISBN 9780099597728

Typeset in Adobe Caslon Pro by
Palimpsest Book Production Limited, Falkirk, Stirlingshire

Printed and bound by Clays Ltd, St Ives plc

Penguin Random House is committed to a sustainable
future for our business, our readers and our planet.
This book is made from Forest Stewardship
Council® certified paper.

For Ricky

I

Barberton – 1976

When Werner Deyer first saw Salvador Dalí's *Christ of St John of the Cross* he was overcome. He was thirteen years old and had spent his life in the rural town of Barberton. He did not know that the painting he was looking at was only a reproduction. It was good. Miss Hammond, the owner of the store, had developed a talent for copying famous artworks and sold these along with furniture and kitchen utensils. Werner noticed that the woman was watching him.

'Do you like the picture?' she asked.

'Yes, miss,' he said in English.

'It's by a famous artist called Salvador Dalí.' Werner nodded. 'He has a great big moustache.'

'Is he still alive?'

'Oh yes.'

'There are no nails. In his hands or his feet.'

'No.'

'I don't think my Sunday-school teacher would like this painting.'

'I suspect not.'

'Is it for sale?'

'Yes.'

'How much?'

'Thirty rand.'

Werner nodded. It seemed an unthinkable sum, but no painting he encountered since had quite the same effect on him.

When Werner returned home he tore blank pages from his maths exercise book and stuck them to the wall of his bedroom. He called his younger brother.

'Marius!'

'Yes, Werner?' his brother said as he walked into the room.

'Take off all your clothes – except your underpants.'

Marius did as he was told because his brother could be cruel. When Werner was eight and Marius six, Werner pushed him off a fence. Their mother watched from afar, helpless to intervene. Marius only had time to put out an arm to break his fall on the sun-hardened earth. Although Werner did not feel guilty, the crack of bone did make him feel something; when his brother's arm snapped, it sent a shiver up his spine and his breathing quickened.

'What are you doing, Werner?' Marius asked.

'We are going to make a work of art.'

'Like a picture?'

'Yes.'

'Why do I have to be in my underpants?'

'Because,' said Werner, 'you're going to be Jesus.'

'Don't say that!'

'Why?'

'Because it's blasphemous.'

'Don't be ridiculous.'

'It is, Werner. We'll go to hell if you say things like that.'

'Stand against the paper and hold your arms out, like this.' Marius submitted as Werner manipulated his arms and legs into an approximation of a crucifixion.

'Don't move,' Werner said, and with a pencil he traced his brother's outline.

Werner and Marius were afforded an unusual degree of privacy because of a family massacre that had taken place the previous week and mesmerised the residents of Barberton, including the boys' parents, who were distantly acquainted with the people at the centre of it all. Petronella sat at the kitchen table, reading.

'Have you seen the newspaper today, Hendrik?'

'What?' he asked. He was busy with an inventory form.

'They say in the paper that the doctors are pessimistic about the Labuschagne boy. He's so unstable they don't even want to take him to Pretoria.'

'I heard.'

'Maybe it's best if he dies. '

'I don't know, Nellie. Life is life.'

'Some lives are not worth it. Sometimes it's better that the Lord says, "*Ag*, shame, he has suffered enough. I will take him." Sometimes it's a mercy to die.' She sipped her tea and skimmed the article again. 'They need to get to the bottom of this.'

'What do you mean?'

'They must do an autopsy on the man. They must check his brain.'

'For what? Rabies?'

'Don't be daft. Tumours. Brain cancer.'

'I don't know about these things. You're the nurse.'

'Why do you have to be like that?'

'Like what, pet?'

'You know what.'

Hendrik put down his pen and removed his glasses. 'Sorry.'

'Maybe all I do now is scrapes and bruises, but I have seen things. A man doesn't take a shotgun to his family unless there is a reason. Maybe he was a schizophrenic.'

Hendrik knew better than to suggest what everyone in town said. If you were looking for an explanation of a family murder, the first place to start was the bank. And if the bank didn't offer any clues, the next place to go looking was his bedroom. The very last place you needed to go digging was inside the man's brain. But Petronella could not abide the fact that within a sane man there was the potential for such violence.

'You know,' she said, 'they're still talking to the maid. She came into the house in the middle of it all.'

'While he was shooting them?'

'That boy at the chemist's told Maria that the maid tried to stop him. I don't believe that.'

'How do we know?'

'If you see a man shooting people, you run away. You don't try and stop him.'

'Maybe.'

'Maria is obsessed with the thing. Every day she says to me, "*Missies*, I can't believe." It's like she thinks I can explain it to her because I'm white. And now she's got this story in her head about the maid. If this boy dies, who can say the maid is lying?'

'Why does it matter?'

'Because it does matter. If someone wants to be a hero, fine – let them be a hero. But let's get the facts first. Otherwise, what's the point?'

5

2

Werner returns from work just after five. He opens the
door to his father's bedroom to see if he is still alive. It is
often difficult to make out the rise and fall of his chest.
On more than one occasion he had been convinced that
his father had finally died, but when he rushed towards
the bed to check, the man opened his two yellow-green
slits a crack and stared at his son with undisguised loathing.
This afternoon Hendrik is definitely sleeping. He has a
chest infection that makes his breath raspy and loud.
Werner considers opening the windows in the hope that
a cold breeze might hasten things, but Pretoria is warm
and the fresh air will only do his father good. He puts
down his briefcase in his bedroom and fetches a glass from
the kitchen. Just outside his father's room he urinates into
the glass. As quietly as he can manage he creeps into the
room, keeping the glass behind his back. Hendrik turns
and makes a noise. Werner stands still and waits. When
the man settles down, he walks to the bed and gently pours

the warm urine over his father's crotch. The smell is sharp. Seeing the yellow stain makes him want to laugh. He hurries out so as not to wake his father.

In the kitchen he pours himself a glass of wine. His mother will be home around six. He wonders who it will be that discovers that his father is dead. If his father dies in the night, it will probably be his mother. She usually checks on him around five-thirty in the morning. If he dies during the day, his mother will get a call from the nurse who leaves at four. For financial reasons Petronella has accepted that there is one hour, between four and five in the afternoon, when Hendrik is without care. So this is the time that Werner hopes his father will die. When he comes home from work, just before his mother's shift ends at the hospital, he will walk into the room and find him dead. Then he will pour himself a glass of wine, ease his bulk into the wicker chair by his father's bed and think about how his life, at the age of thirty-three, can finally begin.

When his mother comes home she asks whether he's checked on his father.

'I popped my head in,' he says.

'You could talk to him, you know. He's lonely.'

'He was sleeping.'

Petronella goes to her room and gets changed. He can hear that his father has woken up. He moans. Werner walks down the passage and peers into his father's room. Hendrik has noticed the wet sheets and, with the half of his body that is still functional, is trying to pull them off. He wants to hide them before Petronella sees. It's funny watching the man struggle like this. He's trying to be quiet, but the frustration is getting the better of him. He moans again.

'Werner,' Petronella calls. 'Please check on your father. Something is not right.'

He walks into his father's room.

'Pa? What's going on? Are you all right?' He looks at the wet sheet in surprise. 'Oh, bugger. Ma!' he calls.

The old man moans and then with his lame mouth says, 'No! Don dell.'

'Don't be silly, Pa. Ma has to know about this stuff. For your own good.'

'No!'

'Ma – you'd better get in here.'

'What is it?' she shouts from the bedroom.

Hendrik looks beseechingly at Werner. 'Lease,' he says.

'Sorry, Pa – I can't understand you.'

'Cun. Fukin. cun!'

He bends down towards his father and says quietly, 'You miserable old fucker. Did you call me a cunt?'

Petronella walks into the room. 'What's going on here?'

Werner points to the wet, twisted sheet.

'*Ag* no,' she says. 'Hendrik? Did the nurse not take you to the toilet today?' He looks out of the window and ignores his wife. 'Hendrik – it's nothing to be ashamed about. I just need to know if I should get a new nurse. These girls are very lazy sometimes.'

'I don't think it's the nurse's fault, Ma,' Werner says. 'She took you, didn't she, Pa?' he asks.

'Cun,' Hendrik says.

'What did he say?' Petronella asks.

'I think he called me a cunt.'

'You watch your mouth.'

'It's what he said.'

'He didn't. And I won't tolerate language like that in my house.'

'I pay half the bills around here.'

'My roof.'

'Jesus!'

'Don't take the Lord's name in vain. Now help me with your father. We need to get this cleaned up.'

Together they lift Hendrik, ease him out of his sodden pyjamas and put him naked in the wheelchair.

'Strip the bed,' Petronella says. 'I'll clean up your father.'

She grabs a handful of moist wipes and starts rubbing him down. She flips his dick from side to side and rubs under his ball-sack. Werner looks at his father's limp cock. Previously his mother would have asked him to leave the room while performing an intimate task, but now they are both so exhausted by it all that neither of them much cares for Hendrik's dignity. Werner remakes the bed. Even though it's his own urine, the soiled sheets disgust him. He's a consummate performer because he believes his own lies.

Werner and his mother stand in the kitchen making macaroni and cheese.

'I think we should put him in nappies,' he says.

'Are you mad? There is no reason to put him in nappies. The nurse must have forgotten to take him to the toilet.'

'I don't want to come home from work every day to change piss-sheets.'

'You won't have to.'

'Let's put him in nappies.'

'No – I'll talk to the doctor.'

Petronella and Werner have an agreement. If he helps care for his father, then Petronella will relinquish all claim to Hendrik's two hundred and fifty thousand rand, to be paid out upon his death. When they came to the agreement it seemed fair. Now Werner regrets ever having contemplated it. At the time he did not think his father would live to see another year. Every month the money is worth less. He has thought about cutting his losses. He could split the money with his mother. If the state medical aid agrees to provide a night-nurse, she might even be persuaded to give him a hundred and fifty thousand rand. It will not be enough, but he cannot wait any longer.

'I'm tired,' he says.

'Go to bed,' she says.

'I'm tired of this.'

'No one is forcing you to stay.'

'I don't have friends any more.'

'I don't understand why you don't go out and meet someone.'

'I'm too old. I'm too fat.'

Petronella says nothing, and by her silence Werner understands that she agrees. She scoops some of the macaroni and cheese into a Tupperware container and walks to Hendrik's room. Werner is left alone in the kitchen. He eats quickly and goes to his bedroom. On the small desk, beside his computer, is a box labelled *Arcadia 235*. He does not wish to be taunted tonight, so he puts the box under his bed. Maybe tonight Hendrik will choke to death on the mac and cheese. It would be better if his mother were not a nurse. His mother is always doing things to keep his father going a little longer. There was a graph he'd learnt about in high-school maths. He couldn't remember its name. The line of the graph approaches the axis; it gets closer and closer and closer, but never touches, until infinity. This is his father's life. He is getting closer and closer to death, but will never die. Werner has given up so much time waiting. Perhaps the old man knows. Perhaps he draws strength in denying him. That would be like him. Werner relents, gets the box from under the bed and starts paging through the notes he's been making all these years. On a loose sheet of paper is a list of artists – recent graduates at the time – that he'd hoped to exhibit at his gallery. Most of them have long since given up on art but, against the odds, two of them are successful, have exhibited overseas, sold paintings, become rich, celebrated, lauded, loved. This is what he wants. It can still happen, but there is so little time. His frustration is eating him up from the inside. He clenches his fists and shakes with rage. 'Die!' he hisses. 'Die. Die. Die.'

3

Hendrik stood in the kitchen with Maria, their maid, sipping coffee while Maria made porridge. With the Labuschagne business, he was having difficulty invoking the persona that would be required for the next ten days: a stern *veld*-school principal. The twelve-year-olds were easy to deal with. To exercise control over sixteen-year-olds coming together from different schools required a level of sustained vigilance that left him drained by the time the last child left. These ten-day camps had become a right of passage for white schoolchildren across the country. The curriculum included a curious blend of survival skills, patriotic lectures, religious sermons and outdoor activities. He had lost any sense of the greater purpose that *veld*-school was supposedly in service of, but believed that ten days in the bushveld was good for anyone.

'Maria, is there any beer left?'

'I think, *baas*, maybe five bottles.'

'Okay, can you ask Petrus to get another two cases?'

'*Ja, baas.*'

'And can I ask you to make me some *vetkoek*?'

'*Ja, baas*, with the jam?'

'Some with jam and some with mince. Is there any mince left?'

'*Ja, baas.*'

'There will be eight teachers tonight.'

'*Yo* – it's too many.'

'*Ja* – I know.'

He looked at the itinerary for the next three days. They were due to go abseiling, but there had been a small mudslide at the site they normally used. He would need to see if it was still safe. He lit a cigarette as he made notes.

'And cigarettes, Maria?'

'Maybe one carton. Must I ask Petrus that he buys some more?'

'No – leave it for now.'

Outside, dogs were playing with a torn rugby ball. He wondered how it was that the family had again adopted a pack. They looked friendly enough. When was it that that *ousie* came to the house selling grass brooms? There was a moment before it happened when everyone knew – even the *ousie* – what was coming. Something about the stance of the staffies; the way they all lifted their heads. He tore the dogs off the woman before she was seriously hurt. Petronella gave her some stitches, bandaged her legs and handed her a bottle of disinfectant to apply twice a day. Each dog yelped when Hendrik shot it. After the first one, the other dogs tucked their tails between their legs and started shaking. By the time he'd killed the third, he'd broken into a sweat. The last dog sat in the corner, whimpering. He raised his gun, took aim and then lowered it again because he couldn't keep his hand steady. He grabbed the dog by the scruff of its neck, pressed the barrel against its head and pulled the trigger. He made a point of remembering the difficulty he had in shooting the last dog. Years before he'd walked into his bedroom with a gun behind his back. He had sufficient rage and despair to shoot his wife, but perhaps not enough to carry on and kill the rest. Maybe only farmers had what it took. Nellie could wring the necks of chickens and slice the throats of lambs. The ease with which she performed these tasks unnerved him, but he admired her brisk efficiency. His ample black maid killed things all the time too – chickens, goats, sheep – with even less sentiment.

He glanced at the newspaper lying on the table. Perhaps the Labuschagne woman had had an affair, which sent the husband into a rage. He could not imagine Petronella having an affair. Moedswill; a strange name for a farm – purposefulness or wilfulness or wantonness? Or was it *moedswillig*? Spiteful? That time in the bedroom, he stood there while his wife was sleeping and considered what he would have to do next. He would shoot Werner. Then Marius. And then he would shoot himself. That was the only thing one could do. But at what point was one's courage likely to fail? After the first child, or the second? When the house was littered with bodies and you had to put the barrel in your own mouth? He was young and drunk. Was the gun even loaded? Labuschagne slaughtered his children as an act of mercy, an act of love. But from where did he get the will? Did the first murder not drain him of his anger and his madness? Did the first murder not make him keel over with shock and grief and horror? Did he not sweat and puke, as Hendrik did after shooting a dog? A dog. Where did this man find the strength, the resolve, to walk through the house executing his children?

Werner and Marius came into the kitchen and joined their mother at the table. She ruffled the boys' hair, but Werner shrugged her off.

'*Ag*, child,' she said, 'is it too much for a mother to touch her son?'

She poured herself a cup of coffee and took a cigarette out of Hendrik's packet. She stood by the kitchen door and smoked. Petronella allowed herself only one cigarette a day, since she read that smoking caused crow's feet. Early in the morning, with her family around her like this, she felt a sense of ease. Petrus was tending to the garden. He had worked for Hendrik since they'd moved here. She was not sure how old he was. Looking at him, you would guess at least sixty. But life out here was hard. She would not be surprised if he was younger. Petrus was the most senior of their servants and, as such, entrusted with ferrying the boys to and from school. The workers' village where the blacks lived was about a hundred metres from the house, tucked away behind a thick clump of wattle trees and bush. She could smell the cooking fires in the village and saw thick plumes of white smoke. Someone had probably thrown a wet branch on the fire. Beyond the thatched huts was a gorge with a small river, which ran into a dam that was used for the *veld*-school activities. Before they moved here, she and Hendrik lived in Pretoria. He taught geography at a local high school and she was a nurse in a state hospital. When the position at the camp was advertised she was not enthusiastic. Petronella believed her husband should have concentrated his efforts on becoming a principal of a *real* school. But over the years she first grew accustomed to, and then fond of, the rhythms of the place.

Steyn, the assistant principal, stepped out of his thatched rondavel and waved to her. Twenty-eight and separated from his wife, he knew the bushveld better than any of them. He was an imposing man and gave the impression of being ill-tempered, which made him a good disciplinarian. There was no child that Steyn could not break. If boys were caught smoking or drinking, Steyn would chase them up the *koppie*, cane in hand, beating their legs, until at least one of them vomited or fainted. But for all his good points, there was no doubt that the man retired to his rondavel and drank. Hendrik said it was none of their business. Petronella worried sometimes that Steyn posed a threat to the girls. In spite of their explicit instructions to all visiting schools that girls NOT WEAR BIKINIS OR OTHER INAPPROPRIATE ITEMS OF CLOTHING, they did so anyway. It was not as if Steyn had done anything, but who knew if he had the wherewithal to suppress his impulses? And one had to wonder, especially with the English girls, if they had the wherewithal to suppress theirs. Petronella stubbed out her cigarette in the empty flowerpot beside the door.

'Boys, finish up and get changed. Petrus is ready to take you to school.'

Werner and Marius sat in the back of the pickup truck, a Datsun *bakkie*, holding their school and tog bags. They pressed against the back of the cab. It was nicer to travel the thirty or so kilometres like this, unless Petrus hit a pothole or a bump in the road. The two steel seats on the side were the most uncomfortable. The morning had turned cool and the boys were wondering whether they shouldn't have got into the cab instead. Marius pulled his jersey over his knees. Werner clipped the side of his head.

'You'll stretch it. Ma will be *bevoetered*.'

'I'm cold.'

'Don't be a baby.'

'Tell Petrus to pull over. I want to get in front.'

'We're nearly there.'

Marius started banging the back of the cab window, but Werner punched him in the arm.

'I'm cold! I'm going to tell Ma!'

Werner kept on punching him. 'You're a big poof. A real *moffie*.'

'I'm not a *moffie*.'

'You're the biggest *moffie* in school – everyone says so.'

'I'll tell Ma you're drawing a picture of Jesus.'

'So?'

'You're not allowed. It's wrong.'

'It's not wrong. You're just a baby.'

'Fine – then I'll tell her and we'll see what she says. We'll see if she says it's wrong.'

'If you tell her, I'll fuck you up. I'll *moer* you.'

'You see! You know Ma will be mad. You know it. That's why you don't want me to say.' Marius turned around and started banging on the back of the cab again. 'Petrus! Stop the *bakkie*!'

Werner lost his temper and grabbed Marius's wrist. He twisted it behind his back and Marius fell on the floor.

'What did I say? Huh? What did I say?'

'Please, Werner! You're hurting me! Please!'

'Are you going to ask Petrus to stop?'

'I won't. Let me go!'

'Swear?'

'I swear! Let me go!'

'Are you going to tell Ma about the picture?' Marius said nothing, so Werner twisted his arm a little more and forced it higher so that the tips of his fingers reached just above his shoulder blade. Marius screamed. 'Are you?'

'No! You're going to break my arm!' He started crying and Werner let him go. Marius, whimpering, squeezed himself into the corner between the cab and the side of the *bakkie*. He pulled his jersey over his knees and wiped his nose on the sleeve. 'I hate you.'

'You don't have to tell Ma everything. There are some things Ma doesn't have to know about.'

'Like what?'

'Like when you go and look at the girls when they're changing in the camp.'

'You showed me that! You showed me where to go.'

'You want me to tell Ma?'

'No.'

'You want me to tell Ma you play with yourself while you watch them?'

'I don't play with myself. My *tottie* was itchy because Maria was using that bantu washing powder.

They travelled in silence for a while.

'Why do you want the picture?' Marius asked.

'Because . . . just because,' Werner said.

Nobody loved Jesus Christ as devoutly as Werner Deyer: Jesus Christ the boy, Jesus Christ the precocious *wunderkind*. 'I was in my father's house,' Jesus said to his parents. *In his father's house*. A boy – no older than Werner – declaring himself the Son of God. All those people fawning. The disciples and Pontius Pilate and King Herod and the crowds of cripples and beggars who reached out just to *touch* him. All that love; all that adoration! Jesus was magnificent. When people exhorted Werner to love Jesus, it was the easiest thing in the world. Jesus is your best friend, they said. You must love Jesus with all your heart. And Werner did. He worshipped Jesus. Jesus was everything he wanted to be. Beautiful. Powerful. Adored. It was hard to love God. What was God? But it didn't matter that he had no affection for God. His love of God was manifest through his intense and passionate devotion to Jesus. But when Marius asked, 'Why do you want that picture?', a thirteen-year-old could not possibly hope to untangle the myriad desires and beliefs that found full expression in *Christ of St John of the Cross*.

In the early evening, before Hendrik came home, the phone rang and Petronella answered. It was Anja.

'Is Steyn there?' she asked.

'No, Anja, he's still working.'

'Oh. Did you give him my message?'

Petronella was annoyed.

'Yes, I did, Anja. But things have been very busy here. I'm sure that he wants to call you. He's just needs to find the right time.'

'I don't understand. We were so happy.'

'You know how it is with young men sometimes. They're very confused. It will work itself out.'

'Every day the boys want to know where their father is. What am I supposed to say to them? What can I tell my sons about their father? Why can't he just talk to me? I need to understand why. Do you think he doesn't love me any more?'

'I'm sure that's not it. Anja, I have to go now. But I will talk to Steyn when he gets in. Tonight, I promise.'

As she put down the phone she heard Hendrik come in.

'That was Anja again,' she said. He shrugged. 'Don't shrug at me. You don't have to put up with the phone calls.'

'What can I do, Nellie? Just tell her to stop calling.'

'Who am I to tell her to stop calling? She wants to talk to her husband. What sort of man is Steyn that he won't even talk to his wife?'

'Why do you think a man would refuse to speak to his wife?'

'I don't know.'

'Think, woman.'

'*Ag* no – that's a terrible thing to say.'

'Well?'

'I'm going to go and talk to Steyn.'

'I'm warning you to stay out of it.'

'I have to give him the message, don't I? I have to tell him his wife phoned.' She walked out of the kitchen door.

'Just give him the message – that's all.' She marched towards Steyn's rondavel and knocked.

'Steyn, can I have a word?'

'Come in,' he said.

'*Ag*, man – no – it's too hot. Come outside and have a cigarette.' He smoked in silence while Petronella thought about what to say. 'Your wife has been on the phone.'

'I'm sorry,' he said.

'Don't say sorry to me.'

'Okay.'

'But it can't carry on like this.'

Steyn blew the smoke out of his nose. He flicked a cigarette butt onto the ground and extinguished it with the toe of his shoe, then kicked it into the grass that was growing underneath the tap.

'What do you want me to do, Nellie?'

'I want you to talk to your wife. I want you to talk to your boys. God knows we've all made mistakes. Even me – I've done some things in my time. Phone your wife and tell her to pack her things and bring the boys. ' He said nothing. 'At least talk to her.'

'It's hot,' Steyn said.

'Are you not listening? Did you not hear what I said?'

'I heard you, Nellie.'

'Well?'

'I wish things were so easy.'

'Do you love your wife?'

'Yes, I love my wife.'

'And your boys?'

'I love them too.'

'Well then – it's easy.'

'Nellie, I will talk to her.'

'When?'

'This week.'

'That's good,' Petronella said. 'Come by the house. Any time. I'll get out of the way.'

Neither Petronella nor Steyn spoke and the silence was filled by the high-pitched hum of the teeming, fecund bushveld.

'Nellie, I will call my wife, but then I don't ever want to talk about this again.'

'Of course,' she said and turned to walk back to the house.

4

Werner has his own office in a building affectionately known as The Ship. It is the administrative building of the University of the Transvaal. He arrives at his office at seven-thirty to review the files. His first appointment is at eight-thirty. His final appointment is at three-thirty. His job is to decide whether applicants are eligible for hardship bursaries. Although he now has some seniority in the department – he is often called upon to review the decisions of his more junior colleagues – he has been doing the same job, more or less, since 1985, the year following his graduation from the same institution that now employs him. With his degree in art history he'd hoped to get a job as an assistant curator at the university's Cultural Bureau. Its then-director, Dr Breedt, said Werner was a man of 'uncommon talent' and that as soon as a suitable position became available he'd be the first to know about it. Werner took a job in administration and waited. The first interview he ever conducted was with the son of a bankrupt farmer. The boy, embarrassed, recounted his family's woes at length; the death of his mother; the failure of his father's crops. Werner nodded and made notes. The boy called Werner *meneer* – sir.

He made sure to walk by the Cultural Bureau regularly so that if Dr Breedt happened to be passing, he could say, 'Morning, Doctor.' In 1988 the doctor resigned, not having made good on his word.

The phone rings.

'Deyer,' he says.

'Werner, I've decided to take your father in for a check-up this afternoon.'

'Why, Ma?'

'His bed-wetting. It's got me worried. I spoke to the day-nurse. She said she took him to the toilet twice. And there's that cough as well.'

'Well, if you think it's necessary.'

'Can you leave work early?'

'Ma – it's not so easy, I have appointments.'

'The medical aid doesn't want to pay for an ambulance to take him for a check-up.'

'Why don't you just get a doctor to come round?'

'Maybe they need to do X-rays.'

'Well can't you ask the doctor to phone the medical aid?'

'That's not his job. Werner, it's a small thing. For once can't you just help me do this?'

'Fine. What time?'

'Three. I've taken the afternoon off.'

He lights a cigarette and looks at his schedule. He will need to cancel two appointments or ask a colleague to cover for him. It's difficult with the blacks. They never have the paperwork needed. 'Where is your birth certificate? Where is your father's death certificate? I know your mother is a maid, but I need proof of her wages. Who is her employer?' When he calls the employers, they are unhelpful. He doesn't care, he explains, if they pay below the minimum wage. 'You don't understand,' they say. 'I do lots of other things for her. I give her food and a place to live. I give her children clothes. I take her to the doctor. I buy her medicine. I'm the one who said the child should go to university.' Werner's facility for sorting out difficult cases is one reason he is valued in the department. He hardly ever deals with white students any more. His life and his mother's life have symmetry. She hardly ever has white patients. Two old-time Boers, accustomed to dealing with blacks in their brusque and paternal manner. 'Listen to me. You have the HIV, *neh*? Do you understand about the HIV? Where is your husband? You must tell him to come into the clinic. We must test him for the HIV.'

Werner and his mother arrive at the flat at the same time. They dress the old man and put him in a wheelchair. Petronella asks the day-nurse to wash more sheets in case there are future accidents.

'That is not my job,' she says and leaves.

'Bitch.' Petronella mutters.

Werner pushes his father's wheelchair into the lift. In the car park he lifts him out of the wheelchair and loads him onto the back seat of his mother's Toyota Corolla.

Hendrik is passive today. He leans his head against the window and stares out.

'Are you okay, Hendrik?' Petronella asks. He ignores her.

'He's bad-tempered, Ma. Leave him.'

Werner folds up the wheelchair and puts it in the boot. His mother drives. It's a government hospital and one wing is reserved for state medical-aid patients. In the waiting room Petronella helps Hendrik drink a Coke.

'You're in a better mood now, huh?' she asks. Hendrik continues to ignore her. 'Fine, be like that.' Werner is reading a copy of *You* magazine. There is an article about a man whose child was eaten by a crocodile. It includes a picture of a poor and forlorn-looking Boer pointing towards some muddy brown water; in the corner is an inset of a blonde twelve-year-old girl with pigtails. The headline reads: *My child was eaten by a crocodile*. It makes Werner giggle.

'What's so funny?' his mother asks.

'This man's child was eaten by a crocodile,' he says.

'*Sies*, man,' Petronella says. 'That's nothing to laugh about.'

He turns to the article about the vet who castrated himself after cheating on his wife. The vet displays the instruments from his surgery that he used. The man's wife is proud of him. It goes to show, she explains, how committed he is to their marriage.

The doctor says the check-up may take a few hours, so Werner tells his mother to phone when he's needed again and leaves. It's been a long time since he's had an afternoon

27

off, but he's not sure what to do. In the car park a group of black teenagers approach him.

'*Baas!*' they say, 'Please, *baas*, we watch the car for *baas*, nice.'

'You weren't here when I arrived,' he says.

'No, *baas* – we see *baas*. We watch the car nice. Please – give us two rand. We are so hungry. We eat nothing.'

'Leave me alone. My father has just died. I don't have the energy for this.'

They slink away. It is wonderful how one can wield death, like an axe, to drive people away, even a pack of street children. He drives back to the flat. Sunnyside used to be a nice suburb, and although there are still many students who live here, there are more and more blacks moving in. On the top floor of their building are two Nigerian men. Petronella is convinced they are drug-dealers. Werner thinks she is probably right. If they do not move soon, they will be trapped in Sunnyside, like the pensioners who are trapped in Hillbrow. This is another reason his father must die soon. His mother has suggested they sell the flat and use the additional money to buy a smaller place somewhere safe, preferably in Pretoria East, which she believes will remain white for the rest of her lifetime. Werner resists this idea. The money is his. He has no desire to buy a flat in which he and his mother will spend the rest of their days. His gallery, he tells her, is a better solution. Once his gallery is up and running, he will be able to buy her a flat wherever she chooses. He may even be able to buy her a house and then she can give up her job in the hospital. She will no longer have to supervise a ward filled with blacks in their death-throes.

At home he watches the news and a soap opera. The characters live in a nice multicultural building. There's a coloured woman who is continually bickering with a racist Afrikaans *tannie* from the *platteland*. Actually they are best friends and would do anything for each other. They are the lovable comic duo. It is anesthetising and he rarely misses an episode. The phone rings. He ignores it. His mother can wait. But two minutes later the phone rings again. Maybe his father is dead. He jumps up and answers.

'Why didn't you answer the first time?'

'I was in the toilet. Do you want me to pick you up?'

'Your father is sick,' she says.

'What's wrong?' he says breathlessly. It's lucky that excitement and concern can sound so much the same. His mother starts crying. 'I'm supposed to be a nurse. The doctor says he has a severe infection.'

'Oh no,' Werner says.

'How could I not know? Why didn't he say something?'

'He's losing his mind, Ma. It's not your fault.'

'He must be in so much pain.'

'I don't think so, Ma.'

She sniffs and stops crying. 'I thought his colour was a bit off.'

'Do you want me to come by?'

'Do you know,' she says, not answering him, 'it's very

29

lucky we took him in when we did. At least we caught things pretty early. Another day or two and he could have been terribly ill.'

'*Ja* – it's lucky,' he says flatly.

'Can you come and pick me up in an hour?'

'Sure, Ma. Wait for me outside. We'll pick up some takeaways on the way home.'

He puts down the phone. 'Fuck!' How much further servitude has his childish impulse bought him? He goes to the kitchen and pours himself a glass of wine. What can he do, short of smothering his father with a pillow, short of outright murder? He lights a cigarette. His mother goes to bed at ten and gets up between five and six. An overdose of morphine? Do they have any morphine? If not, could he buy some? Perhaps the Nigerians upstairs could provide him with heroin? Would the hospital perform an autopsy? Werner shakes his head. Is he really thinking about murdering his father? It's not murder. Euthanasia. It's unlikely that anyone would perform an autopsy. He is a bedridden man with a brain injury, who has suffered multiple strokes. There would be nothing suspicious about his death. It is difficult to imagine injecting a dose of badness. His hand would shake uncontrollably. His father would wake up. He would know what Werner was doing. He would call out. His mother would wake up. She would catch him murdering. It would be worse than the time she caught him masturbating. But a lethal dose of heroin would be a good way to go. What would be a lethal dose anyway? Would the Nigerians upstairs know? How much does heroin cost? He could tell the Nigerians his father is in terrible pain. They can no longer afford the painkillers required. He looks at his watch. He's running late. He hurries downstairs and drives to the hospital.

'Have you been drinking?' Petronella asks as she gets into the car.

'Just a glass of wine,' he says.

'You smell like a brewery. Why do you drink so much?'

'I was worried about Pa.'

'You mustn't drink so much. Do you want to get diabetes?'

'Let it go.'

'Maybe I should drive.'

'Don't be ridiculous. How's Pa?'

'Not good,' she says. 'I'm worried.'

Werner puts his thoughts of murder on hold. Please, God, he thinks, don't force my hand. I'll be really pissed off.

The next day at work a colleague knocks on his door.

'Morning,' she says brightly.

'Morning,' he says.

'Have you heard the news?'

'What?'

'The Bureau has appointed a new assistant curator.'

'Oh.'

'I thought you wanted the job?'

'Not really,' he says. 'It was something I thought about a while ago.'

'Everyone says you wanted to work for the Cultural Bureau.'

'Well – everyone is wrong.'

The woman is disappointed. 'Well, you would never have got the job anyway.'

'Why not?' he says sharply.

The woman narrows her eyes. 'You did want the job.'

'I said not really – but why do you think I couldn't have got it?'

'Affirmative action. They employed some black. A fine-arts graduate. Anyway, you're too old now. Best you stick with this. Some people say if you stick around you'll be head of the department in ten years.'

In the evening they visit his father in hospital. Werner takes some consolation from the fact that the man looks unwell.

'The infection must be getting worse,' his mother says.

'How do you know?'

'The antibiotics,' she says, looking at the drip.

'Have you spoken to the doctor?' he asks.

'Briefly.'

'What did he say?'

'There is nothing to worry about.'

'Then why are you worried?'

'For a doctor there is never anything to worry about when a person is old.'

He hopes this is true.

5

Hendrik walked around the back garden picking up the empty beer bottles, while Maria cleared away the plates.

'Maria, you can have the rest of the *vetkoek*. It's in the kitchen.'

'Thank you, *baas*.'

'There's some foil in the drawer. Take the plate – but bring it back tomorrow morning before the *missies* sees.'

'Yes, *baas*.'

Petronella had gone to bed earlier in the evening and Hendrik had been left to entertain the teachers.

'Maria?'

'Yes, *baas*?'

'Tell me – do you know the maid who used to work for Mrs Labuschagne?'

'Which one?'

'I mean the one who worked in the house.'

Maria turned on the hot-water tap and squeezed some washing-up liquid into the sink.

'Maria?'

'Yes, *baas*?'

'I said do you know her?'

'I think so.'

'What do you mean: you think so?'

'I don't know if you mean this one or that one or that one. There are many, many people on that farm.'

'No, Maria, I mean do you know the lady who worked in the house?'

Maria put the dishes in the soapy water. She was not a talkative woman but was rarely evasive. It was irritating, but he understood it was not insolence, rather the discomfort she felt about discussing the Labuschagnes.

'It's just the *missies* said to me that the maid saw what happened.'

'*Baas*, I don't want to make trouble. This girl – she is a very stupid girl.'

'Do you know her?'

'Her father is my mother's cousin. It's a very bad thing, *baas*.'

'But she's spoken to the police?'

'Yes, *baas*. She tell them everything.'

'Is it true that she tried to stop him? You know, the *baas*.'

'Some people say.'

'Have you not spoken to her?'

'No, *baas*.'

'Have you spoken to her father?'

'Yes.'

'What does he say?'

'He say she is doing nothing. She just sit. She doesn't eat. She doesn't sleep. She sit. He say she doesn't talk.'

'What's her name?'

'Lerato. But the *missies* there, she call her Lettie.'

'I don't know what's going to happen to the farm.'

'No.'

'If his brother takes it, they might not want her to work in the house.'

'Yes.'

'Do you think maybe she should come and work here?'

'I don't know, *baas*.'

Hendrik put the empty beer bottles into a sack, twisted it and tied a knot in the top. He opened the kitchen door and took the bag of beer bottles outside. When he came back into the kitchen he leant against the kitchen counter, crossed his arms and watched Maria wash the dishes.

'Maria?'

'Yes, *baas*?'

'You don't think it will be a nice thing to give this woman a job?'

'I don't know, *baas*.'

'Stop washing the dishes.'

'But the *missies*, she will—'

'Maria, I said stop washing the dishes.'

She dropped the dish in the sink, but remained where she was, with her back to Hendrik.

'Turn around.' She did so. 'Is it not rude in your culture? Huh? To stand with your back to someone when they're talking to you?'

'Sorry, *baas*.'

'I was just thinking. The *missies* told me about the

maid – and I thought: *ag*, shame, this woman is going to lose her job. So I was thinking maybe she wanted to come and work here.'

'In the house, *baas?*'

'No – not in the house. I thought maybe she could work in the kitchens or she could do some cleaning. There is a lot of work to do here.'

'Yes.'

'So you think it's a good idea.'

'If *baas* say so.'

'*Jissus!* Sometimes it's hard to talk to you people.' He poured himself a whisky and lit a cigarette. Maria stood by the sink, staring at the floor. 'You can carry on washing the dishes, Maria.' He laughed. 'You know – you people are so . . . suspicious. I don't know. Here I was thinking you'd be happy. And all you can say is, "I don't know, *baas.*" Not everyone is out to get you. Don't you think I am a good *baas?* If you go down to the farm where we grew up, you'd see the happiest blacks in the world. When I was a *lightie* I used to play with the bantu kids all day. They were my *chommies*. I can't understand why you're so suspicious. Here we are, having a nice conversation – talking – just like any two people.' He took a drag of his cigarette. 'I am going to go down to the farm and I am going to give Lerato a job. I think it's a good idea.'

'Yes, *baas.*'

'Good. Now finish up. I'm going to bed.'

'Yes, *baas.*'

'Incident'. This was how people now referred to it. At

first it was 'massacre', then it was 'murders' and finally they settled upon 'incident' so that, when necessary, it could be discussed without calling to mind the full horror of what had happened. Petronella's interest was like the rest of the town's: tabloid-like and mawkish. As far as she was concerned, what took place there, at Moedswill, was completely other and could only be explained by brain tumours or madness. But Hendrik could feel something in the murders, something dim and shrouded, a distant shape in the recesses of imaginative possibility. It was the risk of unwittingly stumbling not just into the possibility, but the necessity, that made him want to understand what happened. Who would know better than Lerato, an unassuming maid, invisible to the family who would bicker and argue and ultimately murder and remain indifferent to her presence? The truth of the thing would be distorted by the gossip of his wife and the women like her, who would talk about it for years, who might even – in the tangle of rumours and misinformation – come across a strand of the truth, but then cast it aside, for there was nothing left by which to judge its authenticity and, in any event, authenticity was not a measure of a thing's worth to his wife. Did all the white men in the area have the same idea as him? Did all the men not want to find out how to stop themselves before it was too late?

He poured himself another whisky. The only light still burning was the bare bulb above the sink. It was drawing in the mosquitoes. Whites camped outside Lerato's hut engaged in a bidding war to secure the secret of not murdering their families. *Come and work for me, Lerato, and tell me when I'm losing it. Come and be the bantu in the cave of my soul and, when you start choking, squawk, bantu girl, squawk before I fucking kill the lot of them.* The fact that he thought about this: did it make him safer, this self-scrutiny? The pull of death was felt in different places: the train tracks, the rope bridge. The bushveld could be demarcated into areas of instant possibility. The best thing would be to forget it. Forget Lerato. Forget Labuschagne. She could not protect him. She was the danger. Lerato would be a constant reminder that anything was possible. All it took was twenty minutes of doggedness and then the thing was done.

The pupils were taken down to the dam and given oil drums, jerrycans, planks of wood, bamboo and rope with which to make rafts. The teams had two hours in which to construct their vessel. Afterwards they would race to the other side of the dam. It was a good activity. By now Steyn knew the finer points of raft-building. He had watched the students do this so many times that within the first twenty minutes he could predict who would win the race. To prevent the activity from descending into chaos, he went round from group to group, giving advice on how to improve the construction. It was no good if all the rafts disintegrated.

'If you tie the rope like that, it's going to come loose.'

'How should we tie it, *oom*?'

'Think, man – think! When you put the raft into the water, what's going to happen to these jerrycans?'

'They're going to float, *oom*.'

'*Ja*, they're going to float. So they're going to pull up like this.' Steyn tugged on the jerrycan. 'So do you think it's a good idea to put them here?'

'No – maybe here.'

'I don't know. Maybe. Maybe you're not so thick as you look.' The boys laughed.

Werner and Marius came down to the edge of the dam to watch.

'Hey, *lighties*,' Steyn said.

'Hello, *oom*,' the boys said.

'You don't have cricket today?'

'No, it was cancelled,' Marius said. 'We were going to play Fairlands.'

'I heard. They're from Johannesburg?'

'*Ja* – but their bus broke down yesterday.'

'That's a shame. And Werner – why are you so quiet?'

'Nothing, *oom* – just thinking.'

Steyn took a cigarette out of his packet and lit it. 'Mmm, I worry when you think, Werner. It usually means trouble.'

'No, *oom*. No trouble today.'

'Marius, what's your brother thinking about?'

'Girls.' Werner punched his brother and Marius laughed.

'Hey, Werner – have you got a girlfriend?' Steyn asked.

'No. Marius, you're so stupid.'

'Hey, Werner – don't be so ugly, man. He's just a little *lightie*.'

'He has such a big mouth. He always thinks he's being funny.'

'Let me tell you: it's good to have a brother. Maybe he's just a little *lightie* now . . .'

'I'm not a little *lightie*. I'm eleven.'

'*Ja*, Marius. You're right. You two are practically the same age.'

'No, we're not.'

'One day you will see – two years is nothing. Does your ma know you two are down here?'

'*Ja* – what time is *oom* finishing today?' Werner asked.

'I don't know. Maybe three. Why?'

'I was just wondering.'

'You think because I am down here you can go and cause *kak*, huh?'

'No, *oom*.'

Steyn stubbed his cigarette in the gravel. The area around the dam was lush and green and the bush was so thick in places that you'd have to take a machete to carve your way through. He looked at the boys building the rafts with a mixture of jealousy and contempt. Unrelenting exposure to these smooth, brown-limbed Peter Pans, who arrived sullen and self-assured, like the regular striking of the clock, made him feel the slow decay of his body, the sapping of his prowess.

Werner knocked and, when nobody answered, he opened the door. Steyn was lying on his bed.

'Werner?'

Even through the sweetness of the freshly cut thatch, he could smell that Steyn had been drinking, and that sourness mixed with the ripe smell of Steyn's sweat. There were four empty cans of Castle lager on the bedside cabinet.

'What do you want?' Steyn asked.

'I was wondering if *oom* wanted to go rowing.'

Steyn sighed. 'I'm tired, Werner. It's been a long day.'

Werner sat down on one of the three camping chairs that served as the sitting room. There were no pictures or books. Other than his clothes, the only object that belonged to Steyn was a small radio.

'Or maybe we could hike up to the waterfall?'

'Why don't you go with your brother?'

'I don't want to go with my brother.'

Werner wished that Steyn would do something with the rondavel. If he bought some furniture or pictures, if he made the place home, then Werner would know that he was at least planning to stay for a while, a few years perhaps. But Steyn could leave at any time. He could pack his bags, disappear and there would be no trace of him. He could go back to his wife and sons in Pretoria. Werner had eavesdropped on the conversations his mother had had with his father. She said Steyn's wife called, begging to speak to him. His mother said, 'What sort of man leaves his wife?'

Steyn reached for another beer. He opened the can slowly, just a fraction at first, to release any of the excess gas and prevent the beer from foaming on his bed. The can hissed. He pulled back the tin teardrop, tore it from the top of the can and dropped it into his beer.

'Ma says you shouldn't do that,' Werner said.

'Do what?'

'Put the *toppie* in your beer. Ma says all the coolies and bantus have been touching those cans.'

'But you still put your mouth on the can anyway.'

'*Ja* – my mother can talk some real *kak* sometimes.'

Steyn took the box of matches and threw it at Werner's head.

'*Eina!* Sorry, *oom!*' He laughed.

'Anyway,' said Steyn, 'I don't know why you're so worried about a little bit of bantu dirt. I've seen the way you *jol* with bantu kids.'

'*Ag* no, *oom* – playing with bantus like that is for kids.' Werner scratched his leg and looked down at his bare feet. His toenails were dirty, so he curled them under and tucked his legs under the chair. Not that it mattered. Boys were supposed to walk around barefoot and be dirty. Only a *moffie* would worry about dirty toenails. 'Can I have some of *oom*'s beer?'

Steyn had almost drained the can. He took the last swig, belched a little, crumpled the can between his hands and threw it in the dustbin. He reached under the bed, grabbed another beer and gave it to Werner.

'The whole one?' Werner asked.

'Don't be stupid.'

Werner opened the can and sipped the foam off the top.

'That's enough,' Steyn said.

'But, *oom*, I haven't even had a sip! It was just foam.'

'Okay – one sip.'

Werner lifted the can to his mouth and drank deeply. He swallowed as much beer as he could, before Steyn jumped off the bed and grabbed the can.

'Werner! What are you doing?'

'Sorry, *oom* – I'm thirsty.' He belched.

'*Jissus!* What are you doing, huh? I try to be nice. You want to get me fired?' He cuffed Werner on the side of his head.

'Sorry, *oom*.'

'You've had half the fucking can.'

'Sorry, *oom*.'

Steyn drank some beer, slumped on his bed and laughed.

'Let's go to the dam,' Werner said.

'No, Werner, I'm tired. It's been a long day. Anyway, you're not supposed to be in here. How many times must I tell you?'

'Is *oom* mad at me?'

'Of course. What will your mother think? Her son stinking of booze. Huh? She'll have me out of here in two ticks.'

Werner belched and then laughed.

'Here,' Steyn said. He opened his drawer and gave Werner a pick of Wilson's XXX Extra-Strong Spearmints. 'You eat that whole *blarry* packet before you come within a mile of your mother. And if she asks, I am going to tell her you stole my beer. You hear?'

'*Ja, oom*.'

'Don't know what that poor woman did to deserve a kid like you. Get out of here.'

'Okay, *oom*.' Werner was already beginning to feel light-headed. He walked to the river. No one was around. He lay down beneath an acacia tree growing at the edge of the bank and dangled his feet into the water. He was pleasantly dizzy from the beer. He plucked a long blade of glass and tickled his ear, pushing the blade deeper and deeper in, until it hurt a little. But it was nice. He closed his eyes and thought about the day when Jesus would hang in front of his bed and he could stare at him all day long; Jesus rising up into his bedroom, to be by his side.

6

After a week his father is still in hospital. His mother phones to tell Werner that she thinks he could be home next week, or perhaps the week thereafter. Werner goes to the kitchen and pours himself a large glass of wine. He drinks it quickly and pours another. He then has a shot of his mother's gin, walks up the flight of stairs and knocks on the door of the flat above. He waits for a long time. He is about to give up when the door opens a crack; the door-chain is pulled taut.

'Yes,' the man says.

'Hello, my name is Werner. I live downstairs.'

'Yes, I know.'

'Could I have a word?'

'About what?'

'It's about the building.'

The door closes. The man undoes the chain and opens it. He's six foot and powerfully built, though a little over-weight. He wears fine wire-framed glasses that do not suit his face. The arms of his glasses stretch over his large skull. His forehead is shiny in the evening heat. Werner extends his hand. The man shakes it reluctantly.

'Werner Deyer. Nice to meet you.'

'Ezenwa.'

'Nice to meet you, Mr Ezenwa.'

'No,' the man says. 'Ezenwa is my first name.'

'Oh, I'm sorry. So, I wanted to talk to you about the gutters. There have been some problems with the gutters and I was just wondering if . . . you know . . . maybe there have been some leaks in your flat? Sometimes there are problems with maintenance.'

'No leaks.'

'Good. That's good.'

They stand for a few moments saying nothing. The man asks, 'Is that all?'

'I feel like I should apologise to you.'

The man furrows his brow and cocks his head to the side. 'Why?' he asks sharply.

'It's just that you've been living here for a while and I've not made any effort to introduce myself. It's not very neighbourly. My father has been very ill and . . . well . . . you know how things are.'

The man nods. 'I wish your father well,' he says.

'Thank you – that's very kind of you.' Werner turns to walk away. He is not sure about the protocol of negotiating with Nigerian drug-dealers. As the man is closing the door he says, 'Perhaps . . .'

The man opens the door again. 'Yes?'

'Perhaps you'd like to come over for dinner sometime? My mother is an excellent cook.'

'Perhaps,' the man says and closes the door.
'Goodnight.'

He goes downstairs to wait for his mother. He thinks about the dinner party with the drug-dealers. At first it would be awkward, but then he'd open a few bottles of wine. Wine? Africans preferred beer. Did Nigerians drink bantu beer like the South African blacks? Perhaps he could get some Nigerian brands to show how neighbourly he was, unless of course they were important drug-dealers, in which case they might consider that a drink of the peasants. Perhaps Nigerian drug-dealers drink champagne. But neither of the men drives a low-slung BMW with tinted windows. Maybe theirs is a smaller enterprise. Maybe they are keeping a low profile. They aren't showy. They're professionals, squirrelling the money away into Swiss bank accounts. They'd make chicken, because blacks love chicken. Or goat. Nigerians eat a lot of goat. Does his mother know how to prepare goat? He could prepare the goat if necessary, but he isn't sure he'd be able to eat it. He is sure goat will have a horrible taste. The food is not as important as the alcohol. The alcohol will be necessary to make everyone chummy. They'd talk about Nigeria and how they miss the hustle and bustle of Lagos. They'd all get drunk and talk about how ridiculous it is that they've been living in the same building for a year and have barely exchanged a word, and how good it is to eat together, black and white, local and immigrant, and that

South Africa is turning out to be a fine place indeed. And then, to be a good host, Werner would walk them up the flight of stairs and thank them for coming over and they'd say that they should do it again soon. As he turns to take his leave, Ezenwa would say, 'Werner, before you go, would you like a little something?' And Werner would say, 'A little something?' and Ezenwa would say, 'You know – for a good time.' And Werner would say, 'I always want to have a good time,' and Ezenwa would invite him into the flat and make the full Nigerian pharmacy available to Werner; lots of neat Jiffy bags arranged on the table: ecstasy, acid, coke, speed, marijuana. And Werner would say, 'You know, I feel like a bit of heroin.'

In his reverie, he does not hear his mother open the front door. He's sitting on the settee, staring into space.

'Werner,' his mother says for the second time.

'Oh, when did you get in?'

'There's pizza in the kitchen.'

'Thanks, Ma. How's Pa?'

'Better. He's going to be on antibiotics to control the infection for a long time. But he's much better.'

'Good. That's good.'

He piles a plate with pizza, pours the rest of the wine into a glass and joins his mother in the living room. She's watching TV and eating.

'I was thinking about having some people over for dinner.'

She's engrossed in her television programme. 'Huh?' she asks, not looking at him.

'I want to have some people over. For dinner.'

'Who?'

'Our upstairs neighbours.'

'What?'

'Our neighbours. From upstairs.'

'Are you mad?'

'No.'

'They're Nigerians!'

'I've been getting to know them.'

'You listen to me. I'm not having a bunch of drug-dealers in my house. Now shut up – I'm watching this programme.'

He wants to stab her in the head. He slams his plate down on the coffee table.

'What are you doing?' she says. He switches off the television. 'Werner!'

'Enough!' he shouts at her.

'Who do you think you are?'

'Don't tell me to *shut up*. I am an adult. I pay half the bills in this house and, if I want to have someone over for dinner, I will have someone over for dinner, whether you like it or not.'

She shakes her head dismissively and carries on eating her pizza.

'What?' he asks.

'Nothing,' she says softly.

'No – you have something to say.'

'Werner, I can't talk to you when you've been drinking. I know it's not you speaking – it's the alcohol.'

'Don't start with this nonsense.'

'Your father used to be the same. When you drink there is no reasoning with you. Alcohol has ruined this family. The Deyer men? Huh! You're not men. You're boys. Real men don't behave like this. Shouting at an old woman. What's wrong with you? I spend the whole day working at the hospital – then I spend my evenings at my husband's sickbed. I buy food for you – and this is the way you treat me? Please God may I die soon, if this is going to be my life.'

He looks at his mother, small and grey, hunched over her plate. She drains all the venom from him and he feels like a brute. He picks up his pizza and sits down again.

'I don't want to interfere with your social life. If you want to have criminals over for dinner, I don't want to interfere. You must do whatever makes you happy.'

'Ma . . .'

'All I'm asking is that you remember things are not so easy for me. I pray that Jesus takes me soon after your father. Sometimes I look at him at night, and I just want to crawl into bed with him and lie there until we die – in each other's arms. In my head I pretend that I am the sick one, and he is taking care of me for a change. There's no one to take care of me.'

'Ma – I will take care of you.'

'I don't expect anyone to take care of me. I just want some peace and quiet. I want to be treated like a human being.'

During his lunch break Werner goes to the library to look up traditional Nigerian dishes. There are a great number of recipes, but he decides not to prepare goat. Plantains, yams, rice and spicy chicken. He disassociates the act of hosting a dinner party from thoughts of murder. He knows he's incapable of killing his father, but for now the thought of the Nigerians gives his days a sense of dangerous possibility that distracts him from the excruciating decline of his life. After work he drives to the centre of town where there are a number of African food shops. In a bottle store he asks about Nigerian beers and the man behind the counter points him to a small selection. He buys six bottles of Star and six bottles of One Lager. On the way home he stops at another bottle store and buys his mother a sparkling rosé, three bottles of red wine and a one-litre bottle of J&B. When his mother sees the beers in the fridge she asks, 'What's this?'

'It's Nigerian beer, Ma.' She shakes her head but says nothing before leaving for the hospital.

Werner goes upstairs and knocks on the door. Ezenwa opens it.

'Hello,' Werner says.

'Hello.'

'I was wondering if you'd like to come to dinner. This Friday. You and your housemate.'

'Udo.'

'Yes – you and Udo.'

The man looks awkward. There is no polite way to turn down the invitation. 'All right,' he says.

'Say, seven-thirty?'

Ezenwa nods. 'See you at seven-thirty.' He closes the door.

He has, Werner thinks, done something almost un-imaginable. If his mother is going to be difficult he will ask her to spend the evening at the hospital. She phones later that evening to tell him that his father will be coming home on Saturday. Fate is aligning events. Is it possible that he will have to act decisively? He gets his photocopied recipes out of his briefcase and writes a shopping list.

His mother has reconciled herself to the visit from the Nigerians. He makes her practise their names: Ezenwa and Udo. She is either martyring herself or she is certain the evening will be a disaster and is looking forward to the fallout. On Friday afternoon he leaves work early to start preparing the food. His mother has promised to come home to help. They study the photocopied recipes in the kitchen. 'Bantu food,' she says and shakes her head. She has never prepared plantains or yams. The recipe calls for the plantains to be roasted and served with palm oil. The yams are boiled, mashed and mixed with butter. As they prepare the dishes, Werner and his mother taste them and are surprised. 'Not so bad, huh, Ma?' he says.

'For bantu food,' she responds. The chicken is basted with a hot peri-peri sauce. 'What's for dessert?' his mother asks.

Werner had not thought about this. He hurries down

to the corner shop and buys a tub of Neapolitan ice cream.

'Is that what they like in Nigeria?'

'I think everyone likes ice cream.'

By seven the table is set and the food is prepared. When the Nigerians arrive, Petronella will just need to reheat it in the oven. They stand about nervously, not sure what to do.

'Music?' he asks.

Petronella shrugs. He fetches his old cassette player from his bedroom and brings out a selection of classical music tapes that he sometimes plays in his car. At twenty-five-past seven he starts playing a tape and pours himself and his mother a glass of wine. Petronella eyes the television. His soap opera is on and Werner too now regrets having invited the Nigerians. Would it not be better to ease into a life of quiet desperation and bitterness? It would require so little of him. His whole life he has failed to bring about what he most desires. The connection between the action and what he hopes to achieve has become ever more tenuous: dinner with Nigerians to bring about the death of his father. He takes a sip of his wine. It is not just the death of his father. He has wanted to take drugs. This in fact, he tells himself, is the reason he wants to make these people's acquaintance. A successful art-dealer would snort truckloads of cocaine. He would need to provide cocaine to his clients and his artists and his celebrity friends. If he became a successful dealer, a few select guests would retire to the back of the gallery for a private function. Each would be presented with a silver tray with their names spelt out in cocaine. This is what he longs to be: charmingly disreputable. He would dab at his nostrils with his pinkie and say, 'Courtesy of my Nigerian friends.'

The doorbell rings. Petronella hurries to the kitchen; she does not wish to greet the guests at the door. His heart pounds. The arrival of the Nigerians is a moment of consequence. He opens the door and welcomes the two men inside. They are dressed in black suits. Ezenwa gives Werner a box of Cadbury's chocolates. He is touched by the gesture, but perturbed also. It is not the sort of thing he'd expect a real drug-dealer to do. He leads them into the living room and invites them to take a seat. He offers them a choice of Star, One Lager or wine. The two men reply that they'd like water. He goes into the kitchen to pour three glasses of water. He drinks his glass of wine in the kitchen to calm his nerves. As he walks out of the kitchen he can hear the two men speaking quietly in their native tongue. Three glasses of water; spartan, he thinks, but soon they will see all the traditional dishes that have been prepared for them. Werner takes a seat and smiles. They nod and smile. Eventually Ezenwa says, 'You have a very nice home.'

'Thank you. Do you like living in Sunnyside?'

'Yes,' the men say.

'I have lived here for many years,' Werner says. The men nod. His throat is dry and he takes a sip of water. Ezenwa is sweating profusely, but Werner can't be sure it's because of the heat. He is not being a good host, but his throat has constricted and he cannot think of a way to make conversation. Can he ask what brings them to South Africa?

'Excuse me. I just need to lend my mother a hand in the kitchen.' The men nod and drink their water. In the kitchen his mother asks how it is going. 'Fine,' he replies breezily. 'How can I help?'

'Everything is under control,' she says. 'You talk to your guests.'

He puts a selection of wine and beer on the table and puts a new tape in his cassette player. He dims the lights a little and goes to the bathroom to check himself in the mirror. In the kitchen his mother has started dishing up. He carries the plates heaped high with food and places them on the dining-room table. Petronella takes off her apron and hurries to the bathroom to check her make-up while Werner seats Ezenwa and Udo at the table. They are still drinking their glasses of water and decline his offer of beer or wine. Werner introduces his mother and they all sit down to eat. Petronella looks to Werner, not sure if they should pray. Werner extends his hand to Udo on his left and his mother on his right. Udo immediately takes his hand and bows his head. 'For what we are about to receive, may the Lord make us truly thankful.'

'Amen,' the table choruses. They eat their food and say little.

Werner grabs one of the Nigerian beers and opens it. 'Are you sure I can't offer you something to drink?' he asks. The men decline.

'So what brings you two young men to South Africa?' Petronella asks. Werner looks at his mother, but she ignores him.

'We are here to study,' Ezenwa says.

'At the university?' Petronella asks. 'Werner works at the university.'

'No – at the college.'

'Which college?'

'The Bible college. We are missionaries.' After a few minutes Ezenwa says, 'Thank you for the food, Mrs Deyer, it is very tasty.' She nods and smiles.

Werner finishes his bottle of beer and opens another. His mother looks at him sharply. He is capable of embarrassing her even in front of a bunch of foreign bantus. Udo, he thinks, looks far too shifty to be a missionary. Missionaries? What better cover for drug-dealers? How can he signal to these people that he is not a pious Christian, that they should feel free to disclose the truth to him? How can he say: *Please do not concern yourself – I am a future customer.*

'Your Nigerian beer is very good,' Werner says.

'I would not know. I don't drink,' Ezenwa says. Liar, Werner thinks. In the pit of his stomach a rage is brewing. He has gone to considerable effort to make this man and his friend welcome. He has bought them Nigerian beer, a fact that has gone unacknowledged. What did they think? That Star and One Lager were for sale in the local OK store? That he and his mother would have eaten plantains and yams for dinner, irrespective of whether these two men were here? Do they not see that a historical accommodation has been made in having these two men in their flat, at their dining-room table? He pokes his chicken with his fork. He and his mother, in whom he suddenly has a new-found pride, have been brought low, but are living lives of quiet dignity, being servants of the state, mopping up the sick and dying and poor blacks, dragging them through the system, raising them up on their own tired, broken white backs. Do these men not see the quiet grit of the Boer?

He finishes his beer and opens another. All three people at the table look at him. 'It's good,' he says. 'And cheers – to new friends.' Nobody joins him in the toast.

When they have finished eating, Petronella gets up to clear the plates. She tries to take away Werner's half-finished beer, but he wrestles it out of her hand. Udo and Ezenwa look at her sympathetically. Werner scowls and takes another sip. He feels light-headed and indifferent to the hostility he senses. Petronella comes from the kitchen carrying two bowls of Neapolitan ice cream. It is the first time that Udo smiles. Werner gets up to go to the bathroom. He's unsteady on his feet and bangs the table. His bottle of beer falls over. Ezenwa reaches over and quickly rights it. 'Werner!' his mother shouts and runs to the kitchen. The beer runs over the table and starts dripping on the carpet. Werner uses his serviette to try and pool the beer. The two Nigerians pass him their serviettes and he creates a sodden mess of beer-soaked linen. 'Oops,' he says and smiles at the men. Petronella uses a roll of paper towels to mop up the mess and then sits down to finish her ice cream. By eight-thirty dinner is finished. The Nigerians do not want tea or coffee. They sit quietly at the table with their hands folded, waiting to be dismissed. They thank Petronella and Werner for the invitation. As they are about to leave, Werner insists that he walk them to their door. Petronella rolls her eyes, but the men wait for Werner, who goes to the kitchen to take a final swig of wine. He follows them up the stairs. At the flat, Udo takes the keys out of his pocket, unlocks the security gate and front door. He turns uncertainly to Werner. 'Thank you,' he says.

'Yes, thank you,' Ezenwa says.

Werner nods and smiles. Ezenwa gestures to Udo to go inside. Something in Werner breaks. The Nigerians are trying to run away from him. He needs something. Something must come about as a result of tonight. It is not possible to make bold, reckless gestures without something in return. Do they not understand? His life is slipping away from him. Can they not help steer him on a different course? Will they not even accede to friendship? He steadies himself with his left hand. 'Ezenwa?'

'Yes?'

'Do you not have something for me?'

'What?'

He does not know what to say, so he touches his nostril with his right index finger and sniffs. The man walks into the flat and slams the security door behind him, locking it as quickly as he can. Werner stares at him through the bars, pleading.

'Go!' the man shouts.

'Please,' Werner says. Ezenwa slams the door. Werner can hear him locking the door from the inside and speaking anxiously to Udo in his native tongue. 'Ezenwa!' Werner shouts.

'Go away or I will call the police!' the Nigerian replies.

'Arseholes,' Werner mutters and walks down the stairs. The front door of the flat is open. He can hear his mother in the kitchen washing the dishes. He cannot, will not, spend his Friday night with her. But where to? He walks down the stairs, out of the security gate and down their small suburban street. Not far from here are the bars and clubs of Sunnyside where the students spend their evenings. Young men and women are drinking beers and laughing. He looks into one of the bars. A handsome couple are seated at a table. Werner stares at them. The couple notice and look away. Humiliating. This gesture is what is reserved for homeless people. We have seen you and unseen you. Do not approach. Werner keeps staring. Indignity is the emotional napalm of the beautiful; beautiful people knowingly exude great big clouds of it to fuck you up. The boy looks up. Werner is impossible to ignore. He scowls, but Werner smiles. The boy gets up from the table, leaving his beer, and walks towards Werner. 'What the fuck is your problem?' The people in the bar are watching. He thinks about saying, 'I'm sorry. I am an aesthete and you are very beautiful.' But he does not say this and hurries away. 'Fat cunt!' the boy shouts after him. Some people in the bar giggle.

The street, which moments ago seemed joyful and welcoming, is now hostile. Werner's breathing quickens and he feels a panic attack coming on. Ahead, a menacing group of black men walks towards him. He feels afraid, turns around and starts walking home. He walks faster, but the men keep up with him. He must not break into a run for he could not keep up for long. He wonders whether he would be safer going into a bar, but he's left his wallet at home. Home, he thinks, he should get home. He turns right into his street. It's only a few hundred metres to his building. The men behind turn right also and follow him towards his building. He walks quickly towards the security gate. He fumbles with the keys. The men are right behind him. 'Boo!' one of the men shouts. Werner gets a fright and drops his keys. The men laugh and carry on walking. When he gets into the flat he pours himself a large whisky. Measures must be taken against an increasingly hostile world. If he did not drink, he would collapse under the constant aggression, the assault of humanity. He lies on the settee with his head propped up on the armrest, sipping his drink, fantasising about what he'd like to do with that boy.

'What the fuck is your problem?' the boy shouts.

'You are very beautiful,' Werner replies. 'Is it a crime to gaze upon beauty? And I would watch my tone, if I were you.'

'What are you going to do about it, fat cunt?' the boy asks.

Werner reaches out and grabs the boy by the neck. He squeezes and the boy chokes. 'I am a murderer,' he says. 'And I will murder you.' The people in the bar scream as Werner strangles the boy. To be a murderer is no bad thing.

7

Hendrik had only been to Moedswill once before. They'd been invited to a party. He spoke to Labuschagne briefly. They stood by the *braai*, drinking.

The Datsun struggled to maintain speed on the uphill and he geared down to third. The engine whined. '*Ag, fok!*' he said. That was the problem with the Datsun. It didn't have enough power in fourth and it was too slow in third. He changed back into fourth and put his foot flat down on the accelerator. Perhaps he should have taken Maria with him. When he was drunk he would boast about how he could speak Xhosa, but it wasn't really true. Maybe as a *lightie* he could make himself understood, but he certainly couldn't have a conversation any more. But then he couldn't trust Maria. Who knew what she would say to them? Was it foolish to leave Steyn in charge when the man reeked of alcohol? When he'd stopped by the rondavel that morning he could smell that Steyn had sweated through his sheets.

'Steyn – get up, man. *Jissus*, you look rough.'

Steyn sat up in bed and rubbed the back of his neck.

The man was nervous. Hendrik noticed that every time he knocked on Steyn's door, the man looked at him as if he expected to be fired.

'What time is it?'

'It's five. Can you handle things this morning?'

'*Ja.*'

'I need to sort out some stuff.'

'Fine.' He coughed and rubbed his face with his hands. 'Steyn – take a shower, man. And shave.'

Steyn reached for the cigarettes next to his bed.

'What time you back?'

'I don't know. Nine – nine-thirty.'

Steyn swung his legs out of bed, stood up and stretched. Since he'd started working here he'd developed a small roll of fat around his back and sides, but his stomach was flat and hard. He had thick hair on his forearms; his upper arms were smooth and muscled. He turned to see Hendrik still standing in the door and staring at him. 'What?'

'I need you to keep it together, Steyn.'

Hendrik slowed down now behind a truck. There was no way he could overtake. A large white Mercedes drove close behind. '*Jissus* – get off my arse,' he said. The Mercedes pulled into the right lane and overtook both him and the truck on a blind rise. He was annoyed with himself. If he hadn't been thinking about Steyn he would have seen the truck in the distance and picked up enough speed to overtake, but now it was too late. It was easier just to trail the truck all the way to Moedswill. He wasn't really worried about Steyn. He made a big deal of the drinking and the hangovers to keep Steyn in his place. One night Petronella said that Steyn had more feeling for the land in his left pinkie than Hendrik had in his entire body. He knew this was true, but it hurt that Nellie knew it; hurt even more that she said it. If it wasn't for the drama with his wife, Steyn would probably be better at the job. The Labuschagne business put everything else into perspective. If a man just chose to drink too much because his wife cheated on him, it seemed noble in comparison.

Up ahead he could see the turn-off to Moedswill. A long line of traffic had backed up behind him.

'I'm turning soon, man. Just wait.'

The tar gave way to a gravel road. The Labuschagne brother was wealthy. Some people said he was going to turn the place into a game farm. The idea had met with hostility. But it was more likely he'd sell the farm. House, tractors, livestock, bantus. Hendrik didn't care. Perhaps a game farm would be good. He hadn't yet decided what to do if the brother was there. He'd say he had some additional work at the camp and that it might help if he took a worker or two off their hands for a few months. Would that sound like scavenging? If there was one thing South Africa had an excess of, it was blacks. He wouldn't need to drive all the way to Moedswill. If anyone was there, he'd turn around and drive home.

Hendrik pulled up to the main farm gate. It was closed, but not locked. He hopped out of the Datsun, opened it, drove the car past the gate, hopped out again and closed it. He drove slowly towards the farmhouse. All around, on trees, on the *stoep* and to metal stakes in the garden, pieces of broken yellow police tape were tied. When the wind blew they fluttered, like streamers. Labuschagne's old Mercedes was still parked next to the house, but the two Land Rovers were gone. The curtains in the house were drawn. Hendrik parked the car a short distance away and got out. The garden was already overgrown. That's the way it is, he thought. Nature doesn't give a fuck. The taste of spilt blood and she's rising up, ready to tear everything apart and suck it back down into the earth. He walked to the front door and raised his fist to knock, but then thought better of it. In the back garden an open bag of charcoal leant against the *braai*. There was a small mound of grey ash and on the grill bits of burnt meat and fat. He sniffed it and could still make out the smell of *boerewors*. Two outdoor chairs lay on their sides and the remaining six chairs were arranged in a circle. There wasn't any police tape in the back garden. Perhaps it blew away. Perhaps no one was shot here. He bent down to right one of the chairs.

'*Baas?*'

'*Jissus!*' he shouted as he dropped the chair. He turned to see a yellow-toothed bantu standing behind him. The old man was blind in one eye, but he was tall and still looked strong. He leant on his *knobkierrie*. It was not like the hunting clubs they sold in tourist shops. His was crudely made and the heavy knob was weathered and cracked.

'*God*, you nearly gave me a heart attack.' The man said nothing. 'You mustn't creep up on a man like that – you will give me the *horries*: the heebie-jeebies.'

The man put his *knobkierrie* in front of him and pressed on it with both hands.

'Do you work here?' Hendrik asked him.

The man answered in English. 'I am the guard.'

'The what?'

'Security – for the *baas*.'

'Well, don't worry about me. I am here looking for the workers.'

The man pointed to a collection of huts some way beyond the house.

'Do you talk Afrikaans?' Hendrik asked. The man nodded. 'Are those your people?' he asked in Afrikaans.

'Yes. My people.'

'Come with me then. I need to talk to them.' They strolled towards the huts. 'Have you been here a long time?' Hendrik asked.

'I was born here.'

'And when was that?'

'I was born 1897. My father work for *oubaas*'s father.'

'And you? You worked for *oubaas*?'

'I work for *Oubaas* and *Baas* Labuschagne. Foreman.'

'What's your name, chief?'

'Joseph.'

'Always with the Bible names, huh?'

'Yes.'

The women were tending to fires, and the children, barefoot and dirty, were running around chasing each other. When they saw Hendrik approach, the children stopped playing and the women went into the huts to call their husbands. The men, dressed in overalls, came out to see what was going on. They spoke to Joseph, but he just shrugged.

'Joseph, can you tell them I'm looking for Lettie. The one who use to work in the house.'

Another man, wearing yellow overalls and gumboots, stepped forward and said, '*Baas*, is *baas* from the police?'

'The police? No, I'm not from the police. I'm from the camp.' He pointed. 'I'm looking for Lettie. Or maybe you call her Lerato.' The men looked at each other.

'They want to know why for.' It was Joseph. For a moment Hendrik did not know what to say. Why for?

'They want to know why for?' Hendrik said.

'Yes, *baas*. Lerato – her heart is very sore for this thing.'

'*Ja*, no, I understand. Well, the thing is, Joseph, my maid – she is family of Lerato. Maria.'

'Maria?' the man in the yellow overalls said.

'Yes – Maria, you know her. Lerato is her cousin or her niece, I think. Maria is worried about Lerato. So I said to Maria that Lerato could come and work for me. We have a nice job in the kitchen: at the camp. Mmm? Cooking and cleaning. She can live with Maria for a while.'

One of the women spoke to the man in the yellow overalls. He shook his head and said something in return that sounded sharp. She started arguing and he said, '*Haai!*'

'Now listen here. I just came for Maria because she was worried about Lettie. Who knows what's going to happen to this farm now? Joseph, do you know?'

'No, *baas*.'

'I didn't think so. But if she doesn't want a job at the camp – a nice job – that's fine. I don't care.'

'Let me talk to her father,' said Joseph.

'Which one is her father?'

'That one,' he said, pointing to the man in the yellow overalls. 'This thing is too bad. These people are very scared after this thing. Some people say Lerato is telling lies.'

'Which people?'

'The other people.'

'You mean white people?'

Joseph did not answer this directly. He said, 'I explain. I explain you give Lerato a good job. Let me explain these people.'

'Okay – I will wait for you in the car.'

Could they sense his curiosity? Was it vulgar? Was there something unsettling about him insisting on Lerato? He would have to call her Lerato. It might provide some measure of comfort. Or, if she preferred, they could come up with a different name; a new Afrikaans name. Lizelle? Lisbeth? He waited for twenty minutes before Joseph made his way to the *bakkie*. Following a few steps behind was a young black girl who could not have been more than eighteen. She was wearing a cotton dress with a floral print, threadbare and two sizes too small. She carried a small suitcase. Hendrik got out of the car.

'Joseph – is this the girl?' he asked.

'Yes, *baas* – she is a very good girl. This one is a hard worker.'

'But she is so young.'

'Very hard worker. Strong, this one.'

The dress was very short and Hendrik felt a flush of anger. Poverty was not an excuse for impropriety. The girl stared at her bare feet.

'Lerato?'

'Master,' she said, but did not look up.

'Do you want to come and work at the camp?'

'Master.' Joseph spoke to her sharply in Xhosa. 'Yes, *baas*,' she said.

'Good.'

She hopped in the back of the *bakkie*. Hendrik hesitated; such a small, young thing. He wondered whether he should tell her to get in the front. If she did, he could not drive through town. It would be at least twenty kilometres out of his way. She looked up to see what was happening and Hendrik saw her face. She was beautiful. For it to be so evident, in her cheap clothes and all the dust and the dirt, and her tight bantu curls – for it to be so evident here in the bushveld, without all the creams and lotions and Vaseline and hair-straighteners and skin-lighteners and make-up of the city blacks – for Hendrik, who had never been attracted to a black woman before, to instantly be aroused by this slip of a thing, it had to be an uncommon sort of beauty. He wanted her to ride in the cab. Sitting down, her dress would barely cover her panties, if indeed she was wearing any.

Joseph was talking to the girl, but his tone had lost the sharp edge. He was speaking quietly and gently. She said something and he shook his head and wiped a tear from her cheek. Looking at this girl, Hendrik felt ashamed of his first impulse. If he put his hand on her thigh, she would go rigid with fear. If she writhed beneath him, it would not be from pleasure. She would be like an animal caught in barbed wire. This little girl stood up to Labuschagne? No. Perhaps his wife was right. He reached into the cab, grabbed a blanket and passed it to Lerato. 'Hey,' he said, 'you mustn't worry. You'll like it there at the camp. And your auntie will take care of you.'

'Yes, *baas*,' she said. He drove home by the long route, around the town.

Steyn had been up until late, thinking about the call he would make to his wife. He considered ignoring her, but Anja was certain to call again. And then Nellie would come knocking at his door, or else she would dispatch Hendrik. It would be better to end this thing decisively. While the students were having morning tea, he knocked on the door.

'Can I use your phone?' he asked Petronella.

'Of course,' she said, smiling.

'And, Nellie, I'd really like some privacy.'

'Yes, of course. Maria and I will hang up the washing.'

From the window he watched as the woman and her maid carried a basket of laundry to the line. In the middle of the night, drunk, he'd decided what to tell his wife. But now he was having second thoughts. Did he really want to end his marriage like this? Perhaps he was being too hasty. He could tell her that he just needed a bit of time, he was feeling confused. He picked up the phone and checked that Nellie and Maria were out of earshot. He dialled the number and thought: am I really going to do this?

Werner took the picture out of his closet and laid it down in the floor. He fetched his paint and brushes from his desk drawer and filled a glass with some water in the bathroom. The sky was the easiest to paint. The problem was that he could no longer recall exactly what the painting looked like. Next time he was in town he would need to go back to the shop. But for now it didn't matter. He wondered where Marius was. For the last few days his brother had come and sat with him and watched him paint. 'You know Mrs Fourie from Sunday school says it's a sin,' Marius had said. Werner hadn't read the whole Bible, but he knew his brother was wrong. The Catholics not only painted pictures of Jesus, they made statues of him too. It was the Afrikaners who didn't want to paint pictures of Jesus. It was the Afrikaners who decided there was a rule against it. It was better to break an Afrikaner rule than a Bible rule. Werner tried to remember what was beneath the cross. There were clouds and a lake and a boat. Was the boat on the lake? Were there stars in the sky? He closed his eyes and tried to see the painting. He picked up his pencil to start drawing the boat, but then wasn't sure where to put it. He started drawing the clouds, but they looked wrong. He rubbed them out and accidentally tore one of the pages. Werner snapped his pencil in half and shouted the rudest word he knew: '*Fok!*' He decided to go and find Johann. Johann always had a scheme for making money.

His mother disapproved strongly of the boy. 'Johann,' Petronella said, 'is white trash.' His father used to work for the railways. But something happened. Johann told Werner he'd got sick, and wouldn't be drawn further on it. Since then Johann's father had been getting disability cheques. Werner's mother said the family lived off the government. But Werner liked Johann because he was tough and he smoked. 'There are some Afrikaners,' his mother said, 'who just don't want to be helped. They are an embarrassment to the country.' He knew what his mother meant. It wasn't easy to tell the difference between the way Johann and his family lived and the way some bantus lived. When he and Johann once had an argument, Werner said, 'Everyone knows you and your family are half-kaffir anyway.' Johann set upon him with such ferocity Werner thought he might lose his teeth, but Johann kicked him in the balls and punched him in the stomach. He had to be careful what he said around Johann. Johann, he thought, could probably kill him if he got angry enough. Werner didn't blame him. The family had been the target of the town's teenagers for years. Groups of boys would sneak out at night and throw rocks at the house to see Johann's obese mother, who was reputed to have been a stripper and a prostitute. But usually they were met by the father, armed with a shotgun. He was part of the fun.

'Is it boys or girls at the camp this week?' Johann asked when Werner found him breaking off bits of twig and throwing them into the river.

'Boys.'

'When the chicks come again, you must tell me. I haven't seen any pussy in weeks. I'm gonna get blue balls.'

Johann was fourteen. He'd missed nearly a year of school before the authorities intervened. Werner looked at Johann. It was little wonder people said things about the family. He was the darkest white Werner had ever seen. Luckily for him, his hair was straight and his eyes were blue.

'You just wait,' Johann would say, 'I'm just biding my time. Biding my time, man. The day I turn sixteen I'm out of here. Out of school, out of Barberton, out of this whole stinking place.' Werner would ask, 'What you going to do?' and then Johann would say, 'I'm going to move to Durban and then I'm going to open my own bike-shop. Right there on the beach. And then on the weekend I'll just get on my bike and ride, man. I'll ride, from Durban all the way to Richards Bay. Hell, I'll ride all the way to Cape Town. When I've had enough for the day, I'll just pull over and sleep on the beach. Maybe make a nice little *braai* – have a couple of beers, throw some T-bones on the fire. The life, man. And for my ma I'll buy a nice little flat in Durban, there by Shaka's Rock. My ma would love that. And then I'll buy a gun and shoot everyone in Barberton.'

'We need to make some money,' Werner said.

'*Ja* – one day, when I open my bike-shop, I'm gonna need a helluva lot of money.'

'I mean now.'

'Go collect empties.'

'All the bantus get to them before I do. Last week I found two bottles. Two. I nearly walked to Mozambique.'

Johann laughed. 'You know – if you want to make real money, you should start a shebeen. We can brew some bantu beer. You know, if you walk by my house, there's that small clearing in the bush. Nobody ever goes there. Imagine if we built a little bar there. Man, the Afs will come from all over the place. Put out a few chairs – hang up some of those coloured lights, get a record player – like a real shebeen. We will be in the money. We could even make real Af food. Make a big pot of *pap* and chickens.'

'I don't know. Do you want to spend your whole night with bantus?'

'Who cares? Money is money.'

'Do you know how to make bantu beer?'

'I could ask my pa. He'd know. When he was working on the railways they used to drink it when they ran out of money. Ma would go ballistic, hey. "You come into my house reeking of your fuckin' kaffir beer – what must people think of us?" And then Pa would give her a *klap*. Shuddup bitch. Ha! He'd say she's giving herself airs. He'd say she's nothing but a two-bit slut from Benoni.' Johann went quiet. '*Ja*, man – a shebeen,' he said quickly. 'That's how we're going to make money. That's how I am going to get my bike-shop.'

'I need some money now.'

'What's going on with you?'

'Nothing.'

'Well, there's always an easy way to get money.'

'How?'

'Steal it.'

'Don't be stupid.'

'Suit yourself.' Johann took off his *tekkies* and waded into the river while Werner sat on the bank. He took off his shirt, threw it at Werner and shouted, 'Catch!' About halfway across was an eddy, deep enough that he couldn't stand. He did a somersault and, when he surfaced, his hair was slicked back against his head. He grinned. His teeth were slightly irregular and crowded.

'So, who would you steal from?' Werner asked.

'Not me,' Johann said. 'I have enough *kak* in my life. If they caught me stealing, it would be straight to the reformatory. Do not pass Go. Do not collect two hundred rand. But, if I were you, I'd take the money from those Jo'burg *moffies*.'

'You're mad,' Werner said. He couldn't imagine what his father would do if he caught him.

Johann got out and sat next to Werner on the bank. He shivered a little in the breeze. He grabbed a fistful of hair on the back of his head and squeezed out a rivulet that ran down his spine. Werner didn't like swimming with Johann. He was trim and sleek. Werner's little rolls hung over his costume, and small mounds of fat beneath his nipples made them look like the breasts of young girls.

They walked though the bush, past the old obstacle course, which had been replaced the previous year. Johann easily scaled the three-metre climbing wall. He swung his legs over the top, gripped the edge of the wooden plank, dropped his body and, at the moment his momentum had been broken, released his grip and landed cleanly on his haunches. Johann hated Barberton and the bushveld, but he was ideally formed for it. There was no place in the world he could navigate with such ease. Werner plodded, awkwardly pushing branches out of his face and tripping over rocks, while Johann darted and ducked, back and forward, up and down, never tripping or stumbling, covering twice the distance that Werner did, like a dog off its lead. Standing one-legged in the crook of a tree, Johann said, 'There's your brother.'

'Where?'

'With Steyn, by the dam.'

Werner scrambled up the tree and nearly knocked Johann to the ground, who climbed up to the next branch.

'They must have been rowing,' Johann said.

Steyn and Marius were pulling a boat onto the bank. They were both laughing and smiling.

'Let's go over,' Johann said.

'No.'

Steyn and Marius sat down on the bank. Steyn took out a cigarette and lit it. Werner could feel the tears in his eyes. He brushed them away before Johann noticed. He had a pain in his chest. It was difficult to separate all the parts of what he felt: rage, jealousy, sadness. His inability to explain how he had been wronged in no way diminished his hurt. He wanted to take his brother by the head and smash him against a wall. He wanted to kick him in the stomach. He wanted to punch his face until he bled. He wanted to spit on Marius and trample him and beat him. He wanted to smash a beer bottle and drag it across Steyn's face. He wanted to push him in a fire. He wanted to hold his head underwater until he stopped squirming. He wanted to take an oar and break it over his head. This fantasy flowed through him, hot and soothing.

'I hate Steyn,' Werner said.

'Why?' Johann asked.

'Because he's a dirty drunk. He stinks, man. He stinks like a kaffir.'

'*Jissie!*' Johann said. 'I thought you liked him? I always thought he was a nice 'oke.'

'His wife cheated on him. Probably because he couldn't get it up. Nobody gives a shit about him. Or because he stinks. If she wanted to have it off with someone who stinks, she would have fucked a kaffir.'

Johann climbed down the tree. Werner made him uncomfortable.

'I like him,' Johann said.

'Well – you would, wouldn't you?' he said, without taking his eyes off Steyn and his brother.

'What do you mean?' Werner didn't answer. 'I'm going home,' Johann said. He walked off and left Werner alone with his rage, standing in the tree, staring.

8

His mother wakes Werner up at six the next morning. He has a terrible headache. 'Get up,' she says. 'We're going to fetch your father.' He digs around in his bedroom drawers and finds a pack of ibuprofen. He swallows all the remaining pills. While his mother cooks breakfast, he showers and changes into clean clothes. He hopes that she will not discuss last night. He sits down at the table to his plate of bacon and eggs. Petronella is reading the *Pretoria News*. The food settles his stomach. 'Feel better?' his mother asks. He nods.

They arrive at the hospital just after eight in the morning. Werner sits in the waiting room while Petronella speaks to the doctor and goes to the pharmacy to collect Hendrik's medication. An hour later she emerges pushing Hendrik in a wheelchair.

'Hello, Pa,' Werner says and takes over pushing the wheelchair from his mother. He wonders why she is in such good spirits. Did she not enjoy the time away from him? They take the man back to the flat. As Werner helps his father into his pyjamas, he sees a plastic tube that runs directly into Hendrik's chest. 'What's that?' he asks.

'It's a Hickman line. For his antibiotics.' Although the puncture in the skin is neat, the sight of the plastic pipe running into the man is gruesome. There are two connections for drips and syringes, one red and one blue. 'It will make everything a lot easier,' she says. Werner picks up the plastic tube between his thumb and forefinger.

'Leaf!' his father says. Werner smiles at him. 'Nellie!' Hendrik shouts at his wife, who is busy with his pyjama bottoms.

'What, Hendrik?' she says.

'Leaf!'

'Don't be stupid, I'm putting on your pyjama pants.'

Werner is still holding the plastic pipe between thumb and finger, the way you might appreciate the texture of silk.

'Wera leaf! Leaf alo!'

Werner lets go of the plastic tube. 'Pa, what's wrong?' he asks. 'No need to get upset.' He mouths the word 'Fucker' to his father.

'There we go,' Nellie says when she has his pyjama bottoms on. 'Aren't you glad to be home?'

Hendrik covers the Hickman line. He knows, Werner thinks, that it is a tunnel to the very heart of him. This makes him happy – this source of terror to his father. Petronella reaches for a vial of antibiotics. She taps the syringe, takes hold of the line and injects. 'See how much easier?' she asks both of them. 'Your father needs some rest,' she says and walks out of the room.

'Bye, Pa,' Werner says, leaning forward to kiss him on the forehead. The man tries to slap his son away. 'Now, don't be like that.'

After his mother has gone to bed, he takes a glass and a bottle of whisky and creeps into his father's room. The television is on and the blue light reflects off his father's pale face. 'You awake, Pa?' he says quietly. The man is sleeping.

Werner pours himself a whisky and watches the late-night Saturday film. When the credits roll he looks at his father. His eyes are two slits; watching his son.

'*Jissus*, you give me the creeps when you look at me like that.' Hendrik says nothing. 'Do you want some?' Werner asks, holding up the bottle. 'All right – you can have a little. Ma would have the shits – but, Jesus Christ, you need some pleasures in this life, huh?' He pours whisky into the glass and puts the bottle down on the side table. He cradles his father's head with his left hand and holds the glass to his father's lips, gently pouring the whisky into his mouth. Hendrik's false teeth come loose. 'I wish Ma hadn't had all your teeth ripped out. I kind of thought it was excessive. I know they were a bit rotten, but we could have sorted it out.' He smiles and says, 'You're going to choke on those teeth one day.' With his finger he eases the teeth back into place. 'You know, I should probably just inject the whisky straight into you? Wouldn't that be easier?' The old man moans in protest. 'Relax, Pa, I'm not going to do it. I was just saying if you'd prefer.'

The man licks his lips greedily. 'More,' he says.

'You want more? Okay.' Werner pours a little more whisky in the glass and brings it to his father's mouth. The man lets out a satisfied sigh as he swallows. 'You see, Pa, I'm not so bad. You know we had those Nigerians over for dinner last night. What a sight, Pa. Never in my life did I think I would see my mother serving bantus at our dinner table. And not just serving them – she cooked yams and plantains and everything. She was a real star. Ezenwa wishes you well, by the way. He doesn't much care for me. I think I drank a little too much. I think maybe our Nigerians are the happy-clappy sort – you know, like the bantus in the parks. The Zionists. But I'm like you. Apparently Ma says I am my father's son. *Ja*, Nellie doesn't think we're real men. You must really have pissed Ma off. She complains, but I think she much prefers you a cripple. Obviously you can't piss her off as much.' He leans back. 'This is nice, isn't it? Watching TV with my pa.'

His mother knocks on his bedroom door. 'Werner? Werner? Are you coming to church?'

'No, Ma,' he says.

'I think you should. The minister is coming to visit your father. Won't you be embarrassed to see him, if you don't come to church?'

'No, Ma.'

Last night he'd finished almost half the bottle of whisky. His drinking worries him. What if, by the time his father dies, he is an alcoholic? Could he still live a successful life as an alcoholic? It crept up on you, the ease with which you could consume a half – even a whole – bottle of whisky. Lying in bed, Werner hopes he remembered to put the bottle away. His mother will say something. The worst is when she tries to reach out, when she says with concern, 'Werner, I'm worried about your drinking.' In the morning it is easy to promise himself that he won't drink any more, but then in the evening he decides to have a nightcap to help him to go to sleep. If he doesn't have a nightcap he lies awake, fuming. He only wants to drink enough to help him sleep easily. But then he drinks too much and he sweats through his sheets. His fat body is moist with cold perspiration. His head is throbbing. If he lies very still with his eyes closed, the pain subsides. When the headaches are bad, he imagines gently inserting a needle into his head and relieving the pressure; all the blood spurting out and, with it, the pain too. What he needs to do is get up, find four ibuprofen, drink a large glass of water and lie down for half an hour.

He waits until he hears the front door close. He sits up, and the pain, as if untethered from elsewhere, rushes into his head, pools behind his eyes. He puts his hand on the back of his neck to try to staunch the pain and rubs his temples with his other hand. He gets up, goes to the bathroom and rifles through the cabinet. All he can find is an old packet of Disprin. 'Fuck!' He sits down on the toilet. The pain is making him nauseous. He eases himself onto the floor and dry-retches into the toilet bowl. He folds his arms over the back of the toilet seat and rests his head, facing the pool of water. Again his stomach lurches, but there is nothing. He gets up and drinks from the tap. He leans against the bathroom door and holds his head. A wave of nausea forces him back to the toilet and he vomits up the water. He can taste bile. He rests his face against the cool toilet seat. The drinking has caused a migraine. There is an emergency pharmacy that will be open on Sundays in Hatfield, but to drive would be murder. There is his mother's first-aid kit; it's the type paramedics carry around. There might be some OxyContin. The kit is buried under boxes of shoes. He unzips the bag and starts looking through the contents. Everything for a car crash, nothing for a hangover. He leans against the wall, his hand in the bag, fishing for something to take away the pain. He feels a few boxes. He pulls them out: insulin vials. 'Fuck!' He chews five Disprins. He sits with his eyes closed. He can't summon the energy to walk back to his bedroom, so he crawls into his mother's bed to try and sleep off the pain.

His mother comes home and discovers her son in her bed. He's on his back, staring at the ceiling.

'What are you doing?' she asks.

'I have a migraine.'

'Hangover.'

It's still painful to speak.

'Have you taken painkillers?'

'Disprin,' he whispers.

'Go to your own room,' she says. 'I want to get changed.' He doesn't move. He hopes she will take her clothes and get changed in the bathroom. Instead, in an act of defiance, authority – he does not know – he hears her undress in the room. He looks. He does not think of his mother as a fat woman, but there are rolls of flesh that hang over her brown pants, and her bra-straps cut deep into her skin. She bends over to step into her jeans and he can see some coarse black hairs sprouting from the top of her thighs. On her back are spots and fleshy growths. Opening his eyes has made his headache worse, so he covers his face with the cool side of the pillow.

'Can you get me some painkillers? Please, Ma?'

'You've had Disprin.'

'I need something strong. Very strong.'

'Drink water,' she says and walks out of the room.

By the time the minister comes at four o'clock, the pain has subsided to a dull throbbing in the back of his head. He gets out of bed and walks down the passage to greet the man. When the minister asks where Werner was today, he explains that he woke up with a migraine. His mother says nothing. He wonders if she ever discusses her son's 'drinking problem' with the minister. Unlikely. The appearance of rectitude is important to Nellie. They don't have much else. Together the three of them troop into his father's room. He's watching a one-day international: South Africa versus England. South Africa has put up a dismal batting performance. Looking at the score, Petronella seems relieved. She must hope her husband's interest in the game has waned, lest he put up a fuss about the interruption. The minister looks at the television screen. 'Not looking good, huh?'

'Won seary,' Hendrik says.

'He says we've won the series anyway,' Nellie explains. The minister nods. She turns the television off. The minister sits by the bedside and takes Hendrik's hand. 'Nellie tells me you had a bad spell in hospital, brother.' Hendrik grunts. The minister takes out his Bible. He has chosen to read Psalm 54:

> *Save me, O God, by the power of thy name,*
> *And vindicate me through thy might.*
> *O God, hear my prayer,*
> *Listen to my supplication.*
> *Insolent men rise to attack me,*
> *Ruthless men seek my life;*
> *They give no thought to God.*

It is a strange psalm to choose. It seems to bring his father peace. Hendrik closes his eyes and smiles; if, indeed, it is a smile. He cannot always tell because Hendrik's facial muscles are oddly contracted. It was probably the passage the minister read at the morning service; words to console suburban whites afraid of the blacks at their gates. When the minister leaves, his father continues watching the cricket game. Werner sits in the wicker chair and asks himself whether he has the courage – the balls – to be a ruthless man.

In spite of the hangover, he goes into his father's room that night with the bottle of whisky. He pours himself a small shot, downs it and then helps his father to a small sip. The man looks content. 'What a day, Pa,' he says. 'Jesus, I had the worst headache. Ma thinks it was a hangover. It was a fucking migraine. Miserable old bitch wouldn't even get me painkillers.' He thinks about how he rifled through the first-aid kit. Did he put everything away? His mother probably thinks he's a drug addict. No, he is certain he put everything away. For a moment he stops breathing. He looks at his father. Werner knows. He knows with absolute certainty *how* the thing can be done. The only question is *whether* it will be done. He looks at his own hand. He's trembling. His father also looks at his hand. Werner sees that his father sees. 'Drink, huh?' he asks lightly. His throat is dry. 'Why are you looking at me like that? You give me the creeps.' He picks up his glass and the bottle of whisky and walks out of the room. He wants to go back to the day before. He wishes today never happened. He wishes he never had the revelation, but he has, and it cannot be undone. God is testing him: *This is what you prayed for, fucker.*

The university library opens at seven in the morning. It takes fifteen minutes to confirm what he suspects. He buys himself a cappuccino and locks his office door. His father's life stands not only between him and money, but also between him and dignity, him and freedom, him and love, him and sex. His father's half-life has a very great cost. His father's half-life is vampiric, parasitic. It is not a choice between an old man and a young man; it is the choice between a tumour and its host. He bows his head. *Please, God, if I should not do this thing* – he cannot bring himself to say exactly what. It is superstition. God may strike him down if he utters the words, even in his head. God, inasmuch as he believes in God, tolerates human beings only inasmuch as he allows for ambiguity. *If I should not do this thing, send me a sign.* He opens the door to his first appointment for the day: another student benefiting from the university's largesse because his parents are dead. Here, Werner thinks, I will show you the way, I will scurry from room to room, from department to department, to grant you your life so that you can leave me behind, here in this fucking office, where I will help others, carry them to happiness. *God,* he prays again, *his life is in your hands.*

9

Over the next week Hendrik saw less of Lerato. As she was working in the kitchen with all the other women, it was difficult to engineer ways to be near her. He asked Maria how she was doing. Maria was sullen and uncommunicative. She was angry, he thought, for meddling in her affairs. Did they think this woman was bad luck? The unexpected wave of desire he felt for Lerato had opened him to new possibilities. If he felt this way, no doubt Labuschagne did too. If they'd slept together, perhaps the wife found out. Was that in itself sufficient reason? It would be embarrassing, but it was not unusual. Things happened, people gossiped, staff were sacked. He could not explain it, but having Lerato near made him feel comfortable. The woman who knew what had happened belonged to him, and if the truth of that day finally split her open, he'd be there to witness it.

That evening, after collecting Lerato, he tried to have sex with Nellie. She asked what had come over him. Irritated, he got up and poured himself a whisky. He sat in the lounge with an old *Scope* magazine and tried to masturbate over pictures of Afrikaner girls with blue stars over their nipples. He imagined going to Pretoria on a business trip, staying in a hotel and having sex with a teaching student from the university. It was a fantasy that had always pleased him, but his dick went limp. This was an ugly sight, he thought. A man sitting on the couch with his trousers pulled down to his knees. A glistening string of pre-come, like a spider-web thread, ran from the tip of his cock to his stomach. Nellie knew what he was doing. Why could she not do this simple thing for him? They all needed to play their part to keep things together. When she'd seen him doing this before, she made a comment and went back to the room. And when he was done and crept back into bed, she pretended she was sleeping. He finished his whisky. In a minute or two it would dissolve his defences. No, he thought. Something this fresh and this exciting would happen only once. He couldn't risk a rogue thought spoiling everything at the last second.

He pulled up his pants, went to the kitchen and poured himself another drink. He and Lerato were in the forest clearing. He pulled his pants down to his knees, then to his ankles. It wasn't right. He bent down to remove his shoes and his socks and kicked his pants off. If either of the boys woke up and wandered in, there'd be little he could do, but the drink made him reckless. Fuck it, he thought. He took off his shirt and lay naked on the couch. It was dark and cool. He ran his hands over his body and masturbated slowly. He thought about the journey in the car. By the time they arrived at the clearing he couldn't hold back much longer. He thought about fucking her from behind; Lerato on all fours. He groaned and came. It was good. He closed his eyes. In a few minutes he would be ashamed of himself. The come pooled on his stomach. He put his finger in it. He wiped it off with his shirt and slipped on his underpants. No wonder Nellie was snide, he thought. How would he feel if he saw her doing that on the sofa; her clothes piled on the floor, and Nellie writhing and gasping? How much uglier would it be if Nellie could see what was going on inside his head? It was why, in principle, he disapproved of masturbation. It was not the act itself that bothered him, but the boundlessness, the vastness of the imagination; a mind free to skip from eroticism, to perversity, to depravity. He could never be sure whether masturbating fuelled a thing, making the desire more insistent, or lanced it, so that its potency drained away like pus. He told Werner that the desire to touch himself was to be expected, but it was best to refrain from doing so.

Later, in bed, the remorse that overcame him was worse than he expected. It was all the dead Labuschagne children. He was desecrating their witness. He dreamt that he was fucking Lerato in a field. The children, ridden with bullet holes, came running up to them, begging him to stop. 'Please, *oom*,' they said. 'We need Lettie to save us. Please, *oom*.' But he wouldn't stop. He kept thrusting from behind, while Lerato rested her head on her folded arms and cried. He woke up sweating. He was glad he'd had the dream. Now, when there was any danger of his imagination getting carried away, he could summon the dead children to bear witness.

In town he listened for any word about the Labuschagnes. Had anyone yet realised that he'd snuck onto the farm, like a thief, to steal the maid? He was vigilant to any change in attitude. On Saturday morning he drove to the Spar to buy fresh bread. At the checkout he was stopped by a woman he knew from church. Would he be going to the funeral? It hadn't occurred to him. He wanted to attend.

'The brother is in town,' she said.

'Oh, I see.' His throat tightened.

'Yes – he brought the mother. She's eighty-four. Lives in an old people's home in Johannesburg. He pushes her around in a wheelchair. I think the woman is senile, though – a blessing really.'

'I wonder why he brought her?'

'It's her son.'

In the main shopping street he looked out for the family, but they were nowhere to be seen.

Petronella had waited for Steyn to say something after the call. She expected him to come and talk to her about new living arrangements. If they'd made up, Steyn would need to live in a larger house, perhaps something in one of the suburbs of Barberton. He never came. When she finally said something to him, he replied, 'Nellie, we had an agreement.' That morning, when everyone was out, she made herself a cup of tea and phoned the wife.

'Hello, Anja?'

'Hello.' Anja's voice was thick, as if she'd been sleeping.

'It's Nellie.'

'I know.'

'How are you, dear?'

'What do you want?'

'Anja . . . I was calling to find out how you are.'

'I'm fine.'

'Did you talk to Steyn?'

'What do you want? Did he ask you to call?'

'No, no – he doesn't know I'm calling. What did he say, Anja? I thought . . . I thought he was going fix things up.' Anja laughed unpleasantly. '*Ag* no, man. Don't be like this. Aren't we friends?'

'Did you force Steyn to call me?' she asked.

'But . . . I thought you wanted to talk to him. '

'I wish he never called.'

'Anja?'

'Petronella,' the woman said, 'I want you and my husband to fuck off.' She hung up. Petronella stood with the receiver in her hand. It felt like she'd been slapped across the face. Those two little words had come flying down the line so fast she didn't see them coming. They shot out of the receiver and ricocheted in her brain. *Fuck. Off.* Petronella was shaking as she replaced the receiver. The woman was unhinged. How else could she go from weeping on the phone, like a girl, to someone who could say such things? She would need to change her attitude towards Steyn. She would keep an eye out for him.

*   *   *

Werner made a point of avoiding Steyn. He waited for Steyn to come and enquire after him. 'What's wrong, *chommie*? Hey? You don't have time for Steyn any more, huh?' And then Werner would brush him off. He turned cold towards his brother. When his brother asked him something, he just shrugged or ignored him.

'How's your painting going?' Marius asked.

'Mind your own business,' Werner said.

'Can you help me practise my rugby tackles?' Marius asked.

'Why don't you go and ask Steyn?' Werner regretted saying this. If he could hear the jealousy in his own voice, his brother could too. But Marius was not as smart as he was. Werner went into his brother's room and saw a fifty-cent coin lying on his desk, which he took. He waited for his brother to say something, but he didn't. Two days later there were two twenty-cent coins lying on the desk. Again he took them and waited for his brother to say something. Ninety cents. He wanted his brother to ask for it back. Then he could say, 'And where did you get this money?'

On a Monday afternoon Werner crept into one of the dormitories. It was one of the smaller ones that slept only ten students. He was nervous.

'Hello!' he called out. 'Anyone here?' Some boys had small suitcases, but the majority had brought rucksacks, the old army kind sold at the surplus store. Werner opened the nearest rucksack. The owner had stuffed all his dirty clothes in the top. Werner had neither the stomach nor the courage to start pulling out the clothes and dig to the bottom. He opened the side pockets, only to find a selection of toiletries and a folded car magazine. In the bottom pocket on the left-hand side was a rolled-up pair of clean socks. He squeezed it and felt something solid inside. Cigarettes. He quickly removed two, before replacing the socks and cigarettes. I am stealing, Werner thought. I have stolen. I am a thief. The feeling pleased him. Thieving was not what he desired to do, but he was surprised by the ease of it.

He looked at a small brown suitcase that stood next to a lower bunk. He laid the suitcase on its side, unbuckled the leather straps and lifted the lid. The suitcase was neatly packed. He lifted each of the folded shirts individually, deriving pleasure from the ritual of methodical searching, the monumental, irrevocable nature of this transgression and the possibility that somewhere in a suitcase he might find a ten-rand note. There was nothing in the shirts. He removed a pair of jeans and slipped his hand in the right-hand pocket: a fifty-cent coin. As he bent down to put the jeans back, he heard someone at the door. He flung the jeans into the suitcase and crawled under the nearest bunk bed. He pushed himself against the wall and pulled his legs up to his chest. He couldn't see who'd come into the room. Perhaps it was one of the maids. He closed his eyes for a few seconds. Maybe a student had come to change his shirt or fetch a new pair of socks? Whoever had come into the room was being quiet. Perhaps the person was lying on one of the bunk beds. Maybe he was sick and had been told to lie down for a while. As silently as he could manage, Werner inched away from the wall. Even right at the edge of the bed he couldn't see who was in the room. He began to panic. If he didn't get out soon, all the boys would come marching back. He closed his eyes and prayed silently. *Jesus, you're my best friend. Help me get out of this mess. That's what best friends do. Amen.* He stuck his head out as far as he dared. He could see a faded pair of *tekkies* by one of the rucksacks.

'Johann!' he said as he scrambled out from under the bed. Johann dropped the wallet he'd been holding and shouted, '*Jissus!* Werner! *Bliksem*, man – you gave me a fright!'

'What are you doing here?' Werner asked.

'Nothing. Nothing. I'm just . . . looking around.'

'I saw you.'

'Saw me what?'

'You were stealing.'

'I wasn't,' Johann said. He quickly repacked the bag he'd been rifling through. Werner hesitated for a moment, but knew he would have to do the same.

'And what were you doing?' Johann asked. Werner closed the suitcase, fastened the buckles and leant it back against the bed.

'We need to get out of here,' Werner said.

They ran across the camp-ground. Werner felt the spreading tingle of hysteria and excitement across his body, feeding his muscles with a mad energy, so that when they broke into the bushveld he screamed and giggled and whooped. Even Johann laughed, scrambled up a tree, jumped down and did a handstand.

'I thought I was a goner,' Johann said, after he caught his breath. 'I thought it was the reformatory for sure!'

Werner said, '*Ja – you* would have been in big trouble.'

Johann scowled at him. Did Johann not understand that he was compromised? By his poor family, his alcoholic father and his fat mother, who may or may not have been a whore; by his dependence on the state, the fact that he lived too close to the blacks and that he had on occasion been seen playing soccer with them in one of the dusty clearings, during the year he had absconded from school? But when Werner had made his point, when he said pointedly, '*Ja – you* would have been in big trouble,' he saw that his friend was hurt, and Werner didn't feel like fighting. So he offered Johann a cigarette and they smoked and chatted and it was forgotten.

Standing on the *stoep*, Petronella watched Werner and Johann walking along the road that led to the house.

'Werner!' she called. The boys sauntered. Their casual attitude towards her was irritating. Johann was having a malign influence on the boy. It was unfortunate. She did not like to think of a child as being inherently bad, but everyone knew there was a point when a person's character was fixed and there was nothing that could be done about it. Johann's parents were a disgrace. They lived in the bundus, and the too-many children crawled over the old motorbikes and broken-down cars. As for the mother, lying there in the bed like a fat sow, popping out one after the other – there was no other word for it: infestation.

'Werner, when I call you, don't *drentel!*' The boys

quickened their pace. 'Who do you think I am? Huh? When I call you – you *run*, boy.'

'*Ja*, Ma,' Werner said.

'Johann,' she said in greeting.

'Hello, *tannie*.'

'Werner – this is a school day.'

'I know.'

'Have you finished your homework?'

'I don't have any.'

'Johann, I don't know how your parents feel about the matter, but in this house weekdays are for school and homework. Not playing around.'

'*Ja, tannie*,' Johann said.

'Ma – I said I don't have any homework.'

'Don't you backchat me.'

'This is so unfair.'

'Werner! Enough.' She looked at Johann. His shorts were too small; they hardly extended beyond his crotch; so tight they were cutting into his thighs. His T-shirt, with its frayed collar, was stained. Around his ankles were flea-bites. That's what comes from living in a house filled with dogs and cats. She could just imagine them sleeping on the settee and the beds. 'Johann, you need to go home.'

'Bye, *tannie*. Bye, Werner,' Johann said as he turned around to make his way back down the road.

'You – inside!' she said. Werner did not move. She folded her arms. 'Werner?' she asked threateningly.

'You don't like Johann.'

She swallowed. 'It has nothing to do with that.'

'You think you're too good for them.'

'That's enough. I've told you why I don't want you to be friends with Johann.'

'You think they're white kaffirs.'

'I never said that.'

'You think they're dirty white kaffirs. And that makes me a dirty white kaffir-lover.'

'Shut your mouth! Go to your room!'

'No, I won't.'

'Go to your room now!'

'I won't, you old cow!'

Petronella lunged forward and grabbed Werner by his shirt collar. She was deciding whether to slap him across the face or, if she still had the strength, drag him inside the house, put him over her knee and beat him. But she hesitated too long. Werner tore free with such force that she lost her balance and fell over. He sprinted down the road. Petronella got up and started chasing after him. She picked up a tree branch and threw it at her son, but it only travelled a few metres.

'You just wait till your father comes home!' she screamed. 'He will beat you to within an inch of your life!' She picked up a stone and hurled it in the direction of her son, who had by now almost disappeared from view. She wanted to beat that arrogant defiance right out of him She wanted to beat him until he begged her to stop. She wiped her palms on the front of her dress. Her thigh throbbed where she'd fallen awkwardly on the *stoep* and she knew it would leave a bruise. Evidence, she thought. Wait till Hendrik sees that. As she walked back to the house she saw a wide-eyed black girl standing still in the bushes. Typical bantu, she thought. One little white domestic and they stand there like the *blarry* world is going to end.

'What are you looking at?' she said. The girl started walking away quickly. 'Hey – come here!' Petronella called. The girl, head down, walked towards her.

'*Missies*,' she said.

'Who are you?'

'Lerato.'

'Lerato, huh? What are you doing here?'

'I clean, *missies*.'

'Clean here?'

'Yes.'

'But I haven't seen you before. You work here at the camp?'

'Yes, *missies*.'

'Who gave you a job?'

'*Baas* Hendrik.'

'*Baas* Hendrik gave you a job? Cleaning here? I know nothing about this. We don't need any more cleaners. Since when have you been working?'

'Last week.'

'Did you come here asking for a job?'

'No, *missies*. The *baas* he come to the farm.'

'Which farm?'

'Moedswill, *missies*.'

Werner ran. He was certain his mother was still chasing him, so without looking around he cut through the bushveld. Tree branches whipped his legs and his face and his arms, but he didn't stop. When he reached the river he ran along the bank and, when the growth became too thick, he hopped from stone to stone until he came to a small clearing. Finally he stopped to turn around, expecting to see his mother chasing after him, lifting up her dress as she stepped awkwardly from rock to rock. He struggled to catch his breath. His chest was burning and his face and arms were cut. He had a deep gash above his left eyebrow, from which ran a trickle of blood. He splashed his face with water and picked the bits of twig and branch from his shirt. He sat down, leant against a tree and closed his eyes. The vibrating pitch of the bushveld became louder and more insistent. His senses became thick and his movements felt slow and clumsy. He drew his thighs up to his chest, crossed his arms over his knees and rested his head on his forearms. He'd wondered if this wasn't the way in which Jesus spoke. Perhaps he used the sounds of the world – the dogs and tractors and cars and crickets, the sound of the vacuum cleaner and the lawnmower, but also the bushveld and the river and the bantus singing, and the boys at the camp shouting and fighting and playing, and the washing machine and the loud hum of the fridge; Jesus in your ear, speaking in all the frequencies of the world, louder and louder, more and more urgent, in his multi-tonal screech-speech. Werner couldn't stop the noise. He had to sit down until it passed. Even his breathing sounded strange. Even his breathing was talking to him. He sat and he waited with his eyes closed for a long time, until it passed.

There was no point in hurrying home. He was sure that if he went back now, or at midnight, the consequences would be the same. He stood up, brushed himself off and started walking in the direction of Johann's house. Someone, other than his parents, needed to acknowledge his act of rebellion. There could come a point when you simply stopped doing what people told you to.

Petronella sat down on the small bench outside the kitchen door. She sipped a cup of tea and smoked a cigarette. The temptation, when her husband came home, was to talk to him about everything. She did not know what to think about Lerato. She lit another cigarette, breaking her own rule, but these were unusual circumstances. The situation warranted a number of cigarettes. Smoke up the whole packet, she told herself. She heard Marius open one of the kitchen cupboards.

'What are you doing, Marius?' she asked.

'Nothing, Ma.'

'But I can hear you are opening a cupboard.' Marius closed the cupboard. Petronella stood up and went into the kitchen. The boy had a guilty look on his face. 'What are you doing?'

'Nothing.'

'What do you have behind your back?'

Before he could answer, she grabbed his arm and pulled it towards her. In his hands were two slices of white bread that he'd crushed in an attempt to hide them.

'What the hell is wrong with you?' she asked. Marius, wide-eyed, stood still and said nothing. 'How many times do I have to tell you not to eat before dinner? And why do you lie to me? I asked you: What are you doing? "Nothing, Ma." That's what you said. "Nothing, Ma." But you weren't doing nothing, were you? No – you were up to something. Lying and thieving. You and your brother. Do you not get enough food? Huh?' She grabbed the bread out of his hand, a sweaty dough-ball, pushed it into his mouth and smeared it over the side of his face. 'Come on, Marius – eat it up, so that you can be nice and fat like your brother.'

'What's going on here?' Hendrik dropped his bag on the kitchen floor. Petronella turned. He was smiling. 'What's the little bugger done now?' he asked.

She looked at him for a moment and then bent down to pick up the pieces of bread. 'Marius – go to your room.' He darted out of the kitchen.

Hendrik opened the fridge and grabbed a can of beer. He took a large sip, belched and put the beer down on the counter.

'What's going on?' he asked.

'You're late,' she said.

'*Ja* – there were a few things I needed to sort out. Is everything all right?'

'Werner called me an old cow.'

'Oh,' he said.

'He was wild, Hendrik – completely wild. I only told him to come inside and he screamed at me. He pushed me to the ground. Look!' she said. She pointed to a patch of dirt on her dress.

'He pushed you?'

'He's run away. I don't know where he is. It's Johann. That family is trouble – nothing but trouble. Why do they have to live here? Why doesn't the government do something about them? I can't believe Werner did that to me. His own mother! Threw me to the ground. Threw me, Hendrik – like a piece of rubbish.' Petronella started crying.

Hendrik took her into his arms and for a moment she pressed her face against him, took in his smell and surrendered, while he rubbed her back and said, '*Ag*, Nellie – you're just having a bad day. Huh? He's just a kid. You know what they're like. He's becoming a teenager. I'll sort him out. Huh? Come now – don't cry. Don't cry, Nellie.'

She was about to say, 'And what about this Lerato girl?' but thought better of it, pushed her husband away, wiped her tears and said, 'Well – what are you going to do about Werner?'

'Nothing. We're going to have dinner – and then I'll deal with him when he comes home.'

'Are we just going to let him do what he wants?'

'No, Nellie, but I am not going to go chasing after him. I won't let him be a disruption. Eventually, when it starts getting cold, he'll come home.'

'And what if he is with *that* family?'

'He will have to come home eventually.'

Petronella took the chicken out of the fridge, drizzled oil over the skin and rubbed in some salt. She wiped her nose on her sleeve. She looked at her husband. 'Steyn,' she said.

'Huh?'

'Go and check that he's not with Steyn.'

10

In his desk drawer, beneath some papers, Werner has put the three vials of insulin, a syringe and a pack of Ambien. He's not decided whether he will need the sleeping pills; in fact he has not decided upon a course of murder, but he likes to be prepared. He has considered a number of scenarios and even performed some tests. For instance, he thought it might be wise to dose his mother's wine with a sleeping pill and he tested this on himself. The effect of the pill was unmistakeable. His mother would immediately recognise a drug-induced drowsiness. His main concern is that his father wakes up as he's injecting and makes a noise. This will wake his mother. She might catch him, needle-deep. What his mother will actually do is an interesting question. He doubts that she will report him to the police. It is this belief, above all, from which he draws his courage.

Some further groundwork has been laid in that both his mother and father now accept that he often spends a few hours watching television in his father's room. His father has come to relish the visits, for Werner invariably gives the old man some whisky. Now it is simply a question of resolve. He has been having nightmares. In one, a man from campus security collects him from his office. He tells him it's about stolen cellphones. Would Werner accompany him to identify the suspect in a police line-up? Werner protests. He doesn't know anything about this. It doesn't matter. The men behind the glass all have nooses around their necks. There are seven levers in front of him. 'Choose!' the man from campus security yells. He finds he cannot speak. He is compelled to pull a lever. He does so. The trapdoor opens and the man falls. There is a sickening thud as the body pulls the rope taut. The man then leads Werner behind the glass partition and places a noose over his neck. He knows he must not protest. To protest is an admission of guilt. So he stands silently and waits. They bring in the boy from the bar. Werner should not be able to see through the glass, but he can. He must not reveal that he can see the boy. But he stares. He can't stop himself. He stares at the boy, and the boy sees. The boy says, 'That's the fat cunt. He tried to kill me.' He pulls the lever and Werner wakes up. When he has these dreams, he has difficulty in falling asleep. The only thing that calms him is to sit in his father's room, to prove to the universe that he will not kill him tonight. But the agony is such that he knows relief will only come when the thing is finally done. The trauma of the imminent crime is making him unstable.

He is trying to get along with his mother. Every night they watch the soap opera together. He is beginning to wonder whether he has it in him. It is a revelation to discover, after all these years, how well he and his mother can get along. It's not that he enjoys her company. She is a tedious woman, but after a decade of squabbling, peacefulness feels akin to friendship. She has stopped complaining about his drinking. In part he thinks this must have something to do with the time he's spending with his father. Sometimes she smiles when she sees him walk into his father's room. She is careful, though. She does not say, 'I am so glad you are spending time with your father. He's very lonely.' She and her son have never got on well enough for her to know exactly what might upset the balance. One evening as they wash the dishes she says, 'Werner, is there any chance you can help me take your father to hospital next week?'

'What's wrong?' he asks.

'Nothing. He's doing very well. It looks like the infection has cleared up nicely. Just a check-up.'

He nods and clears his throat. He takes a sip of water because his mouth has gone dry. They will remove the line.

'When?' he asks. His voice is shaky.

'Tuesday.'

'Sure,' he says. 'I will ask at work tomorrow.' Tomorrow is Friday. Three days. If it does not happen in three days, it will never happen. It is, he tells himself, for the best. He cannot go on living like this. If it is done, it should be done quickly. Should he do it tonight? His hands start shaking and he's worried that he will drop a dish. He goes to the bathroom and washes his face. Not tonight, he tells himself, then conceals a thought about not intending to do it and then, somehow, getting caught up in the momentum of it all and doing it anyway. This must be the only way a sane person can commit murder: to tell themselves they won't, while admitting the possibility that they may, and then seeing if circumstances open up a pathway of the possible.

He and his mother watch television together. At nine she will go to the bathroom, wash her face and brush her teeth. Then she will get into bed, read her book for fifteen minutes, before switching off the bedside light. Does she fall asleep right away? He does not know. It is rare, though, for his mother to get up in the middle of the night.

Petronella yawns and says, 'I'm going to bed. Don't forget to switch the front light off.' She says this every night.

Normally he just says, 'Night,' but now he says, 'Don't you want to watch a little more TV? There is a new American comedy on.'

'No, thanks.'

He looks to see if she goes into Pa's room to say goodnight to him. She doesn't. Is that something she will regret for the rest of her life? Will he be inflicting unnecessary pain on his mother? He tells himself to stop thinking this way. He's not actually going to kill his father. He's going to sit with him. He is going to sit with him and, even though now there is not only opportunity but urgency too, he will do nothing. He watches the American sitcom. It's about a group of friends living in an apartment building in New York. It makes him smile. He wishes he could have friends like that. He wishes that he lived in New York. At nine-thirty he gets up and stands outside the front door. Now that he and his mother are getting along better, she feels comfortable enough to ask him not to smoke inside. So he stands in the open-air passageway and smokes. Upstairs he can hear the Nigerians. He has managed to avoid them so far, but he knows a time will come when they will walk past each other on the stairs. Or he will call the lift and one or both of them will be inside, and he won't have any choice but to get in with them. He will nod, they will do the same, and nothing else will be said. He hopes the Nigerians leave soon. It is not fair that he feels unwelcome in a building in which he has lived for twenty years.

He flicks his butt over the side of the balcony. It lands in the parking lot below and makes a shower of sparks. He pours himself a double whisky, adds an equal amount of water and stands at the living-room window, sipping his drink. From here he has a good view of the Union buildings. It is not New York, but the view is nice. He finishes his drink and pours himself another. The first did not have the effect that he'd hoped for. He is still feeling anxious. By the time he's finished the second drink he feels much calmer. He takes the bottle of whisky and the glass and goes into his father's room. The television is still on, but the sound has been turned down. It looks like he's sleeping, but Werner has learnt not to assume. Sometimes Hendrik lies with his eyes closed and, even if he is sleeping, he wakes up often. Werner sits down in the wicker chair by Hendrik's bedside and looks out at the city. When he turns to look at his father, the man is awake. Is he smiling?

'Hello, Pa,' he says. The man groans. 'You want some?' He pours his father a whisky and helps him take a sip. He puts the whisky down on the bedside table. On the ten o'clock news there is footage of violence in KwaZulu-Natal: ANC and IFP supporters having it out. He thinks about the last conversation he should have with his father. In the modern parlance, Werner and Hendrik have many unresolved issues. He needs to become more accustomed to the nearness of the deed, so he goes to his room and fetches the syringe, the three vials and a glass of water. He tucks the syringes and vials up the sleeve of his sweater and sits down next to his father. I am sitting by my father, he thinks, with the means to kill him. Should I so choose, the thing could be done in a matter of minutes. If only the bantu who'd hit his father on the head had used a little more force, had inflicted a second blow, he would not be sitting here. The circumstances surrounding the attack remained mysterious, but his mother was stubbornly incurious about it. She said to Werner at the time that she could not concern herself with what happened; what mattered was that it did happen, and what to do next. What mattered was that his father made the fullest recovery possible. Hendrik maintained that the bantu was trying to steal his car. Petronella never seemed interested in the fact that the bantu was arrested, or what happened to him afterwards. And whatever case there was fell apart because Hendrik wasn't well enough to identify the man or testify or anything else; and Werner thought, but did not say, that there was the question of his fitness, but there was also the question of his disinclination – which was not to say that he didn't want the man tried. In fact Hendrik said he wanted the miserable kaffir to hang, which of course he didn't and never would, but he did die in custody and the circumstances around that remained mysterious too. In all probability, Werner thought, the police or the prison guards or the authorities were not of a mind to release a bantu who had attacked a white man, because where would that leave things? He reaches for his whisky and the murder weapons rattle in his sleeve. His father is still awake. He's looking to the whisky bottle. Werner cannot give his father another drink with, and he laughs at the phrase, *everything up his sleeve.*

'Okay, just a minute, Pa, I need to go to the bathroom.' He gets up and goes to his room. If the thing were done, he'd be best to prepare the syringe in his room. It is good to have a dress rehearsal like this. He places the syringe and the vials under his pillow, goes to the bathroom, pees and flushes. The glass of water is still in the room. He has not considered the details of how he performs the secondary operation to remove any trace of evidence. Think about that tomorrow, he tells himself. In his drawer, from beneath his underwear, he takes out a foil pack of sleeping pills, in capsule form. He removes one capsule. Within a few seconds it feels sticky against his fingers. Tonight he will practise dosing his father – see if the thing can be done. His father is still awake, waiting for his whisky. Werner puts the whisky glass on the window sill. He turns his back to his father. His hands shake a little as he breaks the capsule into the whisky glass. Most of the powder dissolves in the moisture, but a small trace remains. In his hurry to hide the evidence he nearly knocks over the whisky bottle. He pours a generous shot and stirs it with his finger.

'Here we go, Pa,' he says as he turns to his father with the glass of whisky. He holds up the man's head and brings the glass to his lips. Hendrik sips greedily. He smacks his lips. 'More?' Werner asks. His father smacks his lips again and says, 'Tathtes thunny.'

'Huh?'

'Tathtes thunny. Whisthky. Thunny.'

'Tastes funny?' he says, trying to keep his voice even. He takes a small sip, opening and closing his mouth with an audible smack to show that he's tasting. He's surprised that the taste of sleeping pill is faintly detectable in the drink, though his father's sense of taste must be more acute than he could have guessed. 'I can't taste anything, Pa. You want some water?' Werner swallows.

'Thunny!' Hendrik shouts.

'Calm down, Pa. I'll get you some water.'

'Thunny! Thunny! Thunny!'

He takes a glass of water and tries to give his father a sip, but the man keeps his mouth closed. 'Pa, look!' Werner says and swallows some of the water. 'You want some water?' The man relents and takes a few sips. 'Jeez, Pa, you'll wake up the whole neighbourhood.' Hendrik leans his head against the pillow and closes his eyes.

Werner is shaking. What, he thinks, is his father feeling now? Can he feel his limbs becoming heavier? What sensation does his father have left in his limbs anyway? Has he, in this rehearsal, gone a step too far? What will happen tomorrow? The garbled accusation, which his mother will piece together eventually – with more interest, more feeling, more understanding, than she ever showed towards the original crime committed by the bantu all those years ago. His father is sleeping. Werner has another shot of whisky. He remembers as a child, standing at the edge of a pool. The water was very cold. He was unable to jump in. His body, in a willed prescience, erupted in goosepimples. Do it, he tells himself. Do it. Do it. Do it now! He does not move. Do it now or never do it. He gets up and goes to his room. He lifts up his pillow. The syringes and the vials are lightly pressed into his duvet. His hands shake uncontrollably. He balls his hands into fists and presses the side of his head. He removes the plastic casing of the syringe. He is still shaking, but somewhat less so. Let's just see, he says to himself, if I can fill the syringe. It is still a rehearsal? A rehearsal? A game! A childish fantasy. He punctures the vial and draws out the insulin. There, it can be done. There is sufficient insulin to be able to throw this syringe away. He places it on his bed. He takes another sip of whisky and closes his eyes. Then he removes the plastic casing of a second syringe and fills it with insulin. He places it next to the first syringe. It is not, he tells himself, by any means certain that he will do the thing tonight. He fills a third syringe. It is strange how he hadn't managed to work out the exact details of the act, given its relative simplicity. He goes to the kitchen, fills a glass with water and returns to his bedroom. He then removes another two syringes, draws a black dot on them with permanent marker and fills them with water. He taps each syringe and squirts out a small amount of water. He gathers up the syringes and walks to his father's room. Before entering, he puts them behind his back. He closes the door. He wants to look at his watch, but the syringes are in his left hand. His mother must be fast asleep by now. He is standing on the edge of the pool. He stares at his father. He wants to laugh. How ridiculous! Is he on the verge of committing murder? Hendrik is in a deep sleep. His skeleton is a body-sized coat hanger on which is draped tissue-thin skin. The drug must be like a fistful of ball bearings coursing through his neurons, extinguishing consciousness. Bam-bam-bam. Lights out. As he has done many times before, he watches the steady rise and fall of the old man's chest, powered by his own life, sucking it dry until all that remains are two brittle shells. Do it. Do it. Do it! He does not move. He closes his eyes and realises how much he's had to drink. He feels unsteady on his feet. Perhaps, he thinks, when he opens his eyes, the man will be dead. And in this thought, in the strange tumult of emotions, he finds a strand of unexpected colour: disappointment. If he opens his eyes and his father is dead, he will be disappointed. He will have lost an opportunity to act decisively and with great consequence. Of course, he would also feel immense relief and joy and sadness and some guilt, but he cannot deny that part of him wants to know whether he is capable of this. If he is capable of this, surely he is capable of anything. He opens his eyes. His father is still breathing. He walks towards the man, places the syringes on the bed; first the three filled with insulin, and then the last two with water. Boy on the edge of the pool. One. Two. Three. He picks up the first syringe. He is shaking terribly again, but he steadies his hands by resting them on the mattress. He puts the needle into the Hickman line. The deed is still not done. His father's eyes flicker. He injects the contents into the tube. He works quickly; for a fraction of a second he enjoys something like the professionalism of the doctor-assassin. He injects the remaining insulin and then the water to clean the line, on the off-chance that someone performs a test. He is not sure how long it will take for his father to fall into a coma, but he is clearly still breathing. Next door he hears his mother stir. He takes a few deep breaths. He takes the spent syringes, the vials, the bottle of whisky and the glasses to his bedroom. He puts the bottle of whisky and the glasses next to his bed; the syringes and vials are hidden at the bottom of his underpants drawer. These he will dispose of tomorrow in a dumpster a few blocks away. He feels nauseous and is shaking again. 'Oh my God,' he whispers. 'O Jesus, O Jesus, O Jesus! What have I done? What have I done?' He lies down on his bed and closes his eyes. Is his father dead yet? Not yet, he thinks, not yet. But soon, very soon, if there is an afterlife, Hendrik will know that his instincts were right and that his son murdered him, but – blessed with supernatural understanding – will forgive him. He must be dead, Werner thinks. He now knows the most important thing of all. No. He knows nothing. He is gone. There is nothing to know. He gets up and takes two sleeping pills out of the foil. He drinks them with whisky. It is set in motion. When he wakes up, things will have progressed further. He cannot sleep. His limbs are heavy. His eyes are scratchy. He lies like that for an hour. Every few minutes he begins shaking uncontrollably. This thing cannot be undone. At three o'clock he gets up. By now, the thing must be done. If he is not dead now, then the insulin vials were filled with water. He is desperate for a cigarette. He opens the window as wide as possible and smokes in his room. He feels faint. He is certain he will be able to sleep now. He wonders: tomorrow, will his mother scream? He lies down on the bed, but sleep does not come. He closes his eyes and thinks about the plastic tube running into his father. He imagines droplets, clearly visible. His mother says, 'Why is the line still moist?' He sits up with a start. Could you see moisture in the line? What did it look like after his mother injected the antibiotics? He begins to panic. Why did he not look? How could he do this thing? He is going to be caught. Only his mother can save him. He is flooded with a deep affection for his mother and with terrible guilt for doing this to her. He has murdered her husband, but still she will hide this from the world, because he is her son and there is nothing to be gained from ruining his life. He tries to calm his breathing. It is five o'clock. His mother will get up in half an hour. Half an hour or an hour? He must sleep. What will she think if he is awake? It will be suspicious. He closes his eyes. The effect of the pills and the whisky is strong. He dozes off. He dreams that his mother walks into his father's room to discover a rotting corpse. She shouts, 'Murder! Murder! It must be murder for it to have happened so fast!' He wakes up and looks at his watch. It's just before six. His eyes are burning and he can feel the beginning of a migraine. Not today, he thinks. Please not today. He can hear his mother get out of bed. She goes to the bathroom. The walls and doors are so thin that he can hear her stream of urine. It's strong. Like a horse, he thinks. Like a horse taking a piss. She flushes and washes her hands. He closes his eyes. His heart is pounding. His mother opens her bedroom door and closes it; the pad of bare feet on the carpet. She opens the door of his father's bedroom. He listens. She makes a noise. He can't hear. He wants to get out of bed and press his ear against the wall. He moves and all he can hear is the rustling of his sheets. But then softly, wafting, like music, he can hear the sound of his mother's sobs next door, and he knows: the thing is done and they are both free. He is overcome by grief and begins to cry too. He turns his head and cries gently into his pillow.

At six-thirty there is a gentle knock on the door. 'Werner, Werner?'

'Mmm,' he says, feigning sleep.

His mother opens the door. Her face is tear-stained. 'Werner, my dear,' she says.

'What?'

'Your father died last night.'

He sits up. 'What?'

She starts crying. 'He died.'

'Oh God,' he says. 'Oh God!'

He runs to the bathroom and vomits. He does not know whether it's the headache or the sleeping pills or the whisky or the shock. Probably it is all of these things. His mother waits outside the bathroom door.

'My darling,' she says. 'My darling, I am so sorry. I'm sorry.'

He has chunks of last night's food in his mouth. 'I'm sorry, Ma,' he shouts into the toilet bowl. He's crying. 'I'm sorry, Ma.' He vomits again.

'I'm going to sit with your father a bit,' she says.

Werner and Petronella sit at the kitchen table. He's had four Disprins and two glasses of water. His mother smells strong. It is something he has noticed more and more as she ages. Her smell has a trace of urine. He wonders if this signals the beginning of incontinence. She has not brushed her teeth and her breath is rank. She has made a large pot of filter coffee and placed a steaming mug in front of Werner. She has a small notebook in which she writes all her important numbers. The telephone is in front of her. For a moment Werner considers that this arrangement is not unlike a scene from a prison film. She sips her coffee, blows her nose and then stuffs the wet tissue back into her dressing-gown pocket. She flips through the notebook, picks up the phone and dials the doctor. They have a brief conversation in which she manages to hold it together. He will come in an hour. She looks at her watch. She calls the undertakers. Again there is a brief conversation and she arranges for them to collect the body at ten. She telephones her hospital to explain. Werner can hear the voice on the line: a black nurse. '*Hau*, my sister! I am so sorry. Oh! This thing is terrible! I pray to God for you, my sister!' His mother's voice is tight. 'Thank you,' she says and puts the phone down. But then she starts crying again. She puts her head in her hands and pushes the phone towards Werner. He calls the university. The conversation is embarrassing. People expressing their condolences is deeply embarrassing. 'Thank you. Thank you. Yes. Thank you very much. No, we're fine, thank you.' He puts the phone down.

'Will you phone your brother?' his mother asks. Werner nods. He looks up the number in her notebook and dials. It rings, but goes straight to answerphone. There is no point in leaving a message. There are other people to be called, but the list is not very long. Petronella says she will go and tidy herself up before the doctor comes. He has not yet been into the room. 'Werner,' she says, 'you should say goodbye to your father.'

Should he? He picks up his coffee and goes to his father's room. His mother has left the door ajar. He hesitates for a moment and walks in. On the floor he sees something glint. He bends down to pick it up. It's a piece of foil from the sleeping pills. He quickly puts it into his pocket. How did the foil get there? He remembers removing the capsule in his own bedroom. This discovery has made him uneasy. How many other pieces of foil are littered around the house, glinting, calling out to his mother, the doctor, 'Murderer! Murderer! Murderer!' He takes a last look at his father. His mother has taped the man's eyes shut and she has used an old scarf to tie his jaw in place. Trussed, he thinks. My father has been trussed. As his body stiffens, those dentures will finally be locked into place. The thing is done. There is nothing else to be done. The thing is done. He goes back to the kitchen to try to reach his brother.

11

Johann and his sister were sitting on the *stoep* eating sandwiches. It was already dark out and the light that hung
from the *afdak* attracted mosquitoes. Every now and then
Johann would slap his neck or his leg, but his sister, being
more squeamish, brushed the insects away. It was nice,
Werner thought, to stand here in the dark just watching
them. The front yard was scattered with old motorbikes
and the rusted shells of two Volksies. Some of the bikes
had begun to sink into the earth. Werner could make out
Johann's father inside the house. He didn't want to go
inside. He'd never spoken to Johann's father, he'd only ever
seen him in town. He would just sit outside here on the
stoep for a while and talk to Johann. Werner stepped
forward. Johann, hearing something, looked up.

'Pa,' Johann shouted.

'What?' the man said.

Werner froze. He thought about the gun. 'Johann,' he
shouted. 'It's me! Werner!'

Johann stood up and shielded his eyes from the light.
He peered into the darkness.

'Werner, where are you?' he called out.

'Here,' Werner said as he clambered over the debris in the garden, waving an arm in the air.

'What are you doing here?' Johann asked.

'I just . . . came to say hello.'

Johann stuffed the rest of the sandwich in his mouth, licked the jam off his hands and leapt over the stairs that led down from the *stoep*. He stood in the middle of the garden, hands on hips, and watched as Werner made his way towards him.

'Who is it?' the man shouted.

'No one, Pa,' Johann called back. The light from the *stoep* cut across Werner's face and Johann saw the gash above his eye.

'What happened to you?'

'Nothing.'

'You can't come here.'

'Why not?'

'Does your mother know where you are?'

Werner shrugged. 'I'm in trouble anyway.'

Johann peered at his friend. 'It's looks like you've been in a helluva fight.' Werner stood by his friend, waiting to be invited in. Eventually Johann said, 'Do you want a sandwich?'

Werner nodded and followed him into the house. It was worse than he'd expected: filthy, with worn carpets that smelt of dog and cat piss. The sitting-room floor was littered with newspapers and empty beer cans that doubled as ashtrays. Johann's father was sitting in an old garden chair trying to tune a radio.

'Who's he?' the man asked.

'Werner, Pa. He's just here for a few minutes.'

'Hello, *oom*,' Werner said. The man said something unintelligible and Werner followed Johann into the kitchen. The little girl who'd been sitting on the *stoep* trailed after them. 'My name is Charlize,' she said.

'Hello, Charlize.'

'Johann is my brother.'

'*Ja*, I know.'

'For my birthday Johann is going to take me to the flicks. Do you want to come?'

Johann reached for an open tin on the counter. The contents were pink and creamy. Werner thought with distaste that mixing the butter with the jam was a bantu thing to do. The melamine counter was crawling with ants. Johann picked a few out of the jam-butter mixture and flicked them on the floor. He looked at his younger sister, who'd sunk down on her haunches and was inspecting a trail of ants that led under the kitchen counter.

'*Sies*, man – get up off the floor,' he said to his sister.

She ignored him and asked Werner, 'So you want to come?'

'Maybe. Depends on what you want to see.'

'Cartoons. *Tom and Jerry*. The ants are eating something. I think there's something dead under there. Maybe a *gogga*.'

Johann handed Werner two slices of thick white bread, slathered in the pink mixture. They even eat like blacks, he thought, without cutting the bread in half or using plates. He tried not to think about Johann's dirty fingers in the jam, the animal hair everywhere, the piss and the ants and the dead thing under the counter. Charlize got down on all fours and peered under the counter.

'What are you doing?' Johann asked.

'I want to see what's under there. I want to see what the ants are eating.'

Her brother grabbed her by the back of her dress and lifted her off the floor.

'Stop it!' she shouted as she slapped his hands.

'You wanna fight, huh?' he said, grinning. She lunged at him, but Johann, too quick, ducked out of the way. He assumed the pose of a boxer, dancing from foot to foot, leant forward and tapped her on the left ear and then on the right. Charlize tried to smack her brother in the balls, but Johann grabbed her wrist. 'Charlize!' he said in mock indignation. 'Who taught you to fight so dirty? *Sies*, man – you mustn't hit a boy in his goonies!'

Charlize turned around and bent down to open a cupboard. Johann playfully kicked her bottom. She grabbed a cast-iron frying pan from the lowest shelf and swung wildly at her brother.

'I am going to bash your head in,' she said.

'Oh, are you now?' Johann said.

Werner backed away from the siblings and pressed himself against the kitchen wall. Johann saw him and smiled. He darted behind Charlize and flicked her ear. She swung at him with the frying pan. The wooden handle was oily. She underestimated the force of her swing and it slipped from her hands. Werner ducked as the pan flew across the kitchen and smashed into the cabinet opposite.

'*Donner!*' Charlize said.

'Charlize!'

'What the fuck is going on?' It was their father.

Johann quickly grabbed the pan and put it back into the cupboard. 'Nothing, Pa – we just dropped something; it's fine.'

'Sounds like you're breaking down the *blarry* house!'

'No, Pa,' he shouted. 'Charlize is just breaking down the bloody kitchen,' he said quietly. He looked at the damaged kitchen cupboard. The wood was cracked.

'*Donner*,' Charlize said. 'I'm in the *kak* now.'

'Ssshhh. Werner, go stand by the door and check for my father.'

While Werner kept a lookout, Johann rummaged in the drawers for a screwdriver. He started unscrewing the hinges of the broken door. Charlize stood by her brother with cupped hands, holding each of the screws as he removed them.

'Someone is coming,' Werner said.

'*Kak!*'

'*Donner.*'

The door now hung awkwardly on one hinge. Johann held it in place with his hand, as he looked to see who was entering the kitchen. Charlize emptied the screws into the front pocket of her dirty white dress, wiped her hands and looked towards the door nervously. Werner, who was looking down, saw two bruised white feet at the end of fat calves.

'Ma,' Johann said. 'Come in quick, close the door.' The woman shuffled into the kitchen. She steadied herself with a walking cane. Charlize darted round the back and closed the door behind her mother.

'What's going on?' the woman whispered. The problem with Johann's mother – the reason that he did not want anyone to visit his house – was not that his mother was fat. And it was unlikely also that she was a whore. The problem with Johann's mother was that she was simple. Werner tried not to gape. For all these years he had been expecting feather boas and snakeskins: the stripper of Benoni; instead, a fat retard, in a pink nightie with a walking stick. She was not a *mongool* – she didn't have a flat face and she didn't talk funny – but there was definitely something wrong.

'Who are you?'

'Werner, *tannie*.'

'He's Johann's friend, Ma,' Charlize said. The woman nodded.

'What happened to your face?'

'I tripped.' She nodded.

'Charlize – watch the door and tell me if he's coming.' The girl was torn between helping Werner with her mother and standing at the door keeping a lookout for her father. Johann hopped onto the kitchen counter and carried on removing the broken door. His mother looked up and saw the kitchen cupboard. She opened her mouth wide, covered it with her hand and then giggled.

'Johann, what have you done?'

'Just a little accident, Ma.'

'If your pa sees that, he's going to be so mad.'

'*Ja*, Ma, that's why we're not going to tell him.' He put the cupboard door on the counter and turned to his mother. 'We're not going to tell him, are we, Ma?' She shook her head. Johann started removing an identical fitting, which, being lower and behind the kitchen door, was mostly hidden from view.

'What's your name again?' she asked Werner.

'Werner, *tannie*.' She nodded.

'Your face looks sore.'

'It's fine – thanks, *tannie*.'

She walked over to the sink, picked up a filthy cloth and put it under the cold water. 'Come here,' she said.

'It's fine, *tannie*, thank you – it's really not bad.' She wiped his face with the cloth. The dirty water ran down his cheeks and into his mouth. It stung.

'There. That's better.' She rubbed the cut above his eye and it started bleeding again. 'Oops. Oops! We must get you a plaster – or maybe some bandages. Charlize, we must get some bandages.'

The woman repulsed Werner. Her crude maternal gestures were like those of a young girl with a doll, stemming from a place of instinct, but a clumsy imitation of the real thing. He took her hands in his own and held them. 'Thank you, *tannie*. It's much better.' She nodded. He could feel the tension in her arms, so he held onto her hands for a while. He did not want her to stick the dirty cloth into his face again. He eventually let go of her hands and wiped his mouth on his sleeve. He blinked away some of the water in his eyes. What must it be like, he wondered, to live with this woman every day?

Johann had finished the top cupboard. He tested the door. His mother clapped her hands. '*Ag*, Johann, that looks beautiful. You're so clever!'

'Thanks, Ma.' He went to work on the lower cupboard, screwing in place the broken door that he hoped his father would only notice a few days from now.

'Johann says he's going to buy us a television one day,' the woman said.

Werner looked at Johann and said, 'Really?' Johann shrugged.

'*Ja*, Ma,' Charlize said. 'But I think maybe he will have to rob a bank.'

'He mustn't rob a bank. The police will hang him if he robs a bank.'

'Don't worry, Ma, I'm not going to rob a bank.'

'Do you know what a television is?' she asked Werner. He nodded. 'It's like having a bioscope in your own house. Then we can watch *Tom and Jerry* cartoons like at the flicks, hey, Charlize?'

'*Ja*, Ma.'

'How much is a television, Johann?'

He closed the bottom door and stepped back to inspect his work. 'I don't know, Ma,' he said distantly. 'A lot.' Johann turned to his sister. 'What do you say?'

'Me?'

'*Ja*.'

'About what?'

'About saving your butt. Again.'

'It's your fault. You know I don't like it when you flick my ears.' Johann put the screwdriver back into the kitchen drawer. Charlize inspected his work. 'It's a bit skew,' she said.

'She's a right little madam, isn't she, Ma?'

Charlize took her mother's hand. 'Come, Ma. Do you want to go to bed?'

'No, I want to stay here with your friend.'

Johann looked at her. 'Ma, Werner has to go now. He's going to be in big trouble if he doesn't go home.'

'Are you leaving?'

'Yes, *tannie*.'

She hugged him and kissed him on the mouth. 'It's so nice to meet Johann's friends. I think you are Johann's best friend.'

'Yes, *tannie*.'

'My name is Sara.'

'*Tannie* Sara,' Werner said.

Charlize grabbed her mother's hand and pulled her out of the kitchen. 'Come, Ma.' Sara followed her seven-year-old daughter to bed.

Werner and Johann sat in embarrassed silence. 'My ma is quite ill,' Johann said. Werner did not know what to do, so he said nothing. 'I don't think she's ever going to get better.' Werner nodded.

It was after ten by the time Werner made his way home. When they left the house they saw that Johann's father had fallen asleep on the couch. They sat in the front garden, smoking cigarettes and drinking the dregs in the beer cans that Johann had found lying around the house. It was good, Werner thought, to be out here, away from his family. The distance that Johann kept from most of his friends – a distance attributable, Werner thought, to his mother and father and the conditions in which they lived – was now broached. Johann's life aroused both sympathy and admiration, and Werner felt bad for the way he sometimes treated his friend. Before he left, Johann gave him a pack of XXX Extra-Strong Spearmints, as Steyn did, to disguise the smell of beer and cigarettes. He walked quickly. He knew the way well, but the bushveld was more menacing at night. He stumbled into a cobweb and brushed the sticky strands from his face. He tugged at his shirt, front and back, in case a spider had fallen on him. From the path he could see the light that spilt from the kitchen. The flowers that grew wild around the outside tap were prettier than anything his mother had managed to grow. Steyn's light was also on. He wondered whether he shouldn't go to Steyn's rondavel, but by now he'd probably heard what had happened and would send Werner straight to his parents anyway. As he approached the house he could hear the clink of dishes in the sink. His mother was drying some pots and his father was sitting at the kitchen table, drinking.

When Werner entered his house, Hendrik regarded his son coolly, waiting for him to say something.

'Pa,' he said in greeting. 'Ma.'

'Where have you been?'

'Outside.'

'Outside where?' his father asked.

'Just by the river.'

'Don't lie to me.'

'And I visited Johann.' Hendrik nodded. He disliked Johann's family too, but there was something unseemly, unmanly, in insisting that Werner stop seeing the boy, as if he were delicate and in need of protection. Hendrik's instinct was to say, 'You know how your mother feels about those people,' but he did not.

'Do you have nothing to say for yourself?' Hendrik asked.

'I'm sorry, Pa.'

'I beg your pardon?'

'I'm *sorry*, Pa.'

'And your mother?'

'Sorry,' he mumbled.

'Sorry *who*?' Hendrik shouted.

'Sorry, *Ma*.'

Petronella carried on washing the dishes and did not turn to face her son.

'Go to your room,' Hendrik said.

Petronella waited for Werner to leave the kitchen before she said, 'I don't know what's wrong with him.'

'There is nothing wrong with him,' Hendrik snapped.

'What are you waiting for?'

'I'm finishing my drink.'

Petronella's rage was suffocating. She needed to hear it

being done. Hendrik slammed his whisky down. He got up and banged the chair against the table.

'Finish your drink. I didn't say you shouldn't finish your drink.'

It was good, this surge of anger he felt for Petronella; it would help fuel the thing. Quickly, before the anger subsided, Hendrik started undoing his belt buckle as he walked to Werner's room. He grabbed the chair from Werner's desk and pointed. Werner bent over the back of the chair and rested his elbows on the seat. Hendrik folded the belt in half, raised his hand just above his shoulder and brought the belt firmly down on Werner's backside. 'Count!' he said.

'One,' Werner said. By the time he reached four, Hendrik could see that tears were coursing down his son's face and dropping onto the wooden seat. His panting was almost inaudible. He does not wish to give me the satisfaction, Hendrik thought and felt proud. But the last two strikes were harder, so that Petronella could hear a cry and Werner would be reminded that he was not a man yet. Afterwards he shook his father's hand, washed his face and went to bed. Hendrik sat down in the kitchen. Petronella was still busy with the dishes.

'There we go. It's over,' he said. She didn't respond. 'What now, Nellie? Are you never satisfied? I said it's over.'

Petronella picked up a dinner dish and smashed it on the floor.

'Nellie? What's going on? Have you gone mad?' he asked. She glared at her husband, but said nothing.

*　　*　　*

The next morning the kitchen was thick with the events of the night before. Everyone ate their breakfast in silence. Marius, who'd been sent to bed before Werner got home, glanced at his brother and his parents. He'd awoken to the crashing of a plate and wondered what Werner had done. The students were due to leave at midday, so Hendrik hurried out of the kitchen to prepare for the final assembly. Petrus was waiting in the *bakkie* to take the boys to school. Petronella handed them their packed lunches. She kissed Marius on the cheek, but when she tried to kiss Werner he turned his face away from her and walked out of the kitchen without saying goodbye.

'Did you see that?' Petronella asked Maria.

'I see, *missies*. He's cheeky, that one.'

'*Ja*.'

'He's becoming a man, *missies*.'

'Huh!'

For a moment Petronella considered asking Maria about Lerato, then decided against it. The bantus already knew too much about them. She did not need Maria to know that her husband had done something without her knowledge. She looked out of the kitchen window as the boys hopped into the back of the *bakkie*. Werner stood, holding the back of the cab, like a chariot-rider. He was forbidden to do this. Marius sat beside his brother, holding his school bag between his legs. She resisted the urge to run behind the *bakkie* and ask her son to sit. He'd just pretend not to hear her. Her anger towards her son quickly dissolved in the imagined horror of an accident. It was too late to do anything about it now. The *bakkie* was nearly out of sight.

Werner began to spend more time at Johann's house. He got used to the dirtiness. *Tannie* Sara was usually in her room, and the father, though bad-tempered, had little interest in what they did so long as they didn't make too much noise or get in his way. Werner met Johann's two older brothers, André and Lourens. Both worked at the motorcycle shop in town and would come home with different bikes that they'd borrowed for the night. Johann told Werner there was nothing his brothers didn't know about bikes, and they were teaching him. Sometimes the boys would watch them service the motorcycles in the back yard. The brothers would explain what they were doing and both Werner and Johann would nod. If they brought home a 50cc, Johann was allowed to drive it around the garden. Werner tried once, but he kept on stalling and the sight of Johann and his brothers giggling made him squirm with embarrassment. Johann said he was sorry for laughing and he'd teach Werner to ride properly if he wanted, but Werner told him he'd make do with his bicycle for now. There was no point in learning to ride a motorbike if he couldn't go further than the back yard.

Petronella suspected where he spent his afternoons and weekends, but Werner was careful to keep Johann away from the house and the camp. What Werner liked about Lourens and André was that they taught him about girls. They told him about what girls liked and what girls didn't like. They told him about what girls could be persuaded to do, if they thought you loved them. And to these lessons Werner paid more attention than anything they said about motorbikes. The brothers told them about a girl's *poes* and a girl's *gat* and that sometimes for special occasions, such as birthdays, a girl could be persuaded to relinquish the latter. This, they assured him, was to be considered the apotheosis of sexual endeavour. Werner was revolted by the idea, but said nothing. Johann was teased for still being a virgin. At his age, the brothers said, they'd lost their virginity to a coloured prostitute from the local township. 'A real Cape coloured,' one brother said. 'Skinny as a rake, with small little tits and a huge arse. But, hell, she taught me a thing or two.' The brothers laughed and Johann blushed. Werner could not believe the ease with which they spoke about sleeping with a coloured woman.

'Werner, look at my brother – such a pretty little face, huh?' André said. 'He could be a real ladies' man, but instead of chasing *poes* all he wants to talk about is bikes. Bikes this, bikes that. Huh, little brother? You can't fuck a bike.'

His mother's assessment of this family was correct, but the lawlessness, the squalor and most of all the joyousness were hard to resist. And there was something else too. Johann was different from his brothers. It was Johann who made Charlize's school lunches and cooked most of the dinners. In this regard he was not skilled, but the care of his younger sister was more central to Johann's existence than Werner had realised. And although Johann spoke often about sex, he did not display the same vulgarity as his brothers. He showed no inclination to visit a prostitute or even to seduce one of the loose girls in the high school. He showed little interest in his brother's magazines or dirty playing cards. It was the contrast with his family that brought Johann's sensitivity into sharp relief.

Werner was tempted to tell Johann about the Jesus picture. Every fortnight, when he went into town with his mother, he stopped by the shop to admire the painting so that he could continue his reproduction at home. Johann might understand his singular obsession. The paper of his painting was thick with layers of poster paint, and although the image showed some improvement, it was far from the thing of beauty that had first transfixed him. He did not want to tell Johann as if it were a confession. He would wait for an opportunity when they were both in town and casually suggest that they walk down various streets until they came to the shop.

The more time he spent with the family, the more adult he felt. With Lourens and André he would talk about bikes and sex, and even smoke a cigarette or take a swig from a beer. He might help Johann make dinner for Charlize or play cards with her or talk about school. He grew fond of Charlize. He laughed every time she said 'Donner!' although Johann told him not to encourage her. 'It's my brothers' fault,' Johann said. 'She's a little girl, but she talks like a mechanic.'

Charlize showed Werner her secret fairy garden, tucked away in the undergrowth not far from the river. Werner pointed to some dolls' heads impaled on coloured pencils. 'What's this?'

'I had to cut off their heads.'

'Why?'

'Because they told Lourens and André about the garden.'

'Oh.'

'I didn't want to cut off their heads, but Brolloks said I had to.' She picked up a dead dung beetle that was perched on an upturned teacup. 'You see this is Brolloks. Johann found him for me. He used to be as big as a dog, but then Johann fought him and did magic on him and now he's small. He wanted to eat Johann, but we're friends now. He's in charge, except when I'm here. But sometimes he can tell me what to do.' Werner nodded. Charlize had tied burnt-out light bulbs with string to the undergrowth, which formed a canopy over the garden. In one corner were dozens of crisp packets, which had been shrunk in the oven. They were neatly arranged in three rows: salt and vinegar, tomato, and cheese and onion. Werner picked one up. He'd forgotten about this trick. The packet was shrunk to about one-fifth of its original size, but the picture and colours were preserved.

'That's the shop,' said Charlize. 'For when people get hungry.'

She warned him never to visit the secret garden without her protection. There was a magic spell on Brolloks and, if Werner did visit, he would grow as big as a dog again and devour him.

'But your brother fought him off,' Werner pointed out.

Charlize considered this for a moment. 'You are not as strong as my brother,' she said.

Werner wondered about *Tannie* Sara. For the most part Lourens and André acted as if she wasn't there, but Johann sometimes spoke of a time when his mother was well – halcyon days in memory at least, if not in fact, when the house was nice and the family ate a roast chicken every Sunday and his mother enquired about school; times, Werner gathered, that Charlize was too young to remember.

Marius sometimes followed him to the house, but he discouraged his brother. Johann was his friend. It made him feel better about Steyn's betrayal. He had seen Marius and Steyn go rowing again together and was surprised that it hurt even more than the first time. He had a suspicion why Steyn was avoiding him and it made him even angrier, because it was not his fault. It was an accident. He even said that. 'I'm sorry, *oom*, it was an accident.' He apologised twice, and not once did Steyn say it was okay. Not once did Steyn accept his apology. He just looked away angrily. He could barely bring himself to speak to Werner that day, and even though he was friendly afterwards, Werner knew everything was different and that Steyn hadn't really forgiven him. But if he couldn't hurt Steyn, he could at least hurt his brother. And he would certainly take all the money.

In the late afternoon, having spent a few hours at Johann's house, Werner made his way home. He'd learnt to vary his routes to avoid his mother. She was always trying to catch him. He was about to walk through the grass clearing in front of the servants' quarters when he saw a man crouching in the bush. With his back turned to him, and through the dense growth, it was difficult to make out who it was. A young black girl was hanging up washing. Quietly Werner walked back up the path so that he could see the man more clearly. It was his father. He'd pulled his pants down and was masturbating. His father was jacking off over a dirty kaffir girl.

12

Werner collects his brother from the airport. He finds the domestic terminal dispiriting. It's provincial, and yet having to collect his brother from the airport speaks to the fact that Marius has grown up, in a way that he himself has failed to do. It's been two years since he's seen Marius. For a moment he looks straight past him. He expects his brother to look more like him; how does this trim young man fit into the equation of his family? He does not know much about his brother's life. He shares a house in Cape Town with a woman they have not met, but he insists they are only friends. His mother does not approve of the arrangement. Since when, she asked, do men and women share houses?

They hug half-heartedly and Werner offers to carry his small bag, but Marius declines. When they get into the car and drive out of the airport, Marius finally says, 'It happened so quickly. Ma didn't say he was so ill.'

'It was a surprise,' Werner says.

'I feel guilty.'

'Why?'

'I didn't make an effort to see him.'

Werner shrugs. The roads are free of traffic and they are soon on the highway to Pretoria.

'I know this might not be the best time,' Marius says, 'but you should know that I'm moving to Australia.'

'When?'

'In about three months. I just got my visa.'

Werner nods. 'That's great,' he says.

'Thanks.'

Werner swallows. 'Where in Australia?'

'Melbourne,' he says. 'I have some friends out there. Once I'm settled, you and Ma should come and visit.'

'Sure. That would be nice.'

'I don't know what the situation is with Pa's money – but don't worry too much about me. Let's just do what we need to for Ma.'

This is why Werner dislikes his brother. He feigns indifference to money, but does not explicitly rule himself out of the inheritance. He takes the high ground, but is not averse to the cash bonus of death. Werner has a meeting with the lawyer on Monday, after the funeral. He will not invite his brother along. His mother is vulnerable. He is certain, faced with her better-looking younger son, that she will renege on their agreement. As for Marius's plans to move to Australia, she will be devastated.

'Perhaps,' Werner says, 'you can wait a while before telling Ma about Australia.' Marius nods.

Werner has never given Australia much thought. People say it is like South Africa, without the difficult politics and the crime. It is, he thinks, so like his brother to choose such an unimaginative destination. Pretoria to Cape Town. Cape Town to Australia. Beaches, nice weather. *A good lifestyle*. As if that is what life is about. As if that is all that matters. Marry a word of absolute profundity – *life!* – to one that designates nothing so much as a hollowing-out, and you get Marius. Lifestyle. That was his brother, a pretty little zombie, cavorting blindly to death. Werner looked at him and thought: I am a murderer. If I am caught, that will blemish your lifestyle.

In the flat they realise they haven't given any thought to the sleeping arrangements. Marius takes a look at his father's bedroom. 'I'm not sleeping in that hospital bed. I'll sleep in the lounge.'

'Don't be ridiculous,' Petronella says. 'You can share Werner's bed. You're *brothers*.'

Marius puts his suitcase in Werner's room and says, 'Don't worry. I'm going to sleep on the settee. I think we're a little old to be sharing a bed.'

Werner shrugs.

In the evening they go out to their local steakhouse. It's part of a Native American-themed chain of restaurants that Werner usually avoids because the waiters are university students. He would find it embarrassing to be served by someone whose financial distress he knows the details of. Marius talks endlessly about Cape Town, about his friends and the house he shares in Fish Hoek. The Internet, he assures them, is the next big thing. Eventually he will abandon print design altogether and focus on websites. Petronella's vague understanding of the Internet does not extend much beyond the idea that it has something to do with computers. All three of them have time off work. They are having a family reunion of sorts. Death brings about unexpected holidays. An expensive midweek meal is also an extravagance that neither Werner nor his mother would normally indulge in. Petronella seems to enjoy the distraction of Marius's talking, so Werner says little. They order a second bottle of wine. When Petronella is a little tipsy, she brings up the question of the eulogy and starts crying.

'Werner was always better with words,' Marius says. The insufferable brat is even too lazy to write a eulogy.

'Let's leave it to the minister, Ma,' Werner says. 'I think it's better that way.'

At the flat, Marius unpacks his suitcase. He wants to hang up his suit so that it's not too creased for the funeral. Werner sits on the bed and watches his brother. He takes off his jeans and T-shirt and stands around in his underwear. Marius has a good body. When he goes down on his haunches to remove the suit, the tendons in his thigh pull tight against his brown skin. Werner thinks he is doing this on purpose. All day he has been flaunting: Australia, the Internet, his body. There is a fussiness to his brother that he finds distasteful. The white Calvin Klein underwear against his sunbed tan, his hair product, his sunglasses, his too-tight T-shirts, the way he folds his jeans, just so. He is an exemplary exemplar of what dull, middle-class, white South Africa aspires to. He will do well in Australia. But he will not see a cent of his father's money. Marius opens the cupboard and pushes the suits aside. He steps back and looks at Werner.

'You still have your Jesus picture,' he says. Werner nods. 'You're not into art any more?' he asks.

'No,' Werner says lamely. 'I still am.'

'Oh,' his brother says. He slips on a pair of loose tracksuit bottoms, but not a shirt. He lights a cigarette. Werner reaches for an ashtray and lights a cigarette too.

'When are you going back to Cape Town?' he asks.

'I can change my flight. When are we going to sort out all the paperwork?'

Werner shrugs. 'I wouldn't wait. I'll call you if there's anything that needs sorting.'

'Ma says you're going to see the lawyer on Monday.'

'Ja.'

'Okay, I'll come with you.'

'There's no money, Marius,' he snaps.

Marius looks at his brother and assesses him coolly. He takes a drag of the cigarette and then stretches to reveal his chest, his flat stomach. He blows out the smoke. The gesture is hostile. 'Sure,' he says. 'Let's see on Monday.'

Why, Werner thinks, should I stop now? My giant meaty hands around that fine neck of his; the rapture in crushing and crushing until he falls, limp and lifeless, on the floor, spent.

The funeral is not well attended. Werner wonders whether the minister is going to ask everyone to move forward, the way a professor might do in a poorly attended lecture. How lucky he has been. There was no talk of an autopsy. He did not even need to insist that his father be cremated. His mother said it was what Hendrik would have preferred. It is the first time he really reflects on his situation, upon the fact that he has, literally, got away with murder. The hyperbole of the phrase has diminished it to the point where it is now used in reference to minor transgressions; the bad behaviour of unruly children. *You're letting him get away with murder.* Does the diminishment of the phrase suggest that for the average person murder is so unimaginable, so far outside their frame of reference, that it becomes sufficiently innocuous to use in the context of a child's behaviour? A mother would not say, 'You're letting him get away with rape.' Perhaps everyone has been too close, in mind or near or actual experience, as victim or perpetrator, to use *that* word in innocence.

There are twenty thousand murders in South Africa every year and, he thinks, there may well be more, for his own contribution will go unrecognised, uncounted. Surely he must pass murderers on the street from time to time, or in the shopping mall or even in church. He glances around. Having snuffed a life, is there a change – psychological, psychic, physiological – that allow murderers to recognise one another in the streets? Will they hold your gaze a moment too long?

Marius has put his arm around his mother. She is crying quietly. The pangs of guilt Werner feels are intermittent, but sharper than he expected. There are times when the momentousness of what he has done makes him dizzy and he is forced to steady himself by holding onto a wall or else by taking a seat. When people see this, they think it is the force of grief or high blood pressure.

There was a viewing before the service. Werner watched from the back of the church as his mother and Marius approached the coffin. Marius bent over and kissed his father on the forehead. Then the coffin was closed for the last time. The world was becoming impatient to dispose of the body, to be done with the rights and rituals, to move on. At the end of the service they file out of the church, leaving the coffin behind. It will be collected and taken to the crematorium.

The lawyer's office is located in Hatfield above the small shopping centre. It's a small practice that deals with wills, estates, divorces and simple conveyancing. The attorney, in his mid-sixties, sees Werner and Marius into his office. He puts on a pair of glasses and removes a file from his desk drawer. The flat is left to Petronella. In addition Petronella, Marius and Werner will each receive a sum of eleven thousand rand. Werner feels dizzy. Is that all? It is all. But what of the life-insurance policy? The lawyer clears his throat. Did Hendrik not discuss the details of the will? The bulk of the money is to be left to Johann Schoeman and Lerato Dlamini.

Werner and his brother sit in stunned silence. After a while Marius asks if it can be contested. It cannot. In

South African law, the will of the testator is absolute. They sign paperwork and leave. On the way home, Werner is unable to speak. When they relay the news to their mother, she bursts into tears. In Hendrik's room she picks up some of his personal effects and smashes them on the floor. She takes framed photographs off the wall and smashes them too. Werner, in shock, watches. He has a vision of going back to the church and beating his father's corpse with his fists; of flinging open the coffin and punching his dead face, over and over again. How he regrets his father's sweet release from the world. He should have cut his throat and watched him bleed to death. He should have stabbed him in the eye. He should have cut off his dick, shoved it down the man's throat and watched him choke to death. After Petronella's hysterical outburst, they sit in the lounge in silence. They have all been undone by the man's duplicity. The only satisfaction that Werner can take is in his brother's evident shock. In spite of everything he'd said, Marius had come to collect his Melbourne money.

'Who is Lerato Dlamini?' Marius asks.

Petronella gets up and looks out the window. 'A kaffir from Barberton,' she eventually says. She turns, kicks one of the photo frames, goes to her bedroom and slams the door.

Marius turns to Werner. 'And now?' he asks.

Werner shrugs.

'I hate this flat,' Marius says.

'Should we go for a drink?' Werner asks.

They walk down the road to a small bar on the corner. The two brothers sip their pints.

'So you reckon Pa was having an affair?' Werner nods. 'Did you know about it?'

'Of course not. We were just kids.'

'You always knew what was going on.' Werner says nothing. 'How much money was it?'

'Two hundred and fifty thousand.'

'*Jissus!*'

Werner thinks about telling his brother the truth. He would say: *Pa didn't just die. I murdered him.* But now the satisfaction of having killed his father is all he has. He has no wish to share it. Better that Marius carries around this anger towards his father, eating him up on the inside, a fury impossible to avenge. Perhaps they should bury the ashes so that every day the three of them can gather around the small grave – the grave of a mouse, of a rat – and spit on it. Or he could keep the ashes in the bathroom and, every time he takes a dump, he could sprinkle the ashes on his shit. There is no desecration he can think of that will relieve the anger. This he will carry with him for a lifetime.

'Do you think Ma can come and stay with you in Cape Town for a bit?' Werner asks.

'Why?'

'For a break. For a bit of a holiday. To get away from it all.'

Marius looks uncomfortable. 'I suppose. If she wants. You know we only have two rooms. I'll have to ask Yolinda.'

If only, Werner thinks, he could turn his life into an artwork. *Werner Deyer: A study in inertia.* Has he not acted with great force upon the world? How is it possible that, after doing this thing, his life has been returned to him essentially unchanged, except perhaps bleaker, with little hope, no hope, but also guilt. Is he overestimating his act? If his father's life was a half-life, then he has committed only a half-murder. He is a co-murderer. He must share the assignation with a now-dead Barberton bantu, who lacked the courage of his convictions. A much better life was only one solid blow away. Good thing the kaffir died in prison. He had no idea the terrible train of events he'd set in motion, which seemed to culminate here, in this dreary pub.

They finish their beers and, for want of anything else to do, order more. They have no desire to go back to the flat. Werner considers the question of suicide, not in the dramatic sense of returning to the flat and hanging himself from the ceiling this evening (although that would have the added bonus of putting a dampener on Marius's departure, would cause inevitable delays), but in a more general sense of something that he may contemplate seriously in the near, or fairly near, future. Did people commit suicide out of a sense of disappointment and boredom? If he were younger things would be different, but the path to a better life now seemed unimaginably arduous. So much money was needed. So much weight had to be lost. It would all take years. At his last visit to the doctor, when he'd been warned about his weight and his smoking, he did consider that there might be something freeing in being allotted a fixed number of days in which nothing he might do – no decision he might take – could militate against the inexorable progress of some unspecified disease (cancer probably, but his imagination preferred something painless); a joy in no longer measuring every vice in slithers of longevity. There could be succour in the freedom from ambition and desire. If the doctor had said to him, 'Werner, I am sorry to say there is nothing we can do for you any more,' he would at least be granted the ecstasy of the incautious life, not because as the English say, 'You have thrown caution to the wind,' but because caution – that shrill school-ma'am following two paces behind, tut-tutting – had finally lost her cane and he was free to push her into a ditch. But then, in murdering his father, had he not already done so, with little consequence? Well, if patricide was a dud, he could be assured that suicide would, for him at least, be something of ultimate consequence.

They drink until quite late. Guiltily they head back to the flat. Their mother is waiting for them in the lounge. She has decided to go and stay with her friend in Port Elizabeth, she tells them. It has been too long since she's seen the sea and she's entitled to a holiday. She has booked a flight for the next day. Werner and Marius both agree this is a good idea. Marius decides that he will return to Cape Town tomorrow and phones the airline to make the necessary arrangements.

'Will you be all right, Werner?' his mother asks.

'I will be fine,' he says. He will not, he thinks, commit suicide while his mother is away. The thought that people may only be alerted to your death because of a bad smell is too undignified, even for an obese failure like him.

13

Steyn's mother called. He had not visited for some time She wanted to know when he would be back in Pretoria. He couldn't face her. Petronella said, 'If your mother wants to visit, she can always stay with us. We have plenty of room in the house.' He thanked her.

The thought of his mother was tightly bound to what happened on that day. He'd polluted her. He thought about his wife; how she used to be when he visited her after their separation. She thought him very cruel to leave her with no explanation. She said to him, 'I don't mind if you had an affair. Please don't leave me.' All he said in response was, 'I have a new job in Barberton. I'll visit the boys.' And when he did, they would sit in the lounge for an hour, making strained conversation. His wife would wear her best dress. She would have been to the hairdresser. She would have spent the week baking. She would be all smiles and laughs, on the verge of tears. Then he and his sons would go out into the garden and play a game of rugby. His wife would stand and watch, staring at him, his every move, waiting for a sign that this episode was over, that he was going to walk into the house and say, 'Mind if I stay for the day?' or 'Would you like to come and live in Barberton with me?' She loved him so much that she trembled when giving him his coffee. He would take this like a man, like a martyr. He would carry on paying the mortgage while he lived in that shitty rondavel, and his wife would eventually hate him for bringing her so low, for even marrying her in the first place, and all this he would take with equanimity. This is what would make him good. If there was a God, he would say that in the end he did the best he could and he did right by his wife and his sons.

Christmas with his mother was the worst. She looked at him, wounded, wondering how he could do this to her. Not to his wife or his sons, but to her. He knew she was sitting there thinking: Wouldn't it be nice, wouldn't it be lovely, if my son could be here with his wife and my grandsons, and all of us be celebrating Christmas like a normal family? And she was thinking, he was sure: If only there were a reason. Even if it was another woman. Even if his wife had cheated on him. But why had he given everything up, for nothing? Why was he living out in the bundus, in the sticks, in a bare little rondavel? The two of them shuffling around in the flat; it was too much to bear.

It had happened on the 16th of December. Ordinarily he would have not have remembered the date, except for the fact that it was Blood River. When he was growing up in Pretoria he always thought that it was the worst day of the year. The schools had closed for the holidays and everything that might be of interest to a boy was shut. Everyone was reverential. Perhaps it had something to do with the fact that the covenant the Afrikaners had made with God was so recent. God intervened and saved their arses from the kaffirs and they promised – they made a very solemn promise – to honour this day for ever. So when he was a kid, he and his mother would sit in the little flat in Sunnyside and get irritable with one another and fight until his mother got upset and shouted, 'This is a *holy* day – what's wrong with you? Don't you have any respect?'

Steyn walked to the dam. He sat down and remembered: on that day he has the cooler filled with beer and some newspapers and a deckchair. He takes his shirt off and drinks two beers. Then he switches on the radio, covers his face with the newspapers and lies in the afternoon sun. Small beads of sweat gather on his shoulders and trickle like tears into the hair on his chest. It is after two when Werner lifts the newspaper off his face and says, 'Is *oom* sleeping?'

'Just resting my eyelids,' he says.

'*Ja* – that's what my father says too.' Werner sits next to him. 'I'm bored.'

'Go for a swim,' he says to the boy.

'I've just eaten.'

'That's an old wives' tale.'

'Let's go rowing!'

He gets up, finishes his beer and walks with Werner towards the camp's rowing boats. Thirty boats are piled up on the bank; each turned upside down so they don't fill with rain.

'Which one should we take?' he asks.

'The blue one – there, the dark-blue one.'

'No, that one is buggered up. It's got a slow leak. I still need to fix it.'

'What about the green one?'

'*Ja* – that's a good one.'

He pulls the boat towards the dam and tips it over. It hits the ground with a crunch. '*Bliksem*,' he says. The oars lie on the ground. Werner fetches them and throws them in. Steyn pushes the boat into the water and wades in behind it. 'I'll hold the boat – go grab me another beer, quick.' Werner runs to fetch a beer and then wades into the water. 'Hop in,' Steyn says.

Werner sits in the bow as Steyn tries to manoeuvre his bulk into the boat without capsizing it. When he manages to get himself in, he puts his back against the stern and slips his legs under the centre thwart.

'And now?' Steyn asks Werner.

'What?'

He opens his beer and drinks. 'You said you wanted to row. I am just going along for the ride.'

'Okay,' Werner says. He gets up too quickly and nearly tips the boat over.

'Watch it, *lightie*! You'll spill my beer.'

'Sorry, *oom*.' Werner sits down on the bench and plants his feet between his shins. He moves the oars awkwardly into the rowlocks. 'Where to?'

'Wherever you want,' Steyn says, and Werner starts rowing slowly but steadily, while Steyn drapes his arms over the transom, tips his head back and closes his eyes. He sees sunspots through his eyelids. On the banks, black children splash and play in the water and women wash clothes. They wave, and he and the boy wave back. He asks Werner to identify various birds and trees, which he does correctly most of the time. Werner says he thinks he sees a fish eagle. '*Ag* – are you stupid, man? That's a vulture.' At the far end of the dam is a troop of baboons. They are playing in the trees that hang over the water. When one of the larger males spots them, the animal bares its teeth and screams. '*Fok* off!' he shouts and the boy laughs. Steyn crushes the beer can between the ends of his palms and tosses it to the front of the boat.

'I'm tired,' Werner says.

'Well, that's a problem,' Steyn says. 'I'm not rowing.'

'Okay – let me just take a little rest. My shoulders are sore.'

They sit quietly for a few minutes while Werner rolls his shoulders. Steyn looks at the boy through half-closed eyes and thinks that it couldn't do any harm. It is such a small thing and he longs to do it, in all innocence. He sits up and puts his hands, ever so gently, on Werner's shoulders and rubs. He starts talking to break the silence; so that the gesture does not seem too intimate. 'Now – if you want to get really good at rowing, you need to do it every day. You need to row right through the pain and the stiffness . . .' His throat catches on the word, but he clears it and carries on. 'And then, when your shoulders are stiff, you rub on Deep Heat. I used to row for the university – and that's what we always used. Deep Heat.' Beneath his thumbs he can feel Werner's shoulder blades. He longs to take off the boy's shirt and kiss them gently, those two little golden wings, but he dares not, so he cups them in his hand for a moment, as he used to cup the breasts of his wife. His finger brushes the little V of hair on the nape of Werner's neck and he leans forward a little, resisting the urge to bury his nose in it and take in a deep breath of boyhood. Werner tenses under his hands. The boy can feel it, he thinks. He can feel my desire. This is all I will do. I will just give him a back-rub and nothing more, and then this thing will be done. He regrets drinking so much. This boy has awoken something dormant in him that will not, for all he tries, wither and die. Is it, he asks himself, the reason he's taken this job? Look, but don't touch. How long will it be before his eyes betray him? He puts his one hand on Werner's neck and the other on the small of his back. His voice is hoarse.

'When you row, you must keep your back straight as you pull out.' Werner straightens his back, but says nothing. Perhaps, Steyn thinks, if he does it once, he will flush this from his system. It is the tension of never actually having done it. It will lose its allure and, failing that, will give him sufficient to live with – a little bit of sweet sexual nectar, sustaining him in sad little sips to the end of his days, keeping this thing contained, satisfied, before it explodes in an act of unspeakable monstrosity.

He rests his hands on Werner's hips. He can still with-draw and leave the moment with sufficient ambiguity that Werner will only suspect, but not know. Werner's hips, those little bones he can feel through the small roll of fat, are the border between a malformed mind and a malformed life. Steyn's breaths are quick and shallow and he knows he can't speak. Werner shifts slightly in his seat and leans back. Steyn's fingers slip to the front of his hips and touch his bare skin. He can still stop. He can say, 'It's getting late,' and row home. He can be in his rondavel in less than half an hour. His fingers search for the top of the boy's underpants. He runs his middle finger along the elasticated band, from right to left. Then he slips the top of his finger just beneath the band, so that he can feel the boy's flesh. He traces back from left to right. Gently back and forth his finger works its way towards the prick. He brushes over the boy's sparse, newly sprouting pubic thatch. For a moment Steyn stops breathing as he touches it. Werner has an erection. His slips his whole hand into the boy's underpants and cups his balls. Be careful, he tells himself. Be careful with the boy's balls. Werner's scrotum has retracted into his body, the skin tight, thick and wrinkled, like fingers that have been in water. His balls are bigger than those of a child and Steyn can feel a few wispy hairs. He takes the shaft of Werner's dick, gently pulls the fore-skin, strokes him, rests his finger on the head, brushing the small piss-hole with his fingertip. Werner sighs. With pleasure? With his left hand Steyn reaches into his own pants and masturbates. He leans his head against Werner's back. Then, just before he finishes, he takes his hand out of Werner's pants, grabs the boy around his chest, pulls Werner towards him and nuzzles his hair. Werner's shirt rides up, and Steyn can feel the boy's skin stick against his chest; slick with sweat. He tries not to, but he groans as he comes. For a few seconds he sits there, emptied of everything. He pulls away from the child and dips his hand into the water to wash it off. He doesn't want the boy to see this. The disgust and loathing sit in his stomach. 'We need to go home. I'll row.' Werner turns around and sits in the back of the boat. Steyn catches a glimpse of the child's face. He looks surprised and uncertain, but not afraid. He will face Werner as he rows. Steyn wants to tell him to sit on the other side. He wants to say, 'Please, Werner, I cannot look at you right now.' Werner is quiet and thoughtful. As they pass one of the small islands they spot a vulture. Werner says, 'Look, a fish eagle.'

'Yes,' he says.

Werner narrows his eyes and stares at him. 'No, it's not – it's a vulture.'

'You're right – it's a vulture.'

Is it better or worse to have done this thing with a child of intelligence and cunning? There is a giddiness to Werner that makes Steyn uncomfortable; the excitement of a child that has learnt an important secret. What did he expect? Tears? Not from Werner. He did not expect Werner to cry. But he did expect him to be embarrassed. He had hoped that Werner would stare at the bottom of the boat, quiet and embarrassed. He did not expect this cheerful

insouciance. He did not expect Werner's cold and calcu-
lating stare and the slightly crooked smile when he said,
'No, it's not – it's a vulture.' So he of the malformed mind,
and now the freshly malformed life, rows back with this
dangerous boy as quickly as he can. As they approach the
bank, Steyn hops out and pulls the boat onto the sand and
Werner sits, like a princeling, like a lover, not moving to
help. He says nothing. Werner climbs out of the boat and
stretches while Steyn drags it further up the bank, then
flips it over. Looking at the boy, he has a flash of anger.
What has he done, after all? Groped him. That's all. He
has groped a boy, as thousands have done before him and
thousands more will continue to do. And, what's more, he
liked it. The boy was a little complicit, wasn't he? Did
Werner tell him to stop? Did he give any indication that
he didn't want this to happen? Did he not lean back into
his hands, pushing his fingers further, encouraging Steyn,
willing him on?

'Bring me the oars,' he says more sharply than he intends.
Werner looks at him and smiles. He saunters over to where
the oars have been left, picks them up and carries them
over, as Steyn holds the boat up on one side. Werner slides
the oars under the boat and Steyn gently lowers it to the
ground. He slaps the sand off his hands. Both turn to walk
to the deckchair, folded newspapers and cooler box further
down the bank. He packs up his things. Werner stands
and watches.

'Your ma is going to wonder where you are.'

'*Ja*,' Werner says.

Steyn wonders whether he can utter those three ghastly words, those predatory words of the pederast, covering his tracks, hiding his scent. Our. Little. Secret. The words all the more awful for dissembling in their childishness, their childlike-ness, not only the fear of crimes just committed, but also the hope of crimes to come. Should he say he is sorry? He can fall to his knees and say, 'Werner, I am very sorry. What I did was terribly wrong. I swear to you it will never happen again.' But is that not even worse? Is it really necessary to burden the child with his crime? Is it necessary for Werner to share in the guilt? The boy may not appreciate the magnitude of what has happened. The child may well be unaware of the enormity of the transgression. And if Steyn apologises, if he falls to his knees, what Werner suspects will be confirmed. But he needs a sign from Werner – anything – to say he understands. He stands facing the boy, thinking about what to say. He reaches into his pocket and finds a fifty-cent coin. He hands it to the boy and says, 'Thank you.' He hopes that Werner understands. In anticipation of nothing further – thank you. Werner accepts the coin as if he'd been expecting it. He smiles and nods and turns to walk home. Now Steyn thinks, there is nothing to do but wait.

As he walks home he decides not to go straight to his rondavel and cuts through the bush instead. He finds himself in small clearing by the river. He washes his face and his hands. Like a baptism, he thinks. Like a christening. Steyn the kiddy fiddler. Steyn the paedo. Steyn the pervert. He takes off his clothes and scrubs his body. He washes between his legs and his thighs over and over again. Then he sits on the riverbank and cries, not for what he still might lose, but for what he has already lost. He cries because God has turned him into a monster. He cries for being given a life not worth living; a life of perverted, thwarted, terrible desire. He cries for his sons. He cries for his wife. He cries for the poison in his veins, which every boy can smell. And when there is nothing left he walks home, sits on his bed and waits. He listens for the sounds of approaching footsteps. He listens for the knock on the door. He listens for Hendrik. What will he say? Pervert – that's what he'll say. He won't knock. He'll kick open the door and say, 'You fucking pervert.' Then he'll hit Steyn. And if this happens, he will take it. He'll lie there on his bed and take it. He won't hold up his hands to shield himself from the blows. He won't apologise, for that will be craven and cowardly. He will have the only kind of dignity a pervert can have. He will say nothing and do nothing. He will take it like a man. And then Hendrik will either call the police or run him off the camp. Whatever he decides to do, there will be no protest. Above all, Steyn will have dignity. So he waits and waits, but Hendrik never comes and he finally dozes off.

The following morning he packed his things and went to Pretoria. His mother was surprised, but happy to see him. It was late afternoon by the time he arrived. She'd bought tickets for a play at the university theatre. Would he not like to join her? He agreed to go along. He was never one for the theatre, but the performance was passable. During the interval he drank two glasses of wine when his mother went to the bathroom. A woman saw him and made a joke about the play not being that bad. From close up, he could see that she was a few years older. Did he want to go for a drink? He did not care about the disapproving way his mother looked at him when he told her he'd be going out afterwards. He and the woman walked to a bar in Hatfield. She knew a place where the students didn't go. She was in no mood for hostel brats. The place had changed since Steyn lived here. The university had built more skyscrapers. He was taking all this in when the woman asked what he thought about the play. He shrugged.

'I don't know much about the theatre.'

'Neither do I,' she said and laughed.

'Did you have anything to do with it?'

'I directed it.'

'In that case, I liked it very much.'

She laughed a little. She was completing her Masters degree in drama. A sure sign, she said, that she was a failed actress. She had different aspirations now. She wanted to be a theatre director or perhaps a playwright. They sat down in a small bar. He ordered a beer and she ordered a glass of wine. 'There are some famous people in the department. Some of South Africa's greatest actors and actresses. Luminaries.' He nodded. And what did he do?

'I teach.'

'What?'

'Geography.'

They had a few more drinks and made small talk. Eventually she said, 'I hope you understand, I'm not loose. I'm liberated.' Steyn nodded. 'I take it you're the strong, silent type,' she said. Steyn shrugged and she laughed. He downed his beer.

They walked back to her apartment. She shared a flat with another postgrad, but she was away. They opened a bottle of wine. By the time she led him to the bedroom he had to steady himself. 'Sorry,' he said. The sex was satisfactory. At one point she put Steyn's hands on her neck and told him to squeeze, just a little. He shook his head and she blushed. Afterwards Steyn had to sit upright in bed, to prevent the room from spinning. He stared at the buildings in Sunnyside. He could see his mother's block, not far away. Eventually he dozed off. He woke just before dawn with a stiff neck. It was drizzling outside and cool. He got out of bed and started getting dressed. The woman stirred.

'Leaving?'

'I have to.'

'Are you married? I don't care if you are.'

'No.'

'I'm not kinky or anything.' Steyn looked at her, not sure what she was referring to. 'I thought you'd want something different from your *popsie* girlfriend.'

'I don't have a girlfriend.'

'Do you want to see me again?'

'Sure, sure.'

'Just wait a minute – I'll make you some coffee.' She got out of bed and put on a robe. He followed her into the kitchen. She made two mugs of instant coffee. 'Damn – I don't have any milk. I spend all the time at the theatre and never do any shopping.'

'It's fine. I like my coffee black. Thank you.' Steyn thought how it could be pleasant to do this. To make love to a nice woman and then stand around in the kitchen, while it was raining outside, sipping coffee. He liked the anonymity of Pretoria. There were many blocks like this, ten, fifteen storeys high, each with dozens of apartments filled with couples and families, all rousing for the morning in flats that smelt of tinsel.

On a notepad she wrote down her full name and address, her home telephone number, her office at the university and her work number.

'Here,' she said.

'Thank you.' He folded the piece of paper and tucked it into his pocket. 'I have to go.'

She nodded and kissed him on the cheek. It was only a little after six. His mother would soon be awake, but he did not want to go back to her flat. So he walked through Arcadia, along the streets he used to play in as a child. He wondered if Werner had said anything yet. Perhaps Hendrik had phoned his mother's flat. Perhaps the police would come knocking on the door. Here in the street he could be an innocent fugitive. *I'm sorry. I didn't know you were looking for me.*

When he went back to the flat, his mother asked him if he had had a nice evening.

'Very nice, thank you.'

'She seemed like a nice girl.'

'Very nice.'

'Are you going to see her again?'

'No.'

'That's good.'

'Why?'

'You know why.'

'The marriage is over.'

'What did you do?'

'Nothing. I did nothing. I was just not meant to be married to her.'

'I don't understand.'

'There is nothing to understand. But if you want to talk about this, I will leave.'

'Please don't leave. I hardly see you.'

'Then stop it.'

'Are you going to see the boys?'

'At Christmas.'

'You were so beautiful together.'

14

Werner has been granted two weeks' compassionate leave. He makes a discreet enquiry about whether it is transferable. Could it not, perhaps, be tacked on to his annual leave? There is stunned silence on the other end of the phone. 'Never mind,' he says to the woman from HR and puts down the receiver. Two weeks of leave is not what he needs now. After he drops his mother and brother off at the airport, he drives home and opens a bottle of wine. He drinks it quickly and smokes half a packet of cigarettes. It is a relief to be rid of his mother.

He has not thought of Johann in many years. Perhaps he has opened his motorbike shop after all. Would Johann understand that Werner's father has committed a gross injustice by leaving the money to him? Could Werner go to Johann and say, 'My mother and I cared for my father for more than a decade. He has left us destitute. Taking this money is not right.' Destitute; a good old-fashioned word, and to make an appeal on behalf of his mother was good too. 'My father has left me and my mother destitute.'

He falls asleep on the settee at seven in the evening and wakes up at around four the next morning. There is nothing to do, so he takes a sleeping pill and goes back to bed. He wakes up at nine, groggy and bad-tempered. There is a knock at the front door. Still half-asleep and smelling of alcohol, he opens the door. It is Ezenwa, the Nigerian missionary. He is holding a bouquet of flowers. Werner invites the man in. Ezenwa takes in the flat: the overflowing ashtrays, the empty bottle of wine, the dirty plates and dishes. Werner quickly tries to clear the worst of it, stacking the plates and removing the ashtray and bottle of wine to the kitchen. He offers Ezenwa tea or coffee, but he declines. He has put the flowers on the dining-room table.

'My mother has gone on holiday. But she will be very grateful for the flowers. Thank you.' The man nods. Werner considers apologising for the other evening, but decides against it. He has suffered a bereavement, which should wipe the slate clean.

'When my father died,' Ezenwa says, 'I was very sad. When I heard, I thought about my own father. And I have been thinking about you and your mother. I have been thinking about how sad you must be.'

Unexpectedly Werner feels a wave of affection for the man. His words bring a lump to his throat and his eyes start tearing up.

'Let us pray,' the man says. He takes both Werner's hands and they sit side by side on the settee. Together they recite the Lord's Prayer. Werner opens his eyes when they say 'Amen', but the man squeezes his hand and recites the prayer again. They repeat the prayer over and over again like an incantation. It is not the religiosity of the gesture so much as its intimacy that touches Werner.

When the man leaves, he sits on the settee for a long time. He cannot simply wait in the apartment for two weeks and then return to work. He telephones the lawyer and asks for Johann's and Lerato's telephone numbers. The lawyer's tone changes. It would be a mistake, he warns Werner, to do anything rash.

'Johann is a childhood friend,' he assures the man. 'I thought it would be nice to get in touch.'

'Really?'

'We are over the initial shock.'

'And Ms Dlamini?' the lawyer asks.

Werner is not sure what to say. He eventually settles on the explanation that he is curious. The lawyer says that, in his experience, it is best to leave the past alone. No need to cause any further pain to his mother.

'You can understand my point of view,' Werner says. 'My father seems to have had an affair with a black woman in 1976. Maybe she was the love of his life. Maybe he was the love of *her* life.'

'I think you are making a serious mistake. I really think you and your family should just move on.'

'I can't.'

The lawyer relents and gives him Johann's telephone number and address. For the woman he only has an address; it's a farm called Moedswill.

'Does she work on the farm?' Werner asks. The lawyer

does not know. He has sent letters to the farm's owner, in an attempt to reach the woman. If she is uneducated or illiterate, then he will look to the farm owner to make suitable arrangements for the management of the money on her behalf. Of course the woman might have left or be dead. There is still a lot of information that he needs to obtain.

'What if the woman cannot be found?' Werner asks.

'We will find the woman.'

'But if you can't?'

'Well, then the money becomes part of the residue.'

'The money comes to us?'

'Your mother.'

'Do you not have a telephone number for the farm?'

'It is a curious situation,' the lawyer says. 'Most of the farm seems to be leased to another company. I believe the owner lives in the farmhouse. But there is no number.'

There is hope that the woman has simply disappeared. Werner would like to know at what point the law finally grows impatient and turns its beneficent gaze back upon him, the rightful heir, but he does not ask. Blacks, as he well knows, without birth certificates, passports or paperwork of any kind, disappear all the time. It would be less of course than he'd hoped for, but something may yet be salvaged. This small bit of news lifts his spirits. He looks at the address. Johann still lives in the same house. Are they all still there – an infestation of rats? What would Johann make of this windfall? He'd spend the money on some ludicrous scheme: a bar, or motorbikes. His father might as well have flushed the money down the toilet. Perhaps he could appeal to Johann's sense of honour; perhaps he could guilt him into fifty grand or so. *I got nothing, Johann. My mother and I got nothing.* He dials Johann's number. A woman answers. She is young, sweet-sounding. He can't speak and puts down the receiver. On the fridge his mother has left the contact details of the friend in Port Elizabeth. He calls his mother. He too has decided to take a holiday. Where? Durban, he lies.

As he drives east towards Mozambique, the landscape becomes greener and lusher. He stops in Emalahleni for breakfast and then again for tea in Machadorp. Free of Pretoria and the flat and his life, his mood improves as he heads towards Barberton. It is extraordinary, he thinks, that he has not been back. But then what was there in Barberton?

When he arrives he experiences the strange intersection of the familiar and the unfamiliar. He parks the car in the main street and finds a small tourist office. He picks up a brochure that lists local hotels and bed and breakfasts. The location of each has been marked on a map. There is a small family hotel near the Lomati dam, within the nature reserve. Studying the map, he sees that it is within walking distance of the camp, which itself has been renamed Mpumalanga Eco Camp. He calls the hotel to check if they have any vacancies and books a room. When the receptionist asks how long for, he hesitates. Would it be extravagant to stay for a week? A week, he tells her.

His hotel room is basic. The furniture is raw pine, but the bed is comfortable and there is the added benefit of a small television. He unpacks his clothes and pushes the suitcase under the bed. And now? It is late afternoon. He has not formulated a plan as such, but he has come here to do things – to get things done. At the back of the hotel, with views of the dam, is a bar and restaurant. He sits down outside, orders a pint and smokes a cigarette. There are only a few guests staying in the hotel. A family with two children, an elderly couple, two women in their late fifties and a few young people that Werner takes to be foreign backpackers. The family, he thinks, are from Germany. They are sitting too far away and talking too quietly to be sure. The view is good, but not magnificent. Can that really be the dam? His dam? It looks smaller, muddier than he remembers. That is the story of his life. Everything is smaller, muddier than it should be. He finishes his beer and then walks towards the dam. He turns round to get his bearings. In the distance he can see a cluster of buildings that must now be the Eco Camp. The receptionist told him that it's a 'private place for rich kids'.

Even though it is now late afternoon, it is still hot and the high-pitched hum of the bushveld is loud and insistent. He swats away a cloud of gnats. The dam is further than it looks and several times he stops to catch his breath and mop his forehead. As he approaches the water he sees a boy, fourteen perhaps, standing on the bank. Werner sits down on an old tree stump and starts undoing his shoelaces. After he has taken one shoe off, he sits up, to catch his breath. The boy, who has not seen him, kicks off his flip-flops and with the insouciance of youth, slips out of his shorts, shirt and underwear to reveal his small hips and firm young arse. Werner blushes. He has intruded on a private moment. He feels like a thirty-three-year-old man who has snuck into a teenager's bedroom to watch him change. Still, he cannot stop staring. The boy puts on a swimming costume and wades into the water. Werner bends down to remove his other shoe; this the protocol he has adopted of a fat man on holiday. It is permissible to remove your shoes, roll your trousers up to mid-calf and stand in the shallows. It would be unacceptable to expose any more. Once the boy has swum some distance out, Werner gets up and walks towards the water, leaving his shoes and socks behind. Here at the dam, where so much happened, he is overcome. Can he feel a panic attack coming on? No, not that, but the urge to cry. Ridiculous! He bends over and splashes his face with water. Did he ever look that beautiful to Steyn? Did he ever make Steyn want to weep, as this boy does him? He cannot imagine it. They were together three times. Together. A strange word for what transpired, but that is how he thinks of it. And after that, Steyn chose his brother instead. Perhaps his brother made Steyn want to weep. But people do not love Werner. He is not beautiful.

In the evening he has dinner outside. It is a little cool but pleasant. The family sit a few tables away. They are later joined by the boy he'd seen swimming. He is transformed into a sullen teenager, wearing baggy jeans, a sweater and a baseball cap. His mother says something to him and the boy shrugs. They are not German. They are Scandinavian. Danes? Swedes? He cannot tell. The father speaks to him and the boy removes his baseball cap. He brushes the long blond fringe out of his eyes and tucks some of his hair behind his ears.

It is unseemly to stare at a teenager. Werner angles his head so that anyone would think he's looking at the views. Nobody here knows he's a failure. What would they think about a fat man holidaying alone in Barberton? He couldn't be a businessman, not in this hotel. A writer perhaps? Or an artist? He settles for being a writer. Should the opportunity arise to talk to the boy's parents, he will say he is a writer. And if they ask about his books he will make something up. Being Swedes or Danes, they are unlikely to know better. Or would they? The problem with the Scandinavians is that they are so cultured. Those two stern-looking adults and their beautiful offspring probably have a lively interest in post-colonial literature; would want to discuss Coetzee and Gordimer and Lessing. He imagines having dinner with the family. He could tell them how he grew up not far from here and how those early years still exert a significant force on his work. In what way? they would ask. Oh, you know, the politics, but also the land. There is something, he would say, about this place that is unforgiving. The adults would nod solemnly. And afterwards he would overhear them say to their son: *You are lucky to have met a writer.*

He thinks these things while he drinks and waits for his food to arrive.

The family finish their dinner quickly and head back into the hotel. Werner realises he is the last remaining diner. It is not late, but it is uncomfortable to have staff waiting around, even if they are trying to be discreet. He would like to sit here and stare at the landscape and continue drinking, but instead signs the bill and heads back to his room.

At sunrise Werner is awake. He looks at his watch. Five-thirty. When did he become this old man who couldn't sleep? It's cool outside. He puts on a jacket and starts walking towards the dam. Once he passes into the thick bush, he takes one of the footpaths that veer left towards the camp. Like the town itself, the bush feels familiar, but he can't be sure it's not just his imagination. Did he, as a child, ever come this far down? At thirteen, Werner felt he knew every square inch of this area and he thought it vast. But children are like that. Perhaps he never strayed more than a few hundred metres from the family home.

The gentle slope gradually becomes steeper. The growth is now so thick that he doesn't know exactly where he is. It's humid, but the clean smell of the bush is invigorating. Eventually he reaches the top of the hill and the path slopes downwards. In a small clearing is a burnt patch of ground, a few charred logs, empty cans of beer and crisp packets. Kids from the camp, he thinks, sneaking out. There are two footpaths that lead from the clearing: one heads left directly towards the camp; the other, deeper into the bush, keeps close to the banks of the dam. He chooses the latter. He's not sure exactly what he's looking for, but he wants to find something positively identifiable. He wants to be able to stand somewhere and say, 'Yes, I was here twenty years ago. I sat on this spot,' or 'I climbed this tree.'

He sees a rough piece of timber, now almost completely overgrown. Thoroughly urbanised, possibly a little effete, but certainly fastidious, he regards the prospect of leaving the path and cutting his way through the thick, wet undergrowth with distaste. Snakes and *goggas*, he thinks. The piece of timber is covered in thick vine. It is the remains of the old obstacle course. Lucky, he thinks, that he caught sight of that piece of timber. In another month it would be invisible. Should he not mark it in some way? Is the world ready to swallow him up? He tears away at the vine. It's tough and he cuts himself. For half an hour he works to clear the spot, exposing the last rotting beams, to buy himself – this memorial – another two or three years. If he wanted to, he could come back in a year and clear it again. It was his father that built the obstacle course. Or at least it was his father who oversaw the construction. It is the last thing left in the world of the man, unless he counts himself. But he does not consider himself a product of his father. Tired and sweaty, he sits down on one of the logs. Ridiculous! Trying to wrestle his childhood from the undergrowth. He remembers the day he came to look for the ants in the blood. The memory gives him the chills; the strange things that children do. His hands and shirt are dirty and he has a few cuts that are bleeding.

He walks back to the hotel, has a quick shower, changes his clothes and has breakfast. From the buffet table he helps himself to a small carton of orange juice, a few apples and a banana. He decides also to borrow one of the hotel's walking sticks. It makes him look more writerly, he thinks, should he encounter the Scandinavians. He sets off in the same direction as he did earlier in the morning. When he reaches the clearing he takes the path that veers left towards the camp. He knows this path. There are certain trees, even, that he recognises. As he reaches the camp he sees that the path now leads to a gate in a fence. So this is what it has come to. Even here in Barberton: fences. He presses his face against the gate and peers in. There is not much he recognises. The dormitories have been rebuilt. The accommodation looks more like luxury villas. The long-drop toilets have been replaced, and in the centre of the camp is a large thatch-covered *lapa*, the likes of which one usually sees in game reserves. From here he cannot see the house. Short of asking someone to let him in, there is no way he could. No matter. He has no desire to see the house. The camp, unlike the forgotten obstacle course, leaves him cold. Perhaps because it has been rebuilt rather than just forgotten. It's not forlorn. But also the obstacle course was where he and Johann would while away hours with their *kak-praat*, as Johann said. Shit-talk. He always thought of it as Johann's place: both good and bad.

The path breaks into the open *veld* as he heads towards

the dam. From here already he can see that the old boats are no more. Where they used to be kept is a large boat-house, built out of breezeblocks. Two black men are cleaning new fibreglass canoes with numbers painted on the side. The canoes, he notices, seat just one. He raises his hand and waves and the men wave back. So, the boats too are gone. His childhood is being wiped away. He should never have cleared the obstacle course. It is still early in the morning and he had planned to drive to Johann's house, but looking around, he thinks he knows how to walk there. He isn't up to speaking to Johann today, but it would be good to see the house. Seeing the house would give him a sense of Johann's circumstances.

He finishes his cigarette, stamps it out underfoot and takes a few sips of the orange juice. After ten minutes of walking he begins to think he's made a mistake. It's clear the path is hardly used and it feels unfamiliar. Surely he should have been there already? Every few steps he thinks he should turn around, but then something up ahead catches his eye and he is drawn deeper into the bush. His fear is not of getting lost; it's of having a heart attack too far away from where anyone could help him. And even if someone did find him, what could they possibly do? What would his mother say? '*Ag*, it was so sad. They basically had to get the whole township of bantus to come and carry him. He was so big, you know? Those poor bantus, I could see the strain on their faces.' His last great indignity – being hauled out of the bush by a pack of blacks.

He takes a handkerchief out of his pocket and mops

his forehead. He's talking himself into a panic. He takes a few deep breaths and walks more slowly because he can feel his heart racing. Up ahead is a large acacia tree. If he doesn't recognise anything there, he will go back. But even before he reaches the tree he does recognise something. It's the dusty clearing, where years ago he sat and watched as Johann played soccer with the local black kids. What was it about that day that he remembers? A confession or intimacy of some kind. Something about Johann's mother. There are more houses dotted around the area. The newer ones are made from unplastered breezeblocks with corrugated-iron roofs. Government housing. Between the houses are a few communal taps. Woman are hanging clothes on washing lines strung up between the houses and children are running around and playing in the dust. A radio standing on a window sill is blaring, and two little girls, one about six and the other no older than four, are practising their dance moves and then collapsing into fits of giggles. Some adults have gathered around them and are clapping, charmed by the dancing child, who is being instructed by her sister. He is struck by the way in which these hamlets erupt out of the bush, colourful outbreaks of semi-squalor, usually a fifteen-minute walk from a pool of white wealth.

He carries on walking. The bush creates a canopy over the path, which has recently been cleared. As the path veers left, he can see Johann's house. For the most part it is unchanged. Rusted pieces of cars and motorbikes are still scattered around the front garden, but they are sunken and overgrown. A woman with a washing basket emerges from the front door, and Werner, feeling exposed, steps back into the bush. He watches as she hangs up the clothes. Someone calls to her from the house and she answers, 'Look under the sink!'

'What?' a man inside shouts.

'The sink!' she shouts back.

When the man comes out onto the *stoep*, Werner knows, without question, it is Johann. Still the same dark skin, and when he laughs there is a boyishness that breaks through the white kaffir face. His shirt is unbuttoned to reveal the leather straps drawn taut across his muscled brown torso, holding in place the prosthetic, terminating in the metal hook that he has never seen. The woman walks towards Johann and embraces him. He takes care to keep the hook away from her and kisses her gently on the forehead. They walk back into the house. For Johann the cripple, Johann the amputee, he feels such tenderness. He could walk over now, knock on the front door and say, 'Johann? It's Werner. Do you recognise me?' And Johann, what would he do? Embrace him, or put the hook through his face?

15

Maria and Lerato were standing in the kitchen. Hendrik's first instinct was to take Maria aside and explain that Lerato could not work in the house. But then it occurred to him that Maria would not have made this decision. She would not want another maid in the house. This must have been Petronella. He wondered how long his wife had known about Lerato and what she made of it. He did not know what to make of it himself.

'Good morning.' The woman turned and greeted him. He acted as if he expected to find the young girl in his kitchen. Maria poured Hendrik a cup of coffee while Lerato stirred the porridge.

'Breakfast is nearly ready, *baas*,' Maria said.

'No hurry.'

Hendrik stared at his coffee and waited for his wife. She came into the kitchen as she did every morning, hair wet from her shower, wearing her nightgown. Maria poured her a cup of coffee and Petronella sat at the table with her husband. She looked at him and smiled. Cunning little bitch, he thought. Maria put two bowls of steaming porridge in front of the pair.

'*Baas, missies.*'

'Thank you, Maria,' Petronella said.

Hendrik heaped two large teaspoons of sugar and half a cup of milk into his porridge. He would wait, he decided, for his wife to say something. Soon the boys would come into the kitchen. Introductions would follow.

'No sugar, Nellie?' he asked.

'No, thanks. I'm on a diet. But actually I can have a banana with my porridge.' She turned in her chair to face Lerato. '*Lettie*, won't you do me a favour and pass me a banana, please.' Hendrik looked at her sharply. She looked back at him and smiled. 'It's not quite the same as sugar,' she said as she took the banana from Lerato. 'But it does add a little sweetness.' She peeled the banana and sliced it into the porridge. When the boys came into the kitchen, Petronella got up and said, 'Boys – this is Lettie. She's going to be helping Maria out in the kitchen and learning about things here. So if Maria goes on holiday, then Lettie will take care of us. Lettie, these are my boys, Werner and Marius.'

'*Kleinbaas, kleinbaas,*' she said to each of the boys.

'Hello, Lettie,' they both said.

'Boys, you must eat quickly. Petrus will be here any minute. I'm going to go and get changed. Maria, will you make sure they take their lunch?'

Hendrik followed her into the bedroom and closed the door. 'What are you doing?' he said quietly.

The pretence of the past few minutes gave way to

Petronella's anger. 'What am *I* doing? When did you go to Moedswill? Why didn't you tell me?'

'Ssshhh. She'll hear us.'

'I don't care! When did you go?'

'A few weeks ago.'

Petronella sat on the bed and lit a cigarette. Hendrik had noticed that his wife no longer restricted herself to a single cigarette in the morning. Lately she'd been smoking everywhere in the house, and a lot too. She sucked hard on the cigarette, and it was ugly.

'You mustn't call her Lettie,' he said.

'Why not? It's her name, isn't it?'

'No, her name is Lerato.'

'That's her bantu name. When she worked in their house, they called her Lettie. And now she's working in my house, so I will call her Lettie.'

'Be fair to the girl,' Hendrik said.

'What do you mean? Do you think because you change her name she's going to forget? No problem, huh. We change your name, give you a new job – good as new.' Petronella was talking louder again.

'Keep your voice down.'

She tilted her head back and blew out a big breath of smoke. 'What do you want with this girl?'

'She's family of Maria.'

'Family?'

'Yes.'

'She doesn't want her here. Did you see Maria's face this morning?'

'Not in the house. She doesn't want Lerato in the house – she thinks she's being replaced.'

'Maybe she is. Who says she will work for us for ever?'

'Don't be stupid, Nellie.'

'I want to know what you want with this girl. I want to know why you drove to Moedswill to go and find her.'

'I told you. I was just trying to help.'

Petronella looked at her husband. She'd waited over a month since finding Lerato. Bringing the girl into the house was her one dramatic flourish, but she had learnt nothing.

'She gives me the *horries*.'

'Have you spoken to her?'

'What am I supposed to say? And I don't think you should talk to her, either. What are we going to say when people find out? What are we going to say when people start asking questions?'

'The truth,' he snapped. 'That she's Maria's family.'

'Whatever you say, Hendrik. You're in charge.' She said this distantly, while looking out of the window.

It seemed to him ludicrously swift, the short space of time in which he and his wife had become adversaries. In the past month they had constantly been squabbling about Werner. He was beginning to agree with his wife that there was something wrong with their son. It was not adolescent rebellion. There was something unsettlingly hostile in Werner's attitude towards them. Perhaps Werner was smoking *dagga*. There was enough of it around. Half his staff smoked it. Its sweet scent would waft down from the staff huts in the evenings, reminding him of his university days, when he and his friends gathered in flats. If any of his bantus had given Werner *dagga*, he would thrash the person to within an inch of his life and then hand him over to the police. He had hoped Steyn might know something. The boy was very fond of Steyn. Natural, of course. Steyn was younger, more exciting. To Werner, Steyn must have seemed like an older brother. But when he asked Steyn, the man looked away, embarrassed. Hendrik understood. It was awkward to discuss these things. But he pushed the issue anyway. Had Steyn noticed anything odd in Werner's behaviour recently? He had not. Well, Hendrik continued, for there was no purpose in hiding anything now, Werner's behaviour was peculiar. He was angry and distant. He was cruel to his younger brother. Steyn nodded. Wasn't it, the man wanted to know, just teenage stuff? Werner was thirteen. Yes, Hendrik conceded. It was possible, but Petronella thought it might have something to do with Johann. She thought he was a bad influence. Didn't Steyn think that perhaps the boys were smoking *dagga*? Steyn doubted it. It pained Hendrik to ask. Could he make an effort with the boy? He would appreciate it if Steyn could talk to him; find out what was going on. Steyn swallowed hard and nodded in a non-committal way. Then he said something about not being very good in these situations. It annoyed Hendrik that Steyn was so evasive. Werner worshipped him. He cut Steyn a great deal of slack. He rarely complained about the drinking, even though it had got steadily worse since the beginning of the year. Hendrik's recollection of the conversation with Steyn was interrupted when Petronella said, 'What's going on with this family?'

'Nothing is *going on* with this family.' The thing to do – the sensible thing to do – was to go and sit beside her on the bed, put his arms around her and say everything was going to be okay. But he was still angry about the ambush in the kitchen. 'If you want, I will take Lerato back.'

'No. The brother is there now. It will just cause a fuss. Leave it.'

Werner carried a Checkers bag filled with coloured light bulbs. He'd found them in one of the storage sheds. It was not long now before the schools would close for the holidays. He and Johann had decided to go camping. They'd hike deep into the bush and set up camp for the week. They'd take tinned food and maybe some *boerewors* too. In the afternoons they'd fish or play cards. It would be a very good holiday, if his mother allowed it. He held the bag of light bulbs away from his body so that they didn't bang his legs. He should have wrapped them in newspaper, but it was too late now. He'd just walk carefully all the way to Johann's house. He used one of the paths that ran through the bushveld. It was a longer route and overgrown, but his mother was less likely to spot him. As he passed the area where the rowing boats were stored, he saw Steyn and Marius dragging the green boat into the water. He considered going down to join them, but changed his mind. He looked at his watch. They'd be an hour at least. He picked up his bag and sprinted to Johann's house. The bag bashed against his body and he heard the tinkle of a few bulbs, but he didn't care. *Tannie* Sara and Charlize where sitting on the *stoep*.

'Hello, Werner,' *Tannie* Sara said.

'Hello, *tannie*; hello, Charlize.'

'Johann is with André at the bike-shop,' Charlize said.

'That's okay. I was looking for you.'

'For me?' she said, jumping up and running towards Werner.

'*Ja* – I brought you these,' he said, holding up the bag. He leant towards her and whispered, 'For the garden.' She peered into the bag.

'*Donner!*' Werner laughed. 'They're beautiful.'

'*Ja* – they're magic,' Werner said.

'I know. The blue ones are special. Will you help me hang them up?'

Werner looked at his watch. 'Sorry, Charlize, I have to go. I'll help you next time. Tell Johann I said hi.'

'What's in the bag?' *Tannie* Sara called from the *stoep*.

'Nothing, Ma – just some stuff to play with.'

'Can I play too?' she asked.

'I have to go, *tannie*,' Werner said. 'Bye, Charlize.'

He sprinted back to hide in the bush by the boats. Half an hour later he could see Steyn and his brother in the distance. Steyn was rowing and Marius was leaning over the side of the boat, trailing his fingers in the water. Werner moved closer to the dam. There was a small spot where he could hide in the dense bush, but still be close enough to the boats to overhear the conversation. Steyn and Marius hopped out of the boat and dragged it onto the bank. Marius said something about baboons and Steyn laughed.

'I've never heard that before,' he said. 'What's your brother up to?' Steyn asked. 'He hasn't been around much.'

It was a very good idea, Werner thought, to hide here. Marius just shrugged.

'Don't you two play together any more?' Steyn asked.

'He's always with Johann,' Marius said.

Steyn nodded and dragged the boat into position and flipped it over. Marius tucked the oars underneath it. They started walking back towards the camp. Werner realised the error he'd made. He'd expected them to stay longer. He wanted to follow them, but the undergrowth he was hiding in was so dense that if he tried to cut through it, they'd be sure to hear him. He'd have to wait until they were further away. Cursing under his breath, he sat and waited. By the time the pair reached the car-track he decided it was safe. He darted through the bush and found the footpath. As quietly as he could manage he ran along the path, looking sideways towards the car-track until at last he could see the two of them strolling towards the camp. He hid behind another clump of bushes. If Steyn was walking back to the house, he'd have to wait for another time. But Steyn turned down one of the footpaths and

Marius kept walking towards the camp. Werner wo[
have to hurry if he was going to catch his brother bef
he reached open ground. He cut through the bush to
car-track and ran after him. Marius heard someth
behind him and turned. Werner grabbed him and put
hand over his brother's mouth and dragged him off
path. Marius tried to bite Werner's hand, but he hel
firmly over his brother's jaw. He started kicking and s
ting and tearing at Werner with his nails. Werner th
him on the ground.

'*Oom* Steyn!' he shouted. 'Help me – *Oom* Steyn.'

'Shut up!' Werner said. He sat on Marius, holdin[
brother's hands on either side of his head.

'Please, Werner, it's sore. There's a rock underneatl
back.'

Werner released one of Marius's hands. 'Get the
he said.

Marius arched his back and brushed away some pe
'What are you doing, Werner? I'm going to tell Ma

With his free hand Marius tried to scratch We
face, but Werner was too quick. He grabbed his bro
hand and held it to the ground. Then, for good me
he put his knees on his brother's thighs and pinned
to the ground with all his weight. Marius scream
pain. Werner stopped because Marius was making so
noise, and put his hand over his brother's face.
covered in snot and tears. 'That will teach you!' h
Marius was still struggling to free himself. 'Stop it!
sit still, I won't hurt you.' He took his hand off his b[

face. Marius was whimpering quietly now. 'Where's your money?'

'What money?'

'Don't lie to me. Where's the money?'

'I don't have any money.'

'Okay, fine.'

Werner thought for a moment. He needed both his hands and legs to pin his brother down. He could lean his forearm over Marius's throat, but it would be difficult to control the force and he'd probably choke him. He decided instead to hold his brother's throat in his hand. If Marius struggled too much, he'd squeeze. He shifted his weight onto Marius's stomach so that he could reach his pockets. With his legs freed, his brother started kicking. Werner squeezed Marius's neck and the boy stopped struggling. He slipped his hand into Marius's left pocket and pulled out a stick of gum. He removed the wrapper with his one hand and stuck it in his mouth.

'My gum!' rasped Marius.

'I'm sorry – what did you say?' said Werner as he tightened his grip. Marius choked again. Werner swopped hands and held his brother's throat with his left hand. It wasn't quite as strong as his right, so he'd need to be quick, although by now Marius was less inclined to do anything rash. Werner thrust his right hand into the other pocket. There was nothing there.

'Where's the money?' By now Marius had become hysterical and was sobbing. 'You're such a baby. You should meet Johann's sister. She's seven and she'd fuck you up.'

Werner was about to let his brother go when he saw a glint in the undergrowth. The money must have fallen out during the struggle, but it was too far to reach. Werner clambered off his brother and grabbed the fifty-cent coin from the ground. Marius tried to run away, but Werner grabbed the back of his shorts and pulled him to the ground. He felt invincible. He didn't know whether this new-found strength was just the adrenalin coursing through his arteries or some miraculous part of adolescence. He felt as if he could pick his brother up by the scruff of his neck and toss him over the trees, over the bushveld into the dam. Werner held the coin between thumb and forefinger. 'Where did you get this?'

'It's not mine,' Marius said between sobs. 'It must have been lying there.'

'Rubbish! The bantu kids would have found it. You got this from Steyn.' Marius said nothing. 'Did you like it? Huh?' Marius shrugged and started crying again. 'I bet you liked it.'

'It's my money,' Marius shouted. '*Oom* Steyn gave it to me.'

'*Ja*, I know he did.'

'You're the one who's been stealing my money! I thought it was Maria.'

'Stealing? No, not stealing. You're paying me to keep your secret. You're going to give me all the money Steyn gives you. Okay? Because if you don't, I'll tell Ma and Pa what you two do in that boat.'

'You've done it too!'

He slapped his brother. 'No I haven't!'

Marius started crying loudly again. 'Then how did you know?' he shouted between sobs.

'I've seen you. You little pervert.' Werner pinned him to the ground again and brought his face close to his brother's, so close that he barely had to whisper. 'I'm watching you, Marius. If Steyn gives you anything, you give it straight to me. I don't care if it's one cent or ten rand.' When he let go of his brother he expected him to run away, but Marius just lay on the ground and cried. 'Grow up,' Werner said and kicked him in the ribs. He looked for the path that Steyn had gone down. It wasn't one he often used, but he knew it led to the small clearing by the river.

By the time he got there Steyn was standing naked in the river, washing himself. His clothes were left on a heap by the bank. The water came midway up Steyn's thighs. He splashed his legs and the top of his stomach. The cold water made his body taut. He looks like Jesus, Werner thought. He looks like my Jesus. He stared at the prominent collarbone that jutted out beneath Steyn's skin, and traced his fingers along the surface of his own, down to his sternum, and let his fingers rest in the middle of his chest.

The sounds of the bush became louder, as did the lapping of the water on the bank. Werner closed his eyes. Perhaps he had been too hard on his brother. Marius hated him. He didn't mean to hurt him. The sounds around him became more urgent. He sighed. He wanted to run towards Steyn and talk to him. He could pretend he'd just walked down to the river. Steyn need not know that he was spying. He closed his eyes and leant against a rock. *Stop being a baby. Stop being a baby. Calm down. Calm down. Calm down.* He sat like this for a few minutes. He hoped Steyn wouldn't leave before he calmed down. Then he heard the shout. It was very loud and angry. It seemed as if the whole of the bushveld was screaming: 'Werner!'

Steyn slipped on his underpants even though he was still wet. He was in no mood to be caught naked, but he would have to sit in the remaining sun to dry off. He reached into his pocket for his cigarettes and lit one. He was ashamed it had happened again with Marius. The third time with Werner, the boy came in his hand and he got scared. He was fucking the boy up. The boy kept on apologising, but Steyn didn't know what to say. Then Werner kept on coming round to the rondavel. He thought about taking the boy rowing and not doing anything, just to show that it was over – that everything could go back to the way it was – but he didn't trust himself. Perhaps it was just the money. Werner was happy to take the money. He always seemed to have a fifty-cent coin in his pocket now.

When Hendrik came to ask him about Werner, Steyn's stomach lurched. What was it he said? *Werner is extremely fond of you. Werner is very close to you. Do you think those two are smoking* dagga? He spoke in that scandalised way that only people like Hendrik, who had never taken anything in their lives, could. That was the trouble with Hendrik. He was one of those people you couldn't relate to, because you could just tell there wasn't much going on. He was one more *Christen-Boer* – *vir volk en fokken vaderland* – for nation and fucking fatherland – utterly demon-less, with that plain, interfering Boer wife. It wasn't unlikely the boys were smoking *dagga*. The family was rough. No doubt the older brothers smoked all the time. Two idiots at the bike-shop. Steyn had wandered around the showroom and they tried to sell him a clapped-out 250cc. It only took a glance at the engine to see they'd fucked it up. As for their brother, well, something about that boy made him ache inside. He'd like to sit down with that boy and strip a motorbike, piece by piece, and show him how to really fix a thing. But Johann was dangerous. He couldn't trust himself around Johann. If anyone could turn him into a monster, it was Johann. Steyn sat with his knees up against his chest and stubbed the cigarette on the rock. A loud cry startled him. He turned around to where it was coming from. It was Hendrik shouting. 'Werner!'

Hendrik eventually found him by the river. Werner said he'd fallen asleep. Hendrik grabbed him by the back of his shirt and dragged him back to the house. Werner struggled under his father's grip. 'I can walk by myself.'

'Walk then,' his father said, pushing him forward. Werner expected to see his mother sitting in the kitchen, but the only person there was Lerato, staring wide-eyed as Hendrik dragged Werner to Marius's bedroom. He opened the door. His mother was sitting on the edge of the bed where Marius was lying. He was wearing a T-shirt and underpants, facing the wall. His mother had lifted up his shirt and was rubbing some cream into Marius's back. Werner could see the deep-purple bruises.

'Turn around, Marius,' Hendrik said.

'Please, Pa, I don't want to,' Marius said.

Petronella stroked her son's head. 'Come now, boy, just for a moment. I want your brother to see what he's done.' Werner's heart pounded and his mouth went dry. He thought he'd just roughed up his brother a little; nothing worse than usual. Marius turned on his side. He didn't want to look Werner in the eye, so he stared at the floor. Werner felt dizzy. Marius's neck was badly bruised and the right side of his face, where he'd slapped him, was swollen. His brother's eyes were red, but he'd stopped crying. There were two black bruises on Marius's thighs, where Werner had pinned him to the ground with his knees. Marius turned on his side to face the wall. Petronella squeezed more ointment into her hand and looked away from her son. 'Please, Hendrik, I don't want to see him.' Hendrik grabbed Werner by the neck, shoved him out the room and closed the door behind him. His father's temper scared Werner. How was he to explain that this was not nearly as bad as it looked? He hadn't really meant to hurt Marius. Perhaps he'd gone a little far, he could see that now, but his parents were carrying on as if he'd beaten him. Hendrik grabbed his son and threw him against the wall.

'Why? Why did you do that to your brother?' Werner said nothing. 'There must be a reason. He must have done something to you! Please tell me he did something.' Werner tried to think of something that would assuage his father's anger, but it was difficult to think with him shouting and pounding him against the wall. 'Why?' his father shouted again. Werner could hear his brother start whimpering in the room, devastated no doubt that he was the cause of all this, and Werner smiled at the thought of his soft little brother. 'You think it's funny? I will give you something to smile about!' He struck his son across the face.

'Pa, please! I didn't mean it.'

Hendrik dragged his son into the kitchen and started fumbling with his belt. 'Bend!' he shouted. He couldn't get his belt undone. 'Fucking belt!' He reached for a wooden spoon and broke it across Werner's buttocks.

Werner shouted in pain. 'Pa! Please, Pa! It was an accident!'

'Accident?' he muttered, fiddling with his belt again. 'Let me show you an accident.' He grabbed the end of the belt and ripped it with as much force as he could muster. It snaked through the trouser loops and, as the tip of the belt escaped, caught Werner on the side of the face. Werner winced, but Hendrik didn't notice. He brought the belt down as hard as he could. He misjudged his swing and caught the boy on his lower back. Werner crumpled in pain. Hendrik stepped back and dropped the belt on the floor. Werner was on all fours, arching to escape the burn. He started crying. Hendrik looked up from his son on the floor. Lerato was standing in the kitchen. She was shaking.

'Lerato! Calm down.'

Werner took in a deep breath and let out another wail. Hendrik noticed some blood on the side of the boy's face. He wasn't sure how that happened. Fuck, he thought. Werner bawling like a dog on the floor and a crazy *meid* having a breakdown in my kitchen. What a mess! This was how it started. Before you knew it, you were hitting and beating and kicking and shooting everything in sight to make things okay again. Lerato ran out of the kitchen. Hendrik looked at his son and said, 'Ok – enough of the dramatics. Get up,' and followed Lerato out into the garden.

'Lerato! Lerato! Wait.' Lerato, he supposed, wanted to run all the way back to Moedswill. 'Don't be scared,' he said. 'I'm sorry you had to see that. You understand?' The girl looked at the ground. 'Werner is a little bit wild at the moment. Lerato, look at me.' With some reluctance she looked up, but her eyes still didn't meet his. 'What happened there – in Moedswill – it's not going to happen here. You understand?'

Hendrik heard Petronella in the kitchen. 'Where's your father?' she asked Werner.

'Chasing after his *kaffirmeid*!'

He heard a door slam and wasn't sure whether it was his wife or his son.

'Lerato,' he said. 'Are you okay?'

Petronella came out of the back door. 'Hendrik,' she shouted. 'Leave her!'

'Lerato, it's all going to be fine. Just go back to your room, okay?' She nodded. Hendrik turned to talk to his wife.

16

Werner sits in the bush for over an hour peering at the house, waiting for Johann to come out again. He wants one more look before he leaves. He wants to drink Johann in. With that hook, he is remarkable. Someone should paint him: naked with a hook. Then Werner would lie in bed and stare at him, and Johann would suck up all the sound in the room and whisper it back into his ear, 'Calm down, calm down.' He hears a car door slam shut and the vehicle pull away. He tries to see who is inside, but the car is gone. If he were certain they'd both left, he'd peer into the house for clues as to what Johann has been doing for the last twenty years.

He walks back to the hotel. When he emerges from the bush he sees the boy standing by one of the service entrances of the hotel talking to a staff member. Werner stands and watches. The boy gives the man a wad of cash and the man hands him a little bag. How embarrassing that a boy, in a foreign country, could do what Werner, a native of thirty-three, could not. The boy looks at Werner and realises there has been a witness to the transaction. His eyes narrow.

He expects the boy to shout, 'What are you looking at, you fat cunt?' Instead the boy pockets the drugs and ambles in Werner's direction. Though excited by the imminent contact, he feels caught. Should he continue walking to the hotel? This would look as if he was walking towards the boy. On the other hand, he can't simply stand and wait. He does not want to create the impression that the boy needs to explain himself. Without turning away, he takes a seat at one of tables. Immediately a waiter appears. Werner looks at his watch. It's a little after noon, so he orders a beer. The boy stands close to his table and gazes out at the dam. He shields his eyes. Werner is a little breathless. The boy is wondering how to tackle the conversation. The waiter returns with a beer and Werner signs the receipt.

'Hello,' the boy says shyly.

'Hello,' Werner says. He is embarrassed of his own thick accent. Not *hello*, but *hullo*. Werner knows what the words should sound like, but his guttural vernacular has twisted the muscles in his tongue so that it grates and rasps at the English words; words that have been smoothed and weathered like small beach pebbles over centuries.

'It's hot today,' the boy says. Werner nods. And then, 'Are you going to tell my parents?'

'No,' Werner replies. The boy nods; not a question then, but an instruction. 'I'm Aleksander.'

'Werner.'

Again he nods, as if he knew this.

'This is the most boring place in the world. There's nothing to do.'

'I know. I grew up here.'

'Where?'

Werner points to the buildings in the distance. 'My father used to run that camp. Are you here on holiday?'

'Sort of,' he says ambiguously.

'Where are you from?' Werner asks. It feels improper to talk to this boy. It feels like he is doing something dirty.

'Denmark – but I haven't lived there for a long time. First we stayed in London and then in Boston. And now here.'

Werner nods as if these are places he knows well, though he has never left South Africa. He has barely been outside the borders of the old Transvaal; painful the way a child can make him feel so benighted.

'I'm going for a swim,' Aleksander says. 'You want to come?'

Werner does not know what to say. He thinks for a moment. What will it look like, viewed from the hotel, this fat man following a boy into the bushveld? He has, for the most part, given up guarding against indignity, though he does what he can. He is careful, however, about appearing obscene.

'Well,' Werner says, 'I might dip my toes in the water.' Immediately he regrets the words. They sound avuncular. As they walk down the path the boy says little. He has the self-possession of the beautiful. Werner sits on what he has come to think of as his tree stump and removes his shoes. He tries not to look as the boy

strips off his clothes. This time the boy does not bother
to put on his swimming costume and wades into the
water naked. When the water is up to his knees he turns
around to face Werner. Aleksander is at that point in
adolescence when he still has the body of a boy, slim
hips and shoulders, a slight softness between his nipples
and his armpits that is rapidly being absorbed, with the
cock of a man, like an organ borrowed from the future,
so that he can play at being his father or his coming
self. There between his thighs is the epicentre of change
rippling through his body. Werner knows the boy is
offering himself for a moment, as a token of thanks. He
thinks that if this were a photo, it would be considered
objectionable, possibly illegal. It is a good thing the police
cannot see into his mind. They would find a good deal
there, other than murder, which is not to their liking. If
the gesture is strange, it is, he thinks, in keeping with
the man-boy who makes it. Only a boy, a child, could
believe that the whole world of adults has his welfare at
heart; that Werner had any intention of taking his parents
aside and warning them, for Aleksander's own good, of
what he was up to. If the boy was buying heroin from
North African drug-dealers and injecting himself with
needles from the rubbish dump, Werner doubts it would
have moved him to intervene. And yet from their brief
encounter – from some gesture Werner made, from something in his eyes – the boy knew instinctively that there
was something darker about Werner's interest in him;
hence his standing here naked, in thanks. Is that not the

understanding of an adult? Does that not speak to a certain kind of sophistication? Perhaps not. If there is one thing we are born knowing about, it is sex. The boy turns around and dives under the water.

Werner takes a nap to escape the heat. His dreams are vivid. He is living in the apartment with his father and Aleksander, except that the boy is called Johann. When he is told this, there is a moment of recognition and he wonders why he did not realise before. Of course, he thinks, it is Johann. That's why the boy was looking at me like that. His father says, 'Thank God you injected that adrenalin. You turned my life around.' When Werner asks where his mother is, his father says, 'Don't be silly. She's living in East London now.' And Werner remembers that this is true too. Adrenalin, he thinks. At least he is not a murderer, and he feels a surge of relief. He thinks to himself that the relief is like adrenalin, and this makes sense too. There is an order and a logic to these things. It is nice that Johann is living with them, but he wonders why his father now likes the boy. That must be why his mother is in East London. She refused to live with white trash. When they sit down to eat lunch, he sees that Johann has a prosthetic arm. 'What's that?' Werner asks.

'He had to have it,' his father said.

'Why?'

'To protect him from you.'

Johann raises his prosthetic arm above the table.

He snaps the hook open and shut in front of Werner's face. '*Ja*,' he says, 'to protect myself from you.'

His father laughs. 'You'd better watch out, Werner. He'll tear your little *tottie* right off with that thing!'

The boy laughs and Werner smiles at this little joke, though they have hurt his feelings. He was happy to have Johann here – why is the boy being so cruel to him? When they return to the table for dinner, the boy grins to reveal his sharp steel teeth. 'What have you done?' Werner asks.

His father says, 'He insisted. He asked me to do it. We went to Boston. The man there put them in for him. Top-of-the-range. It's the only way he feels safe.'

When the boy speaks, his words are slurred by the sharp, ill-fitting, steel dentures. He spits and hisses and cuts his tongue and lips. A little trickle of blood runs down his chin. '*Ja*, you'd better watch out, Werner. I'll bite your *tottie* right off with these things.' He grins and his teeth glint with spit and blood.

Werner starts crying at the table. 'Please,' he begs them, 'where are Johann's teeth? There is still time to put them back. Why are you doing this?'

'Don't be silly Werner,' his father says. 'Look what you did to me. Who knows what you'll do to the boy? He'll get used to his teeth in time.'

Werner knows he cannot argue with this. He did kill his father, after all. He is still a murderer. When he wakes up he is drenched in sweat. He gets up and looks out of the window. It is strange how in dreams there is an implac-able logic, even in the illogical, so that his father sitting before him, living, breathing, could remind him that he was murdered. The vision of the boy with the prosthesis will stick to Aleksander and be conjured up next time they meet. He takes a shower, shaves and puts on clean clothes. He puts gel in his hair and sprinkles himself with cologne. I'm not going on a date, he thinks. *Soos a fokken laventelhaan* – like a fucking dandy. He takes a towel and tries to rub it off. He can still smell the cologne, but it's not as strong. He runs his hand through his hair to try and hide the fact that he has dressed up. He decides to walk. This will help clear his head.

The bushveld smells good: burnt grass and flowers and rain. Fresh. He had forgotten how good it smells. On the way he passes tourists who have been out for a hike; they smile at this man, dressed in his best trousers and a white shirt – reeking, he worries, of cologne. As he approaches Johann's house he gets nervous. It is not clear what he is doing here, or what he is going to say. He peers through the bush. Johann, wearing an old pair of jeans but no shirt, is working on a motorbike. 'Still a piece of white trash,' he says to himself. He takes a breath and steps out into the clearing. Johann does not see him. He remembers the danger in doing this previously, when the old man had a gun. He must be careful not to startle Johann. No doubt he carries a gun too. When he is a couple of metres away, Werner clears his throat and says, 'Hello.'

Johann turns around and shields his eyes from the sun. 'Hello,' he says. He wipes his hands on his jeans and gets up. He squints a little as he looks into Werner's face.

'Werner?' he asks. Werner nods. '*Fok*, man – Werner! How long has it been?'

'A long time.'

'Shit, man. It's good to see you.' His face breaks into a broad grin and Johann extends his hand. Werner shakes it. He can feel his own face is hot and he is smiling too, beaming perhaps, at the sight of his old friend. Johann's shirt is hanging over the seat of the bike. He takes it and slips it on. He puts his nose by his armpit and takes a whiff. 'Whoa! I'm a bit ripe, man. It's so fuckin' hot.' Using one hand he does up three of the buttons. 'Come inside. Let me get you a beer.'

He follows Johann into the house. Not much has changed. There is a new settee, but some of the old *riempie* chairs from before are still there. The place is tidier, though. The floor is not scattered with rubbish and the carpets no longer smell. Johann is living a life of dignified poverty. He first goes into the bathroom and Werner can hear him take a long piss as he lets out a sigh of relief. Werner is unused to these situations; being with another man who can unselfconsciously take a leak while still continuing a conversation: 'Make yourself at home, *boet*.' The intimacy is exciting. The pop of a deodorant can being removed is followed by the hiss of the spray. When Johann comes out of the bathroom, Werner sees that he's even fixed his hair. He goes into the kitchen and returns with two cans of Castle lager.

They sit on the *stoep* and crack open the beers. 'Werner,' Johann says with real feeling, 'I heard about your pa, man.

I'm so sorry. I wanted to phone, you know – but . . . it's been so long I didn't know what to say.' Werner shakes his head, dismissing the necessity for an explanation, but Johann continues. 'No, man, I feel bad. I should have found your number. I should have called.'

Sitting heavily between them is the question of the money. There is a great big wad of cash in Johann's throat, making it difficult to speak. He drinks his beer thirstily and goes to the kitchen for another two. Werner asks about Johann's family. The parents are both dead. His mother died only two years after Werner last saw her. His father drank himself to death before Johann finished high school. Is it reassuring or frightening, when a person's life takes the course you expect it to, that the unexpected direction is so rare? And of his own life? Is he living the life people expected? Would Johann at least have the good grace to be disappointed with how things have turned out for him? Werner keeps his answers vague. He works for the university, he tells Johann. 'The university, huh? You always were the clever one.' And what of Charlize? Pregnant in high school to one of Johann's friends. '*Jissus*, I wanted to kill that guy.' Johann shakes his head. 'I had him, man – right there – up against the wall.' He points to the wall. 'I was going to punch his fucking lights out, but Charlize was screaming.' Johann imitates her girlish hysteria: '"I love him! Leave him alone, you arsehole!"' He shakes his head and laughs. 'She always had a mouth on her. Anyway this guy says – no, he wants to take care of the baby. He's going to take care of Charlie. All the usual *kak*. Of course, after the baby is born, that *poes* is gone. I told her. I told her that *'oke* is a *fokken drol* – a real piece of shit. She's all right now. She's trying to get her *kak* together in Durban – four kids – huh?' He laughs. 'You know I told her: Don't be like your fuckin' family. Don't marry some *blarry* stupid mechanic. You know – not even a real mechanic, just some fucking arsehole that can hardly do an oil change. Worse than her useless brothers.' He lights a Chesterfield and offers one to Werner.

Johann makes a living fixing bikes, working in the shop and delivering drink to shebeens around the area. His tone is rueful. He fetches another two beers. He hands one to Werner and then ruffles his hair, laughs. 'It's so good to see you, man.' It is a strange gesture, more paternal than brotherly and one that could only be done after a few drinks, but it brings forth such a powerful surge of affection and longing that Werner has to turn away. Johann belches and laughs. How good it is, to have a friend again. How very good. He takes a sip of beer. They both laugh. How good it is, to be touched like that. They sit quietly for a while. This is what happens when old friends are reunited; they must both take stock, trot out the narrative each has constructed of the last twenty years. It is frightening how little remains, frightening that one can so easily give an account *of everything*. To turn twenty minutes into twenty years, all they need add is: *I got up. I went to bed. I brushed my teeth. I boiled some potatoes. I watched television. I read the newspaper. I cleaned the car. I mowed the lawn. I slept. I slept. I slept.* When Johann says, 'So, I suppose you've come to talk about the money?' it is as if he has coughed up that wad of cash; it lies there between them, covered in spit and phlegm and a little blood, this distasteful thing, lying there between two friends, that had to come out. What would it take, to reach down and pick it up? What would Johann do? He looks his friend in the eye. What an intimate thing it is to do. How difficult it is not to blush and smile. 'No,' Werner says. 'I haven't come about the money.' What has he done? *No, I have not come about the money. I have come about my life. I have come about the life that was taken from me. It just so happens that my life coincides with that money, it coincides with that money which my feckless fuck of a father, so thoughtlessly, so cruelly, gave to you – the one person I know who could conceivably give it back; the same person I cannot bear to take it from.*

Johann insists that, unless Werner has other important business to attend to, he stays for supper. He tries to reach Marleen at the supermarket where she works, but by the time he phones she's already left for the day. 'No worries, *boet* – Marleen can whip something up.' He takes a shower while Werner waits in the lounge. Werner hears a car pull up outside and a car door slam. Marleen, he guesses, must be in her early thirties. She is pretty enough, but there is a hardness around her eyes and mouth. The roots of her hair are a mousy brown. She struggles with grocery bags and keys. Werner opens the door for her. 'Hello – can I give you a hand?'

'Who are you?' she asks.

'Werner. I'm a friend of Johann.'

'Oh – Werner. Hello.'

They shake hands.

'Can I help?'

'Please. Can you take these?' she asks, handing him some of the bags. 'Just put them there.'

Johann comes into the kitchen showered and shaven. He grabs Marleen from behind and nuzzles her neck. 'Hon, this is Werner,' he says, letting her go.

'*Ja* – we've met,' she says. 'Are you staying for dinner?' she asks Werner. Werner looks to his friend.

'Of course he is,' Johann says.

'Seems like you two have been having a good time already.' She picks up the empty beer cans and stuffs them into the rubbish bin.

'Couple of beers, *skattie* – my little treasure.'

She unpacks the groceries. 'Well, I was going to make spaghetti with mince.'

Johann pulls a face and opens the chest freezer. 'Let's have a *braai*. There must be some stuff in here. Couple of steaks or some *wors*. Or maybe some lamb chops.' He digs amongst the bags of frozen vegetables and fish fingers to find some meat.

'You're making a mess,' she says. 'Why don't you go and make a fire and I'll find something.'

'*Bliksem* – we don't have any charcoal. Werner, you want to come with me? We'll go to the shop quick.'

'Sure,' Werner says.

Marleen shoots a glance at Johann. 'Why doesn't Werner stay here with me? He can help me make the salad.'

'*Ag*, man – he's the guest. He doesn't have to do anything.'

'Johann, it will be nice for me to get to know Werner a bit. Werner, you don't mind, do you?'

'Of course not. Let me help with the salad.'

Johann sighs. 'Okay, I'll be ten minutes. Werner, grab yourself a beer. Hon, you want me to pour you a glass of wine?'

'I'll help myself – thank you,' she says. Johann stands, beaming at the two of them. 'Go and get the charcoal, Johann. We want to eat before midnight.'

He takes his car keys and goes out of the front door. Werner smiles at Marleen. She turns to the fridge to take out some tomatoes, lettuce and onions.

'Would you like me to chop those for you?' Werner asks.

'No, I am fine. Let me get you a beer.' She puts down a can of Castle on the kitchen counter and pulls back the tab. The beer foams over the side of the can and pools on the counter. He grabs a cloth and mops it up. 'Werner,' she says as she arranges lettuce leaves into a bowl, 'I'm sorry to hear about your father.'

'Thank you.'

'It's never easy, losing a parent. It doesn't matter how old you are.'

'No, I suppose not. But my father had been ill for a long time.'

She nods. 'So what are you doing back in Barberton?'

'I don't know really. I guess, after my father died, I thought it would be good to see the place again.'

'I see.'

'And Johann, of course. I thought it would be good to see Johann.'

She turns the tap and fills the bowl of lettuce leaves with water. 'Now you want to see him?' she asks. Werner is cautious. She is smiling, but there is a note of anger in her voice.

'Yes. I want to see him.'

'For all these years you don't ever come to visit him – you don't phone him – now suddenly you want to be *chommies* again?'

How does he explain this, to this woman? He remembers a day in Pretoria walking down the street with his father. Hendrik was half-paralysed and dragged his foot as he walked. Some children from Werner's new school walked past and his father greeted them in his slurred speech. 'Come, Pa,' Werner said. 'Come.' The boys stared and said nothing, but the next day the children in his standard were walking around dragging their feet, drooling into the dry Pretoria earth and shouting, 'Weernaaah! Weernaah! Ima weeeeetaard!' How can this mousy little woman know what it is like to leave your home and your school and your friends, and everything you've known and loved, and find yourself in a cramped flat – your father transformed, disfigured, revolting; your mother so full of rage that her days are an endless cycle of stony silence and hysterical screaming, and your own mind, twisted and bitter with grief for your former life? This woman is angry at a child who no longer exists; a child who died twenty years ago.

'I don't know what you want me to say, Marleen.'

'I don't want you to stand here in my kitchen and pretend that you want to be friends with Johann.' She slices the tomatoes with such ferocity that she cuts herself. 'Fuck!' she says, scooping up those with blood on them and throwing them in the bin. She runs her hand under the cold tap and then sucks the cut finger.

'You'll need a plaster,' he says.

'I can see that.'

'Let me finish. Go and put a plaster on your finger.'

He chops the remaining tomatoes and onions while he thinks about what to say to Marleen. *Of course I want the money. I need the money. But I want Johann too. I love Johann. You love him, she says. Like a brother, he says. I love him like a brother.*

Marleen comes back into the kitchen with a plaster on her finger. She pours herself a glass of wine. 'What I am saying is: I want you to be honest, so that everyone knows where you stand. I spoke to the man from Pretoria. I asked him straight. I said: Mister, you tell me now, can the family take this money away from Johann? And he said no. He said that's the law.' Werner nods. 'But the problem is, the lawyer doesn't really know Johann. And you do. When he heard, Johann said, "This is not right. I can't take this money. This is Werner's money. This is the *tannie*'s money." Can you imagine – a grown man saying that? The *tannie*'s money. A thirty-four-year-old man. But it is right, Werner. You know it. I know it. You've got your fancy life in Pretoria. What does Johann have? Nothing. You know – he raised Charlie.'

'I know – I was there.'

'You were not there. Not after. And when his father was sick, where do you think his brothers were? Out *jolling*.'

'I know. Things were hard for us too.'

'I'm sorry – it's not like me to speak ill of the dead, but your father was a *blarry* madman. He was not right, Werner. And now he has done this one good thing. Don't take that away. With this money Johann can have a bit of a life. He can have a second chance. Maybe he can give Charlie a bit of money. God knows that girl has had it rough too.'

Now she has gone too far. Werner puts down the knife. 'I don't know why you are carrying on like this. As you've told me – we can't get it back. And it isn't even why I came.'

'If you care for Johann, you'll go. You just being here makes him feel guilty.' Werner is astonished by her hostility. 'I'm sorry,' she adds quickly. 'That was unfair. I'm sorry. I'm upset.'

They hear Johann pulling into the driveway. He walks through the front door with a pack of charcoal over his shoulder.

'Werner, grab me a beer and come outside.'

Marleen opens the fridge and takes out two beers. She

looks past Werner to see that Johann is out of earshot. 'He's a good guy.' She passes him the beers.

After dinner Johann offers to drive Werner back to the hotel, but Marleen objects that he is far too drunk. Instead Johann says he will walk Werner. The criss-cross of paths through the bush is an old neural network flickering to life. Here and there Werner stumbles into patches of concentrated familiarity and unleashes little bursts of memories. They avoid the old obstacle course, but walk by some of the camp's new developments. 'It's changed a lot, huh?' Johann asks.

Werner nods, but then says, '*Ja* and no.'

'I never thought I would still be living here,' Johann says. Does he regret this or has he reconciled himself to a life here, which surely can't be all bad? Has he found happiness in that? At the new boathouse they stop and gaze out over the water. 'They built that about three years ago. You know, they were still using some of the old boats up until then. Every inch was patched.'

'What happened to Steyn?' Werner asks. Johann shrugs. It is difficult to understand what his gesture conveys. Is he indifferent to the man's fate, or is this something he does not want to talk about? Johann lights a cigarette and Werner does the same. They walk in silence along the bank until they come to the path that leads to the hotel. Johann stops to gaze out over the water again. They are standing close together, still drunk, but the cool breeze that has picked up is sobering.

Johann turns to Werner and puts his hand on his shoulder. 'Werner, are we okay?'

'*Ja*, of course.'

Johann nods. 'Just follow that path,' he says.

'You want to come up for a drink?'

'Next time.'

Werner starts walking up the path. He turns around to see Johann still standing there. He raises his hands in farewell, but Johann has his back to him and does not see.

17

Lerato looked at the floor and Maria glared. Petronella had summoned them both to the kitchen. 'I've been thinking,' she said, 'that Lettie needs to learn how to be a proper maid. Lettie, you must learn how to do things nicely, like Maria.' The two women standing in front of her did not react to this news and Petronella was emboldened. 'This week, Maria, I want Lettie to work with me in the house and you can work in the camp.'

'But, *missies*, I am the maid here. I work in this house for fifteen years.'

'Yes, Maria – you're a very good maid. But I need Lettie to learn about these things too. She's not going to learn by cleaning the dormitories. And I need her to learn to make proper food.'

'*Missies*, this is not right, *missies*. This is my job, *missies*.' Lerato shuffled uncomfortably and Maria muttered something in her native tongue.

'Maria,' Petronella said sharply. 'I'm not asking you – I am telling you.'

'But *missies* wants to give my job to this one. I tell the *baas* this girl is not good. This one she is not right.'

'What are you trying to say, Maria?'

'This one she is too young. She know nothing. She is a little girl. And she make big trouble there.'

'Where? Big trouble where?'

'There. *Missies* knows.'

'At Moedswill?' Maria said nothing. 'Now you listen here, Maria – I won't have any of your bantu nonsense here. If you have something to say, say it.' Maria shook her head and muttered something under her breath. 'Maria, I don't like your attitude. You're getting a little white, huh? You'd better not forget who is in charge around here. And if you don't like it, you can pack your things. Do I make myself clear?'

'Yes,' Maria said.

'Yes, who?'

'Yes, *missies*.'

As Maria walked out through the kitchen door to join the other camp cleaners, Petronella called out, 'And, Maria, if you see Johann or any of those other children around, I want you to come and tell me.' Maria said nothing and Petronella turned to Lerato. 'So, what would you like me to call you. Lettie or Lerato?' The girl shrugged and looked at the floor. 'How can we carry on like this? Every time I ask you something you just shrug. I want to settle this business once and for all – is it Lettie or Lerato?'

The girl spoke so softly that Petronella had to lean in to hear her. 'Whatever *missies* want.'

'Whatever *missies* want,' Petronella repeated. 'I think Lettie is a lovely name. We should call you Lettie. Are you okay with that? If I call you Lettie?' The girl nodded. 'Now, I've been into town and bought you some proper maid's outfits. Some nice overalls and a nice *kopdoek*. We are going to make you look like a proper servant – not some little *piccanin* running around barefoot in the *veld*.' She opened the cupboard where the cleaning materials were kept and handed the girl a bag. 'Now there are two sets in there – a blue one and a pink one. You see,' she said, removing one of the dresses, 'it's got proper white trim and everything. Now – I want you to wash these every day. Blue one day and pink the next – *neh*? And I want it clean. Every day.' The girl nodded. 'What do you say?'

'Thank you, *missies*.'

'You are really going to have to learn to speak up, if we're going to get on. I can't have you whispering the whole time. Well, go and put one on – let's see what you look like. You can wear those *tekkies* for now, but we will have to get you new shoes at some point.' Lerato didn't move. 'Well, what are you waiting for, girl?'

'Which one, *missies*?'

'Well, whichever one you want. Did your old *missies* dress you every morning? Lord, Lettie! Whichever one you want – pink or blue: you decide. Come, hurry up now. We have lots to do. And you can tell Maria that if I see her skulking around the house, and not cleaning dormitories or cooking food, there will be hell to pay. *Neh*?'

Petronella placed the ingredients for the morning's cooking lesson on the counter: pumpkin, flour, eggs, sugar, milk, cinnamon and vegetable oil. Marius stood in the kitchen door watching his mother.

'Good morning,' she said to her son.

'Morning, Ma,' Marius said. It was his second day at home since the fight with Werner.

'You look better,' she said. 'Come here.' His face was less swollen than it had been yesterday. She lifted his shirt and looked at his back. The bruises were yellowing. 'I think you can go back to school tomorrow,' she said.

'What are you doing?' he asked, pointing to the ingredients.

'I'm teaching Lettie how to cook.'

'Why?'

'Because she's a maid and needs to know how to cook. You're worse than your father. *Blarry* ridiculous.'

'Sorry, Ma.'

With her fingers she brushed her son's hair off his forehead. 'I'll need to give you a haircut.' He shook his head. 'Don't be silly,' she said. 'Are you ever going to tell me what you and Werner fought about?'

'It was nothing, Ma. We were just fighting.'

'Has your brother made up with you?' Marius nodded vaguely. 'I suppose not,' she said. 'I don't know what I'm going to do with the two of you.' She poured breakfast cereal and milk into a bowl and put it on the kitchen table. Lerato appeared at the door, wearing the pink uniform. 'Look at you,' Petronella said. 'Mmm? Much better. Don't you think?'

'Yes, *missies.*'

'Maybe it's a little big, but you will grow into it. Have you got the *kopdoek*?' Lerato held the headscarf up in her hand. 'Put it on. I don't want to see you without the *kopdoek*. It's part of your uniform. Now, we're going to make some pumpkin fritters. Every Sunday we eat roast lamb, pumpkin fritters, roast potatoes, beans and cauliflower with cheese sauce. Come here, girl – don't stand around like I'm going to bite you.'

Marius ate his cereal as he watched his mother instruct her new charge in the art of making *boerekos*.

Petronella was not one for a great deal of introspection, but as they waited for the pumpkin to cook she wondered what exactly she hoped to achieve by taking this young girl under her wing. It had been so long, she told herself, since she'd last instructed a maid that there was pleasure to be had in doing it again. Besides, when she taught Maria she was barely a woman herself; newly married and wet behind the ears. With Maria, older then herself, she worried that the woman would think her a fool. Back then she was too free and easy with servants. In the early days of their marriage, Maria had seen her cry from loneliness or boredom, or after a quarrel with her husband. Perhaps this was why Maria was not as good a servant as she could have been. Now to start again, to be able to tell someone – without fear of what they may think – that you like things just so, was satisfying. It was good to have a project again. But Petronella knew it was unlikely she'd be doing this, if

Werner had not said to her that Hendrik was outside with *his kaffirmeid*. And when she went outside and saw the way Hendrik was standing there talking to Lerato, so gently, imploring her to come back, there was such tenderness in him – tenderness the like of which she had not seen for many years – it made her frightened. She thought, No, my boy, not *his kaffirmeid* – *my kaffirmeid*, because she had a way with bantus that Hendrik didn't and, if he felt something for this girl, she would draw her in close and twist it and make it something else completely.

Steyn was barely concentrating on the young girls learning to row on the dam. One of their teachers, a pretty woman in her mid-twenties, came to sit next to him.

'Can I bum a cigarette?' she asked, pulling her hair back and retying the elastic around her ponytail.

'Sure.' He took the packet out of his pocket and offered her one. She put the cigarette in her mouth and leant forward, waiting for him to light it. She crossed her legs and ran her fingers over her thighs. She was probably a netball or hockey coach at school.

'I shouldn't really smoke in front of the girls, but I saw you there and I knew I was just dying for a cigarette.'

Steyn had not been sleeping well. The fight between Werner and Marius was keeping him up. He was shocked when he saw the evidence of Werner's rage towards his brother. It was only a matter of time, he thought, until he was exposed. He needed to get Werner onside again.

'So how come you live at the camp?'

'Sorry?'

'I said how come you live at the camp?'

'It's part of the job. Someone needs to be next to the dormitories.'

'And what about your girlfriend?'

'I don't have one.'

'Someone said you had a girlfriend.'

'Who?' he asked.

'Oh, I don't know,' she laughed. 'Must have been one of the other teachers, I guess.'

'Your friends are looking at us,' he said, indicating with a slight nod of the head some of the staff by the water's edge, who had turned to watch their colleague.

'Let them look,' she said. 'You've never come across such a lot of old prudes in your life.' Steyn laughed. 'Listen here – you wouldn't have any booze, would you?'

'*Ja*, in my room. Would you like to come round for a drink tonight?'

'Is it a date?'

'It's a date.'

She got up and walked back to the other teachers. She smiled at them and they knew she'd got what she wanted. The ugly teachers shook their heads dismissively.

It was easy to be normal. Tonight the pretty young teacher would come round and they'd drink. It would be good. He thought about calling his wife. For the first time since he arrived, he wanted to go home, away from Werner and Marius. He regretted ending the thing so decisively. He wanted to go home to her, so that she could hold him and tell him that everything would be okay, and that this would pass, and that it was not his fault. It might still be possible to convince her that he'd changed. He'd said the army had unleashed in him perverted desires and that he didn't trust himself. He could tell her that it was better now, that he was returning to normal. But then he thought about what he'd done the previous day with Marius and became aroused. He started thinking about who, if he could choose, he might spend one night with. His wife? Perhaps. A night with his wife would be more restorative than anything he could imagine. They could drink and smoke and talk until the sun came up. She would try to wrap both hands around his biceps and talk about how much she missed his body. She'd bite his nipple and run her fingers through his chest hair and nuzzle him. There was succour in a woman's desire. And Werner? No. He could not imagine Werner spending the night in his bed. The boy's desire was unsettling; as unnatural as his own. And his haughtiness, when the thing was done. Unbearable. He looked at you with those pale-blue eyes as if you'd suddenly revealed yourself, as if he had in no way participated in what had just happened. He'd be demanding and stroppy. He'd ask for beer and cigarettes. His every word and gesture would be blackmail. To spend the night with Werner would be to spend the night captive; pleading, begging, cajoling, bribing.

'Steyn!' someone shouted, but he didn't hear. He

thought about spending the night with Marius, his arms wrapped around the warm naked body of the boy, drawing him in tight, gently caressing him and kissing him until they fell asleep. But if he could choose, above all it would be Johann.

'Steyn! Steyn!' A teacher was running towards him. His date for the evening had waded into the dam and was making her way towards a capsized boat.

'Fuck!' he said. He took off his shirt, ran into the dam and started swimming towards the boat. He quickly overtook the blonde teacher. When he reached the boat there was no sign of the girl who'd been rowing. He dived under it, to find the young girl holding onto the side of the boat, crying.

'Are you all right?' His voice echoed. The girl sobbed. 'Don't worry – it's fine. I'm going to take this life jacket off, so that you can go under. Okay?' The girl, still frightened and sobbing, nodded. Steyn undid the buckles of her life jacket, which cut across her budding breasts. This is what people worry about, he thought. Moments of intimacy like this with young girls. Perhaps, if the girl wasn't crying and she didn't have snot all over her face, he might have felt a flicker of desire. 'Okay, I'm going to count to three, and then we're going to duck under, okay? One, two, three.' They surfaced on the other side of the boat. 'Now hold onto the boat. I'm going to get your life jacket.' A few seconds later Steyn returned with the life jacket and strapped her back into it. The boats were old and heavy. It would take a lot of effort to right it in the water. The blonde teacher had nearly reached them.

'Lourien!' she shouted. 'Lourien! Are you okay?'

'I'm fine, miss,' she said. '*Oom* Steyn saved me, miss.'

The teacher's relief gave way to fury. 'I told you! I told you not to get up and mess around – didn't I! You could have knocked yourself out and drowned!'

'I'm sorry, miss.'

'You are going to be very sorry,' she said.

'Let's get everyone back to shore and we can talk about it there,' Steyn said. He helped the girl get on top of the capsized boat. He gripped the rim of the bow and started paddling awkwardly back to shore.

'Let me help,' the teacher said. Holding opposite sides of the bow, they made their way back to shore, occasionally kicking each other underwater. At first they apologised to each other, but halfway back they were too exhausted to speak. By the time they reached the bank, their chests were heaving. They dragged the boat onto shore and the girl jumped off and ran to her friends. Steyn looked at the woman.

'I'm so sorry,' he said. 'I was distracted.'

'It's okay. She's fine.'

His arms and legs were aching. 'I'm sorry.'

'It's fine.'

'Still on for that drink tonight?'

'Of course.'

Werner didn't even bother to go home any more. He told Petrus to drop him and Johann at the turn-off and from there walked straight to Johann's house. Petrus argued with him. '*Kleinbaas*, this is not right. The *missies* will ask me where you are.'

'She knows where I am,' Werner said.

'You make big trouble for me.'

'Don't worry, Petrus,' Werner said, as he walked off. 'My mother knows.' Petrus shook his head, put the car into gear and drove back to the camp.

The days were becoming milder, though it was still hot. It would be several months before the headmaster finally relented and instructed the caretaker to fire up the boiler of the school's old heating system. Werner had tied his blazer around his waist, but it kept on coming loose, so he threaded his finger through the loop in the collar and draped it over his back, though it made a sweat-patch. Johann's parents couldn't afford to buy him a school blazer. If he needed one for special assemblies or sports days, he'd rifle through the lost-property box and borrow a blazer for the day. As they walked along the dirt road to Johann's house they scanned the *veld* for empties.

'There's girls at the camp now,' Werner said.

'*Ja*? Standard five or standard eight?' Johann asked.

'Standard five.'

'I prefer the standard eights,' Johann said. 'Still, even the chicks in standard five can be hot sometimes. But they have small titties.'

'*Ja*.'

'We should go and check them out. Can you still see them shower?'

'*Ja*. Except Marius is there the whole time, pulling his wire.'

'That kid is such a pervert.'

When they reached the edge of the property, where the bushveld thinned out into the clearing in front of the house, they saw Johann's mother wearing a swimming costume, a swimming cap and a large elasticated skirt. Johann's brothers and Charlize were trying to coax her back into the house. 'But I want to go swimming!' she shouted. 'I want to go to the swimming pool in town! Everyone else can go swimming – why can't I go?' Johann's father walked out of the house. 'Tell that woman to shut the fuck up!'

'Come,' Johann said, 'let's go.'

'Where?' Werner asked without moving. He watched the scene unfold with interest. Johann grabbed him by the wrist and pulled him away. 'Come on!' he said. Werner followed.

'You don't have to be embarrassed,' Werner said.

'I'm not embarrassed.'

'It's not your fault that your ma is *getik*. I know she's not right in the head.' Johann pushed Werner up against the tree. 'She's not *getik*!'

'Yes, she is,' Werner said. 'She's *getik*.'

Johann gripped Werner even tighter and pushed his body up against him. 'She's not.'

'What happened to her?' Werner asked.

Johann let Werner go and carried on walking. Werner felt flushed and excited. He wanted to share everything with Johann. He wanted Johann to talk about his mother and his father. He wanted to tell Johann about the Jesus picture and how it was the most beautiful thing in the world. He wanted to tell Johann about Steyn. But Johann looked defeated. Werner was sure Johann was going to tell him to go away.

'Johann,' he said, 'I'm sorry. Your ma isn't *getik*. She's sick. That's all.'

Johann said nothing and sat down beneath one of the acacia trees. From here he could see the black boys playing soccer on the dusty clearing. 'She didn't used to be like that,' Johann said.

'What happened?'

Johann picked up a stick and started scratching in the dirt. His knee-high school socks had fallen down around his ankles. 'Just after Charlize was born – no, maybe a year after – Ma and Pa had a fight.'

'What about?'

'It doesn't matter. My brothers were still in school. So Ma packed her things and said she was leaving. She said she was going to go back to Benoni and would find a new job. She was going to come and fetch us, and we were all going to live with her. We had to watch out for Charlize, because Charlize was only a little baby. And then she left. She was walking down the street with her suitcase and Pa was shouting at her – but she didn't even turn around.' He couldn't look at Werner.

'And then?'

'She missed my birthday,' he continued. 'I remember

because after she left, my brothers said she'd be back in time for my birthday. She must have forgotten. And then one day we got a phone call from my *ouma*. She said my mother was in hospital. The police had found her in the street. Something happened. She had an accident. My father went to go and fetch her. When he was at the hospital he phoned us and told us Ma was sick. He said she wasn't quite *lekker* in the head. Sometimes my ma is like a little kid. When *ouma* phones she says she wants to go home. She says she misses her mum. I don't really understand. She knows we're her children, but she thinks she's a child too.' He looked at Werner. 'You know what everyone says about her is not true. She wasn't a stripper. She was working in a bar. *Ouma* said she was saving her tips for a deposit on a flat.' Werner had an urge to give something in return, but he had nothing comparable with which to eviscerate himself. So all he could do was nod. Johann got up and started walking towards the clearing where the black boys were playing soccer, and Werner followed. The black boys gestured towards Johann. '*Kleinbaas! Kom! Kom speel!* Come play!' Johann broke out into a grin. 'Come on,' he said to Werner. But Werner declined.

Johann ran onto the makeshift field. The goals were demarcated with little piles of stones. Werner could not make out who was on which team – if there were any teams at all. The Africans made a half-hearted gesture to include Werner in their game, but he could see there was no real feeling in it. It made him jealous. He was jealous of Johann for the ease he had with these people. And although he had no desire to play soccer, he was jealous of how happy they made Johann.

'Johann,' he called.

'What?' Johann shouted while still playing.

'Come, man – let's go for a swim or something. I don't like soccer.'

'It's fun, man. You should play with us.'

Previously, Werner would have dismissed him as a white kaffir and left him to it. But Johann was making him helpless. So he sat down in the grass and watched his friend play.

Steyn was sitting inside his rondavel when he saw Werner walk towards the house. It was dark out. He went outside to smoke a cigarette and called the boy over. 'Werner.' The boy pretended not to hear and carried on walking. 'Werner!' he called a little louder.

'*Oom?*' he said without walking closer.

'Come here, man. *Jissus!*' Werner hesitated for a few moments and then slowly walked towards the rondavel. Steyn was wearing a pair of jeans, a plaid shirt, which he'd tucked in, boots and a black belt with a silver buckle. He was freshly shaven and had slicked back his hair with Brylcreem.

'Hey, *lightie*,' Steyn said. Werner looked at his feet. 'What's up with you? Come inside.' Werner followed Steyn inside the rondavel. Steyn opened a beer and took a sip. 'You want some?' He held out the can. Werner shrugged. 'Hey, *boet*, come now. You can talk to me. We're both men – huh?' He held out the can again. Werner took the can, had a small sip of beer and passed it back.

'Sit,' Steyn said. Werner sat, but looked away from Steyn. The room smelt strongly of Old Spice. Steyn had tidied the place and made his bed. 'I've got a date tonight. What do you think?' he asked, indicating his outfit. Werner nodded, looked up at Steyn and held his gaze. Steyn cleared his throat. 'So . . . you and Marius had a big fight.' Werner nodded. Steyn laughed uncomfortably. 'What's wrong with you, *lightie*? Normally I can't shut you up.' Werner said nothing. Steyn took another sip of beer and held the can out to Werner. This time he took the can and drank deeply; enough to make him light-headed. Outside they heard footsteps.

Hendrik said, 'Steyn?' as he knocked on the door. Werner put the beer beside the chair, out of sight. Hendrik came into the room and saw his son. 'Oh, I didn't know you were here.' He looked at Steyn and smiled. 'Sorry, I didn't mean to interrupt. But we need to talk about what happened at the dam today. We might have to file a report – everyone says you're a hero or something.' Steyn shook his head. 'Werner, I'll ask Ma to put your dinner aside for you.' Hendrik looked at his son. There was a scab on the side of his face where the belt had caught him. 'Are we okay, my boy?' Werner shrugged.

Steyn waited until he heard the kitchen door close before saying anything.

'So, what were you and Marius fighting about?'

Werner reached for the packet of cigarettes lying on the bedside table. He removed a cigarette and held it to his mouth.

'Werner,' Steyn warned.

'Does *oom* have matches?'

Steyn considered this. 'If I give you a light, will you talk to me?' Werner nodded. 'And if your father or your mother comes, you'll put the cigarette out?' Again Werner nodded. Steyn passed him the matches.

Werner, smoking a cigarette and occasionally taking a swig of beer, was a grotesque mimicry of adulthood. Steyn's clothes, his newly ironed jeans and shirt, the smell of aftershave and Brylcreem thick in the air made him the adult supplicant-lover of a smoking child in shorts and T-shirt.

'Why did you fight with your brother?'

'Because my brother is a *poepol.*'

'Are you angry with me or your brother?' Werner shrugged. 'You're angry with me.' Again Werner shrugged. 'I'm sorry, Werner. What do you want me to do?' Werner fixed him with a stare, but said nothing. 'Do you want me to leave? I should resign. I think that would be for the best.'

'No,' Werner said. 'Don't go. Please.'

'What do you want me to do, Werner?'

For a long time the boy said nothing. He tried to find the words to express the ineffable thing he wanted. He tried to find the courage also. The beer was doing its work. He could not look Steyn in the eyes when he said the shameful thing. If Steyn had paid attention he might have noticed that the boy was on the verge of tears when, while looking out of the window, he said, 'I want you to take me rowing.'

18

Werner cannot sleep. The reunion with Johann has been too unsettling. He is trapped in a loveless relationship with the apotheosis of Afrikaner mediocrity. It is only a matter of time until the money is siphoned off by the demands of the sister, dull holidays by the seaside, and the endless mewing of the spawn that is sure to come, until Johann, like his father before him, retreats into a corner of the house and drinks himself to death – sucked dry, devoured, by his own family. The money will not be his salvation. It will be his undoing. Johann is too precious for that. When Johann ruffled his hair, Werner thought for a moment that Johann's hand might slide down, around the back of his neck, and caress him. He closes his eyes and thinks about it. What is Johann doing now? Is Johann thinking about him too? Marleen is lying in the corner of the bed, as far from Johann as possible – a coiled spring of resentment and anger, dangerous to the touch. What would he give to be that woman for a night; to turn and face Johann, to run his hand down the shoulder blade to the point where it ended in a smooth, rounded stub, coloured the same deep olive as the rest of his body, caressing it, cupping it in his hand, like a breast or a buttock, kissing it. Werner's strokes quicken and he ejaculates on his stomach. This is not why he came here. He did not come to rekindle an adolescent crush. His chest hurts. Is it love or a heart attack?

He wakes the next morning still thinking about his friend. He dreamt about him again, but this time Johann had not possessed the body of a fourteen-year-old Dane, nor did he threaten to bite off Werner's dick with a set of steel dentures. Werner was living in the house with him and Marleen. Whenever Werner and Johann were alone, Marleen would burst in on them and demand to know what they were doing. It was a good dream, to be conspiring with Johann. Marleen said, 'I know you want each other. There is no point in pretending.'

He eats breakfast outside; the gloom has lifted. He does not know how, but he is certain that his life is going to change. He consults his map and plans his route to Moedswill.

The farm is about a forty-minute drive from his hotel; perhaps a little closer to Nelspruit than to Barberton, but almost equidistant. He turns off the main road. The farm gate is open and just beyond it he can see a sprawling squatter camp. He stops the car on the dirt track. Something catastrophic has come to pass here. His heart is pounding. He has never driven through a squatter camp before. Black men and women are milling around the shanty houses, going about their daily business. Is it possible that the farm has been occupied? Beyond the shanty houses is a ten-foot fence, the top of which is covered in razor wire. And just beyond the fence he can make out rows of fruit trees. The people seem indifferent to him, but should something go wrong there is no room to turn the car around; the houses are too close to the road. He will need to reverse out. For a moment he considers driving back and asking Johann to accompany him. Except, of course, that would be impossible. Johann cannot be a witness to what he has come to do today. *Get the fucking money*, he thinks to himself. *You came for the fucking money.* Werner puts the car into first and drives slowly up the track. The camp, by the standards of those in Johannesburg or Cape Town, is small, but there must be hundreds – if not thousands – of people who now live on this narrow strip of land between the barbed-wire fences. There are spaza shops, a hairdresser, a witch doctor, a place from which to make telephone calls, women selling fruit and vegetables, others selling cooked meat. There are goats tethered to poles, though he does not see where they might graze. Loosely strung from poles are coloured festoon lights that he remembers from his youth. Electrical cables run from house to house to a point far beyond. There are at least four shebeens, where even now, early in the day, men are gathered drinking. They are sitting on white plastic garden chairs, the kind you buy from OK Bazaars, and there are umbrellas emblazoned with the brand names of cold-drink and ice cream companies.

Brightly coloured memories of his youth have been churned into this slum in the middle of the Eastern Transvaal; a great big shitty streak of 1970s Pretoria, as if two decades ago the city had wiped its arse on the bush-veld. He has never seen anything like it. He notices too that some of the women walking along the track are wearing short skirts and wigs. Their faces are heavily made up. When they see Werner they put their hands on their hips and gyrate. The track bends to the left, and in the distance he can make out the old farmhouse. The shanty town extends to within a few metres of the front door. There is nowhere for him to park but directly in front of the house, surrounded on both sides by tin dwellings.

He gets out and knocks. A maid opens the door and says, 'Yes?'

'Hello,' Werner says, 'I wonder if I can talk to the *baas*, please?'

'Are you from the company?'

'The company?'

She points to the orchards in the distance. 'That one. Stefan, he says he does not want to talk to you. If you want something you must talk to his lawyer. This is his property. He do what he likes. They must *fok off*, all of them.'

Werner is distracted by something he sees in the house: a canvas, propped against the wall. At a guess, it would be eight feet high. Maybe more. Painted in meticulous detail is a girl, standing in her school uniform staring knowingly at him, smiling. She is not pretty, but has a kind, open face. The maid, seeing that he is looking into the house, closes the door a little and steps towards him.

'You say these people are stealing the fruit. How do you know?' she asks. 'How do you know it is these people? Maybe one of the children, he is playing there – but so what? I tell them they must not play there. I tell them. It is not the people here that are stealing the fruit. It is other people. These people, they know – if they steal the fruit, then Stefan, he will kick them out. Ask them. You ask them what *Baas* Stefan say.' She stops talking, steps directly in front of Werner and asks, 'What you looking at?'

'I am not from the company,' Werner says, without looking away from the picture.

'I say what you looking at?'

He can still make out the head of the schoolgirl and the top of her blazer. The braiding on the blazer has been rendered with an exactitude that brings back memories of his own school days.

'I'm sorry,' he says. 'I need to speak to the *baas*.' He reaches into his pocket and takes out a sheet of paper on which he's written the details provided by the lawyer. 'Stefan Labuschagne.'

'Yes. Stefan. *Baas* Stefan.'

'It is about a legal matter. It has nothing to do with the company. I've come from Pretoria.'

She nods. 'Wait here.'

'Can I wait inside?'

'No – wait here.' She closes the door and leaves him

standing outside. He waits a long time before the door is opened again. This time a man in a wheelchair has accompanied the maid.

'Who are you?'

'Mr Labuschagne?' Werner asks the man.

'Yes?'

'My name is Werner Deyer. I have come to speak to you about a legal matter. Could I come inside?'

The man in the wheelchair nods and Werner steps into the house. Now he can see the whole painting. He stops a short way from the front door to take it in. It is ineffably beautiful and sad. The girl is standing in the very room he is now standing in, producing an unsettling mimicry. Behind the girl stands a man, pointing a shotgun at her head. Stefan clears his throat to get Werner's attention.

'That is an extraordinary painting,' Werner says.

'You say you've come about a legal matter?' Stefan says, indicating the settee and waiting for Werner to take a seat.

'Yes.'

'Well?'

'Has a law firm in Pretoria been in contact with you?'

'Are you from the firm?'

'No. My name is Werner *Deyer*.'

The man narrows his eyes. 'Oh – Deyer. Of course.'

'I'm his son.'

'What is it that you want, Mr Deyer?'

'Please – call me Werner. My mother and I cared for my father for the last twenty years of his life. Unfortunately he has put us in a rather difficult position. You see, my mother was counting on that money for her retirement.'

'I expect so.'

'I was wondering whether you'd found the woman. Lerato Dlamini. She used to work on this farm.'

The man smirks. 'And what do you plan to do, if you find her? Tell her your sob story?'

'I wasn't sure she would be found. In which case my mother gets the money. But it would be good to know, either way. For my mother's sake. I am sure you understand that this entire affair is a cause of considerable pain to her.' Stefan nods, but says nothing. 'Have you found her?'

'What do you know of Lerato Dlamini?' Stefan asks.

'Nothing.'

'Do you remember a woman called Lettie?'

'Yes, I do. She worked for my mother for a short time.'

'Well – they are one in the same.'

'I see,' he says. He remembers the young black girl. If he is surprised it is only inasmuch as he's just made the connection; something his mother must know, but chose not to share. 'I remember her,' Werner says. 'She still lives on the farm?'

'Yes.'

His heart sinks. He was a fool, desperately clinging to the last hope. Everyone has been found and accounted for; in fact she probably has been found for days. The answering machine must have stored on it a recorded message: *Mr Deyer, I am phoning to let you know that we have located Ms Lerato Dlamini since we last spoke.* It is only now that he recognises the extent of his delusion. He puts his head in his hands. He cannot bring himself to say anything. He sits up and rubs the back of his neck. He looks at the hollow-cheeked man sitting in the wheelchair. He knows that the man sitting before him must be in his late thirties, but his face is sunken, which makes him look older. He looks at the painting again.

'It's extraordinary.' The man shrugs. Werner gets up and walks towards it. 'It really is extraordinary.' He leans in close to inspect the brushstrokes. 'I remember the murders.' He says this not matter-of-factly, but tenderly. 'Everyone thought you were going to die. I remember that.' Stefan looks away and sighs. 'I'm sorry,' Werner says. 'I was being rude.' Stefan shrugs. 'You see, when I was young I thought I was going to be a curator. That was always my dream. And you know, as dreams go, I thought it was modest. I didn't want to become a famous movie star or a millionaire or anything. And somehow, even with your most modest ambitions, life just gets in the way.' He turns to face Stefan. 'You painted this?'

'I did.'

'You are very talented. I'm curious – how do you paint such large canvases?'

'I was quite busy when you interrupted.'

'You were busy painting?'

'Yes.'

'Would you mind?'

'What?'

'If I watched you work.'

Stefan sighs. He does not strike Werner as a kind man, but perhaps his own small tragedy might soften him in this instance. It is a small request.

'I suppose.'

He leads Werner into the adjoining room, which in the past must have been the dining area. Scattered on the floor are tubes of oil paint, brushes and a piece of hardboard that's being used as a palette. A large, nearly complete canvas is propped against the wall. This one is of a man putting a shotgun in his mouth. His eyes are stretched wild and mad; as if he's being attacked by the gun. It is a difficult picture to look at. It is not beautiful, though it is beautifully executed. Immediately in front of the painting, hanging a metre off the ground, is a wooden chair suspended by three ropes that run to steel pulleys fixed to the adjacent and back walls. Beneath the pulleys are steel stays. There are three black men, neatly dressed in white overalls, standing at the back of the room. Stefan points to an old *riempie* chair. His manner is imperious and Werner understands that this is where he is being instructed to sit. The men lift Stefan out of the wheelchair and slide the wooden chair beneath him. Leather straps hold him in place. He indicates the height he wishes to be raised to and the men, seemingly practised at this, gently raise him two metres off the ground so that his head is level with the face of the man. They then secure the ropes to the steel stays beneath the pulleys. Two men stand on either side of the painting and move it left or right, as required. Another man passes Stefan brushes and paints and occasionally holds the palette when Stefan's arms tire. After half an hour he instructs one of the men to put on some music. 'CD six,' he says. It's a selection of Bach concertos.

Werner watches Stefan paint the area around the man's nostrils for a full two hours. During that time Stefan speaks only to give instructions to his staff. Sometimes he puts his head back and closes his eyes. Then, at one o'clock, he says, 'I need a rest.' One of the men takes the brush and palette from him and he is gently lowered into his wheelchair. His brow is wet with sweat. He takes a handkerchief out of his pocket and mops his forehead and the back of his neck. He drinks water and eats an apple in silence. 'Go, go,' he says to the men and dismisses them with a wave of his hand. 'One day the people on this farm will kill me.'

'Why?'

'They would love to get me out of the way. And who can blame them? I can barely afford to pay them. Some of them work in lieu of rent.'

'For squatting here?'

He nods and takes another bite of apple.

'Why don't you get rid of the squatters?' Werner asks.

'These are the people from the farm. I couldn't tell them to leave. Where would they go? They don't have anywhere else. And if I can't give them work, I must at least give them a place to stay. At first there weren't so many – maybe a hundred. But then they had children and their families came and, before you know it, I'm king of the township. King Stefan Labuschagne, ruler of Moedswill.'

'Well then, I suppose it's in their interests to keep you alive. If you died, what would happen to them?'

'I wonder how long it would take anyone to notice?' He takes another bite of apple and muses as he chews. He swallows and then says, 'I don't think anyone would, really. Maybe the hospital would want to know why I missed appointments. But then they have enough to keep them busy, without worrying about some mad paraplegic. My death will go unremarked. These people will bury me beneath their shit and rubbish. It will happen.'

'Why don't you move to the city?'

'The city?'

'Yes – I am sure a studio could be adapted so that you could paint. You wouldn't need as much help. You wouldn't be so . . . isolated.'

'Why don't I move to the city and paint pictures?' he asks.

'Well . . . it would be easier. Don't you think?'

'Because this is my farm! This farm is my birthright!' Stefan sips some water and then says quietly, 'Or at least what is left of it. It's time!' he shouts at the door. 'Get off your fat arses!' The men wearing white overalls file into the room. One of them approaches Stefan and says, '*Baas* Stefan?'

'What?'

'*Baas* say I can have the afternoon off. I must go with my sister to the clinic.'

'When?'

'Today, *baas*. *Baas* say I can go today.'

'No – when did you ask me?'

'Last week.'

'I don't remember.'

'Please, *baas*.'

'What am I supposed to do, huh? What am *I* supposed to do when you go off to the clinic? Clinic, my arse! Shebeen, more like! You are such a bunch of ungrateful old kaffirs!'

'*Haai, baas*! *Baas* mustn't say these things.'

'You are! All of you! I'm just a useless cripple who can't do anything, so you all take advantage of me. I have so little time to finish my work. Now you want the afternoon off.'

Werner says, 'I could help out. If you wanted.'

The man turns to Werner and says, 'Thank you.' Without waiting for Stefan to agree, he leaves.

'Never mind,' Stefan says dismissively. 'You can go.'

'No, please,' Werner says, 'I'd like to help.'

Stefan sighs. 'You will need an overall – for your clothes.'

'Don't worry about that. I'll be careful.'

'Listen to these two,' he says. 'They'll tell you what to do.' One of the men reties the leather straps and buckles that hold Stefan in place, then Werner, as instructed, takes his position beneath the far pulley. It would not do to tip the man over. Hand over hand, they slowly raise Stefan the two metres. 'That's good, stop there,' he commands. 'Help him tie the rope,' Stefan says. 'If it comes undone, I'll fuck up the painting.'

One of the men takes the rope from Werner and ties it.

'Werner, you can help with the paints. Come stand here – to my right.'

Werner does as instructed. He passes Stefan the palette. He's already mixed most of the colour he needs for the day, but occasionally he will ask Werner to pass him a tube of paint. How long has it taken to paint this canvas? And how many others are there? Stefan paints for a further three hours, uninterrupted. Werner's back and feet ache. But there is pleasure in watching the man work.

As Stefan leans forward, a soccer ball hits one of the windowpanes, startling Stefan and Werner. He jerks his brush and smudges some paint. 'Fucking kids!' He leans back in his chair and passes Werner his brush.

'Don't you worry about all these people? Living here?' Werner asks again. It is unimaginable to him to be surrounded by squatters.

Stefan is still leaning back with his eyes closed. He picks up a cloth, leans forward and wipes off some of the paint. 'I need a break.' They lower him into the wheelchair and Stefan dismisses his assistants. He wipes his forehead. Stefan sits with his eyes closed and Werner wonders whether he's taking a nap, but then he starts speaking.

'About two years ago – or maybe it was three – I'd just come home from the hospital. It was a Friday night. I was sitting here, reading a book, drinking. I heard something in the house.' He tilts his head back and rubs his neck with the back of his hand. 'There was someone in the house. I thought it was children, looking for sweets or cold drinks. So I go into the kitchen. There are three men.

In their twenties, I'd guess. They're busy stealing my microwave. I don't recognise them. They don't live here. They're not even startled. Or maybe they are startled, but they don't care. They're completely indifferent. It's the way things are now – isn't it? So I tell them to get out. It must have looked pretty funny. This skinny little mad Boer in a wheelchair. "Get out – get out of my house!" Like a grandmother, I suppose. And they start laughing. In the way blacks laugh. In the way black *men* laugh. Black women – well, you know, there's something joyous about them. But black men – young black men – that's something else. Maybe it has something to do with what we did to them. What is it the English say? *There's no such thing as a free lunch. The chickens are coming home to roost. Just desserts.* They have a lot of ways to say: You'll get what's coming to you eventually. So these men think that maybe they can have some fun with a skinny Boer in a wheelchair. They lift me up and they put me on the ground. Then they piss on me. You know the way kaffir piss smells? It's very strong. It smells like animal piss. Very oily. I guess we make a big deal about that. About being pissed on. Really it is not such a terrible thing. There are people who take pleasure in it. They get off by being pissed on. It was unpleasant, but not so terrible. Then they start kicking me and hitting me. And I realise this is how I am going to die. I am not embarrassed to tell you that I started crying. Good story for the papers. *Paralysed man beaten to death in his own home.*' He stops talking.

Werner wonders if Stefan is going to say something

about being press-fodder for the second time; if he's going to say something about how the prurient interests of an insatiable public would be excited by the compounded horror of his tragedy. *In the same house.* Stefan takes a bite of an apple and chews it thoughtfully. Werner wonders whether the story is finished. 'Did they leave?' he asks.

'No. I think they meant to kill me.' The light in the room is fading. Outside they can hear the children playing soccer. They whoop and shout and laugh. 'Can you imagine what would have happened? If the police came here and found me in this house? With these paintings? Freak! But *my* people – *my* blacks – realised something was wrong. So they came into the house. They tried to grab them, but two of the men broke free. They caught one. And they start beating him. Someone else is helping me back into my chair – and my bantus are busy beating this man. So you see, really I am quite unfair to them. They weren't beating this man out of a sense of obedience – they were beating him out of pure rage. Out of love for me. Maybe affection. Or familiarity. I think perhaps they thought that if anyone is going to kill me, that is *their* right. Not some strange out-of-town kaffirs who were just taking a chance with a cripple. But to watch them beat that man – it was a beautiful sight. A very beautiful thing to feel so loved, and protected. And of course I was very angry with that man. When someone makes you cry with fear, I can't tell you how strong the hate is. It was unfortunate for this man. I think that maybe, for my people, once they'd beaten him a bit, knocked out some of his teeth, the anger would

have dissipated. After the adrenalin rush. I don't know –
I'm guessing here – but I think it would be fair to say that
after you've beaten a man quite badly, there would come
a time when the excitement of it fades. Maybe you'd pick
him up by the scruff of his neck and toss him out on to
the street. But they kept at it. And every now and then
they glanced at me. They were doing this for me – giving
it to me. They were waiting for me to give the sign. But
I felt such love *from* them – not for them, but I suppose
that too – and such hate for this man. I was always on
the verge of saying, *Enough!* But how often does the world
give you a chance for revenge? And then eventually they
all stopped, and I thought: Thank God; thank God they
stopped of their own volition, because really I don't know
if I had the strength to stop them myself. But also I felt:
How dare you stop? How dare you? If I wanted, you should
have beaten this man to death before my very eyes. You
have given me much tonight, but I would like to know
how much more you could give, if needed. That night I
slept better than I had in many, many years. It was the
first time in a long time that I felt safe. I could lie in bed
thinking: Whoever comes in here will not only be thrown
out, but beaten, maybe killed. And it was the first time in
my life that I got revenge.'

'What happened?'

'What do you mean?'

'To the man?'

'I don't know. They took him outside.'

Stefan sips water. Werner says nothing. Stefan calls for

his assistants. He looks out of the window. There is enough light, he says, and continues for another two hours. By the time they lower him back into the wheelchair, Werner's back is aching. The festoon lights have been switched on outside the house and men and women have gathered in the shebeens. Music blares from stereo systems. People are dancing and clapping. The unmistakeable smell of marijuana wafts through the house.

'There's no point in keeping them here much longer,' Stefan says of his assistants. 'When things become like this, they itch to get outside and drink and smoke. I've tried to keep them painting late into the night, but they get careless.' He opens the drinks cabinet and pours himself and Werner a whisky. He lights a cigarette and Werner does the same. 'Why don't you come again tomorrow? It's nice to have some company.'

19

Hendrik did not know what to make of his wife and Lettie. All he knew was that this was part of a war she was waging against him. She no longer kept up the pretence that the arrangement was temporary. Maria had become a full-time, if resentful, member of the camp staff.

'*Baas*, why the *missies* give Lerato my job?' she'd asked. He did not know what to say. Because, Maria, this has nothing to do with you and everything to do with me. Because, Maria, the *missies* is fighting with me in the only way she knows how.

'Maria – don't be silly now. The *missies* is just showing Lerato how to cook and clean.'

'But why, *baas*? Why must she show her these things? The girl knows how to clean.'

'Yes, but not the way the *missies* likes. Huh? You know – she likes things to be just so.'

'Yes, *baas*. I know. That is why I must do it. I must work in the house. I am the *baas's meid*.'

'*Ag*, come now, Maria. Why can't someone else learn? This will help Lerato get a good job.'

'*Baas* – the *missies* she say to me maybe it is few days. But now it is two weeks. I work very hard for the *baas*. Fifteen years. When Werner is a little baby I carry him on my back. *Baas*, this is my job. This thing is not right.' And with that she just shook her head and walked off.

Hendrik felt a stab of guilt. Petronella was casting Maria aside, a loyal servant whose grievance was fair. And he, the master of the house, could do little about it. Or could he? Could he not assert the proper authority over his wife? He thought about walking into the kitchen, grabbing his wife by the hair and dragging her into the bedroom. *Enough, you cruel, relentless bitch! Give me a fucking break!* And for a moment he thinks again about taking a gun to her head. If these fantasies have become less common, it is because he can see that whatever venom this woman has stems not from malice, but from small-mindedness, from a complete failure to understand the world on any terms but her own. Still, it didn't change the fact that she was a bitch. But *not* without intuition. She could smell how much he wanted to fuck Lerato. Shit, even Werner knew how much he wanted to fuck that girl. Maybe Werner knew because he wanted to fuck her as well. He would not put anything past that boy. Was that why the kid was acting up? And, by bringing her into the house, did Petronalla mean to tempt Hendrik, tease him? Or was she hoping to turn her into a proper *meid*. Did she think him incapable of fucking the *ousie*? It would be good to leave the woman. But it would never be over. She would always be there. Sulking. Resentful. Bitter.

He lit a cigarette and asked Lerato to pass him an ashtray. He picked up the newspaper. There'd been some trouble in Soweto. Some kid was shot by the police and the bantus were going wild. Riots all over the place. He would have to keep an eye on things. On the whole it was the urban blacks who were more of a problem. The urban blacks were influenced by foreigners and intellectuals and Russians. The rural blacks never really complained. But sometimes, when things got out of control in the cities, the rural blacks became restless. They got drunk, started fights. Some would argue with their bosses, demand higher wages, new schools. He skimmed through the article. *Riots spreading across the country . . . hundreds of arrests.* On one of the pages they'd reproduced a picture that had originally been printed in *Drum* magazine: a teenager, running down the street, carrying the body of a young boy. He turned the page. On the bottom right-hand side of the page was a small headline: **Labuschagne boy survives shooting.** He skimmed the article. *A miracle that Stefan Labuschagne (16) survived gunshot wound in the back . . . likely to be paralysed for life . . . transferred to a specialist unit in Pretoria . . . Uncle says they thank God . . .*

He looked up at Lerato, who was washing dishes. 'Lerato?'

'Yes, *baas*?'

'Can you read?'

'A little, *baas*.'

'Here,' he said. 'Take this to your room. There is something there you will want to know about it.' He handed her the paper.

'*Baas* – the *missies* she wants to read the paper.'

'Never mind. Take it. Go put it in your room now.'

She took the paper, but as she turned to leave Petronella walked into the kitchen and said, 'Where are you going with that newspaper, Lettie?' She turned to Hendrik. He looked down at his coffee. 'Give it here,' Petronella said. Lerato passed her the newspaper. 'I would like a cup of coffee, please.'

Petronella sat down at the breakfast table and started paging through the newspaper.

'So what do you find so interesting?' she asked as she flipped the pages. 'You shouldn't be reading about what's going on in Soweto, Lettie. It's terrible. I don't understand why they want to burn down the schools. Where are they going to get, without an education?' She turned the page. 'Did you want some of these coupons? If you want coupons, it's fine – but you must ask me first. Maybe I need the coupons too. We're not made of money.' Lerato put the cup of coffee down on the table. Petronella took a few sips while she looked at the coupons. 'Twenty-five cents off washing powder. That's quite good actually.'

'Enough!' Hendrik whispered across the table.

'Enough what, Hendrik?' she asked. She flipped the page and saw the article. She looked up at Hendrik. 'I see,' she said. 'I don't think you should worry about these things, Lettie. The uncle is taking care of everything now.'

'Lettie,' Hendrik said, 'when the *missies* is finished reading, you can take the newspaper.'

Petronella got up, tucked the newspaper under her arm and went back to her bedroom.

Steyn was waiting for Werner in his rondavel. He had a long break while the girls were being given a lecture about the insects of the *veld*. He'd resisted at first, but then he thought this could all be part of his recovery. He'd slept with the pretty young teacher and it was nice. He thought about masturbating before they went rowing, but that felt like cheating. Someone knocked at the door. It was the teacher.

'I snuck out of the lecture.'

'Hey,' he said. She leant forward and gave him a kiss, then grabbed his crotch. 'Have you got some time?' She unbuttoned his fly and rubbed his cock.

He laughed. 'I'd love to. But I can't. Please don't make me horny.' She went down on her knees, wrestled his dick out of his underpants and took him in her mouth. He tilted his head back and enjoyed this for a few seconds. 'No,' he said, pulling away. 'I can't.'

'I want you,' she said, crawling towards him on her hands and knees. She thought it was a game. She lifted up her dress and put her hand in her panties.

'Get up,' he snapped. 'Someone is coming.'

She adjusted her panties and stood up. 'Where?' she asked, turning around.

'Hendrik's son is coming round.'

'Oh,' she said, smoothing down her dress with her hands. There was a note of irritation in her voice.

'I'm sorry,' he said.

'Why do you sound so angry? I just wanted to have a little fun.'

'I promised to take him rowing.'

'Take him some other time.'

'I can't. I promised. Come round tonight.'

She walked out and slammed the door behind her. By the time Werner arrived, Steyn was still feeling angry and aroused. It is, he told himself, part of the test.

'Are we going rowing?' Werner asked.

'Sure.' As Steyn turned to collect his things, he closed his eyes and said a prayer. *Please God, help me get through this. Please God, make me right.*

They walked to the dam in silence. Werner tried his best to be sweet and compliant. He suggested which boat they should take, and when he realised that Steyn hadn't brought any beer along, offered to go back to his room to fetch some.

'No thanks, Werner, I still have work to do after.'

Steyn offered to row, but Werner insisted. Werner tried to make small talk. He pointed to the baboons and the birds.

'Look, it's a fish eagle,' he said.

'No. That's a vulture.'

'Oh *ja* – that's right,' Werner said and smiled.

They rowed past the island and Werner called out at the baboons on the far bank. As they rounded the island, Werner stopped rowing.

'I'm tired,' he said. He waited for a few seconds, but Steyn just stared out at the water. 'My shoulders are sore.'

'Let me row,' Steyn said.

'No – I'm fine. I just want to rest a bit.' Werner started rubbing his shoulders. '*Oom* said I should put some Deep Heat on.'

'Mmm.'

Bird calls echoed across the lake. The water lapped at the side of the boat, making a gentle hollow sound. It was cool, but not cold. Steyn was sitting in the front of the boat. Werner sat on the thwart with his back towards Steyn. He rolled his shoulders.

'Hey, *lightie*, are we going to sit here all day?'

'No, *oom*,' Werner said, but he did not move.

'Either you start rowing or I will.'

Werner grabbed the oars and started rowing to shore. Steyn sighed. It felt good. It felt almost like everything wrong had been washed away. He was glad he had done this. Werner rowed back in silence. As they reached the shore, Werner jumped out of the boat and started walking away.

'Hey, *lightie* – where are you going?'

'Home.'

'You're not going to help me with the boat?'

'I'm late.'

'Werner – come here.' The boy stopped walking, but didn't turn around. 'Werner, get your arse back here. I'm not asking you – I'm telling you.'

He waited long enough to make Steyn wonder whether he was going to defy him. Werner turned round and walked back. He watched Steyn drag the boat on shore.

'What's going on with you?' Werner shrugged. Steyn reached into his pocket and held out a fifty-cent coin. Werner did not take it. 'Here,' Steyn said.

'What for?' the boy asked.

'For doing such a good job with the rowing.'

Werner took the coin and marched off without a word. Steyn dragged the boat into place and flipped it over. He sat on the stern of the upturned boat and ran his hands through his hair. He was trying to make things right. If God decided it was not good enough, if Werner decided to destroy him, there was nothing he could do.

Werner felt wild with fury and hurt. Why was Steyn being so cruel to him? Steyn did not love him any more. He could not go home; not to his mother; not to Marius. Where have you been? she'd ask. Rowing with Steyn. How nice, she'd say. And Marius would look at him and smile. And that would make it worse. He walked to Johann's house. Johann was sitting outside with his brothers. They were trying to fix a motorbike. The brothers were covered with grease and cursing.

'You weren't at school today,' Werner said to Johann.

'No. I'm helping them with the bike.'

Werner nodded. He did not feel like feigning an interest in the bike, so got up to look for Charlize. She was in her secret garden at the end of the property.

'Charlize,' he called. 'It's Werner – can I come in?'

'*Ja* – just one second. I need to do some magic.' She made magical noises and then said, 'Okay, you can come now.'

'Charlize,' he said, 'look at you! You're filthy.' The girl was covered in dirt. Her fingernails were black and her hair was wild. She tried to wipe her face with her dress.

'There's no hot water. Because the thing is broken. And Johann says I must have a cold bath until Pa fixes it. He tried to put me in the bath, but I ran away. That's why I am going to live here. See,' she said, pointing to a pile of clothes and a sleeping bag. 'I even have some crisps and some bread. Look – three packets of tomato-sauce crisps, because it's my favourite. And if anyone comes to get me I'll do magic on them.'

'You can't sleep out here. You'll get cold.'

'I can. I'm tough.'

They heard someone walking towards them. 'Who's there?' Charlize asked.

'Charlize!'

'Go away, Johann. I'll do magic on you.'

'Is Werner here?' Johann pulled back the dense growth. '*Jissie*, girl – look at the state of you? Have you been rolling around in the dirt like a dog?'

Charlize looked at her feet. 'It's not my fault,' she said.

'It's bad enough you don't bath, and then you roll around in the dirt.' He grabbed her by the wrist. 'Come – you are getting in the bath right now.'

'No,' she shouted. 'It's cold! I'm not bathing!' She twisted and tried to break free. Johann grabbed her other wrist and yanked her up. His anger came from shame. 'You're hurting me! Stop it!' she shouted.

'Enough!' he snapped. 'Why do you think everyone calls

us white kaffirs? Huh?' he said, dragging her out of the bush. 'Because you're disgusting!'

Charlize struggled and cried. 'Werner – he's hurting me.'

'Johann, be careful, man. Don't hurt her.'

'I'm going to chuck her in the dam.'

Charlize broke free with one hand and smacked him in the balls. Johann bent over double from pain and let go of her other hand. Charlize ran into the bush and scrambled up a tree.

'You brat!' Johann shouted. He crossed his arms over his stomach and bent over. 'I'm going to *moer* you! In the *blarry* goonies!'

'You were hurting me,' she shouted as she climbed higher up the tree.

'If you keep climbing you're going to get stuck and I won't help you down!'

'I won't get stuck.'

'I'm going to fucking pull you out of the tree!' Johann, like an animal, darted between the bushes and clambered up the tree.

She looked down at her brother, who was quickly gaining on her, and screamed. The adrenalin made her reckless.

'Johann,' Werner called, 'you're scaring her.'

'You come down now!' he screamed.

Charlize looked down and saw how high she'd climbed. She wrapped her arms around a secondary trunk and started crying. 'I'm scared.'

'Christ!' Johann said. 'I told you this would happen.'

He began to give his sister instructions on how to get down from the branch, but she refused to move.

Werner called up. 'Charlize, if you come down, I promise you don't have to have a cold bath.'

'What are you saying?' Johann said.

'I've got a plan,' Werner replied.

'Promise?' Charlize asked.

'I promise,' Werner said.

Foothold by foothold, hand by hand, Johann and Werner guided her down the tree. About a metre from the ground she jumped down and tried to run away, but Johann grabbed her by the back of the dress. 'Where are you going?'

'She can shower at the camp,' Werner said.

'Are you mad?' Johann said.

Charlize shook her head. 'I'm not going to the camp.'

'But the water is hot.'

'Johann says your ma is mean.'

Werner blushed. 'It's not true.' Johann clipped his sister around the back of the head.

'And if she sees me, she will see how dirty I am. And then Johann will be embarrassed and shout at me.'

Johann clipped his sister again. Werner reached into his pocket and took out the fifty-cent coin. 'Do you want this?'

Charlize reached to grab it.

'Fifty cents? Are you crazy?' Johann asked.

Werner turned to Charlize. 'Shower first, though.'

'For fifty cents she'll take a cold bath.'

'No, I won't,' she said.

They walked back to the house to get soap and a towel.

The brothers were agape at the state of their sister.

'*Skorrie fokken morrie!*'

'If Pa sees her, he will go ballistic! Look at her!'

'Fuck you, guys!' Charlize said.

The two brothers jumped up to take their little sister in hand, but Johann quickly moved between them and pushed them away. 'Leave her alone.'

They walked in silence. At the camp perimeter Werner told them to wait. The girls were on a sunset walk with Steyn and his father. They'd be back in about half an hour. He looked around for his mother. She was busy reading a magazine in the lounge. He gestured for them to follow. Johann and Charlize darted out of the bush and followed him to the ablutions block. Werner took a tentative step into the bathroom to see if anyone was there. Maria was mopping the floor.

'Hi, Maria,' he said.

'Werner – what you doing here?' she asked. Her voice was indifferent.

'Maria, my friend's bathroom is broken. His sister needs to take a shower. Is that okay?' Maria shrugged.

When Charlize walked into the bathroom, Maria put her hands on her hips. 'Werner – this one is too dirty. What, you want I must mop again? I have just cleaned.'

'I'll clean, Maria.'

'Yes – you say, but you won't. I know you.'

'Charlize,' Johann commanded, 'go shower now.'

'Not with everyone watching,' she said.

Maria, Johann and Werner stood outside the bathroom

and waited for Charlize to finish. After a minute they could make out singing coming from the shower.

'When are you coming back to the house, Maria?' Werner asked.

'Ah – you mother doesn't want. She want a new *ousie*.'

Johann called in to the bathroom, 'Charlize, hurry up.'

'I'm hurrying,' she shouted back. 'But I'm very dirty.'

'This little girl is sweet,' Maria said. 'I like that you take care of her. But why her mother let her get so dirty.'

'That's why we brought her here,' Werner said quickly. 'Her mother would be angry if she saw her.' Maria nodded sceptically.

Petronella must have seen Maria from the house, standing by the ablutions block, mop in hand, not doing anything. They heard her shout before they saw her.

'Maria, what are you doing just standing around? Huh? You think I can't see you from the house?' Maria turned to face the boys. 'And you two?' Petronella asked. 'What are you two doing here? There are girls in the camp this week. I don't want you hanging around the ablutions block.'

'Ma, let me explain,' Werner said.

Charlize had finished showering, but, afraid of Petronella, waited at the entrance to the ablutions block.

'Who is she?'

'It's my sister, *tannie*,' Johann said.

'Ma – their geyser is broken. I said—'

Petronella cut over her son. 'Come here, girl.' Charlize edged towards the woman, but then stood behind Johann, holding her dirty clothes and wet towel to her chest. 'I'm not going to bite. What's your name?'

'Charlize,' Werner answered for her.

'Charlize, come here.'

She stepped towards Petronella.

'*Nee God!* This girl is still filthy! Johann, what is your mother playing at? Huh? Come, girl. You are going to have a proper bath.' She grabbed Charlize by the wrist, but before walking away she turned to Maria. 'Maria, I don't know what's going on with you. You think because you're not working in the house any more you can just stand around all day doing nothing?'

Maria started shaking her head. '*Aaai, missies*, this is not right. These boys ask for this little girl to shower . . .'

'Don't you backchat me! Who do you think I am? Huh? I am not one of your bantu friends! I am your *missies*. I am your *baas!*'

'*Baas* Hendrik is my *baas* – you are nothing,' Maria said.

Petronella had forgotten that she was still holding Charlize by the wrist. She took a step towards Maria, twisting the girl's arm.

'*Donner!*' Charlize cried. Petronella turned to the child, exasperated. 'Charlize!' Johann said.

'Never in my life . . .' Petronella muttered, looking at Charlize. She turned to Maria. 'Now, you listen here. I have had it with you, *meid*. You go back to your room and pack your things. Because when I tell the *baas* what you said, you will be out of here. You and your husband and your *blarry* kids too. You understand? Now get out of my sight!' Maria dropped her mop where it was and walked back to her room. Petronella turned to Johann. 'And as for you,' she said, yanking Charlize by the wrist, 'I am going to have words with your mother about what's going on. This is not the way you raise children. I have half a mind to call the welfare. Come,' she said as she turned to the house, dragging Charlize behind her.

'Fuck, Werner,' Johann said.

'I'm sorry. Just let her calm down. Wait till my dad gets back. He'll sort it out, I promise. It will be fine.'

It was dark and the girls were returning to camp to shower before dinner. Werner suggested they walk to the dam or the obstacle course, but Johann didn't want to leave his sister.

'We can't hang around here,' Werner said. 'If my father sees us he'll think we're spying.'

'Where's your ma? Do you think she'll take Charlize home?'

'I don't think so.'

'If my dad has been drinking and you ma turns up and shouts at him, there'll be big shit.'

They walked towards the house. Steyn was standing in the doorway of his rondavel.

'Hey, *lighties*,' he said, 'what you up to?'

'Hello, *oom*,' Johann said. Werner ignored him. Johann bit his bottom lip.

'Are you all right, Johann? What's going on?'

'The *tannie* is . . .' Johann looked to Werner, but Werner

looked away. '*Tannie* Nellie got real mad about my sister using the shower.'

'Why was she using the shower, Johann?' Steyn asked.

'Because the geyser is broken, *oom*. She was playing in the bush – that's why she was dirty. And then, when I tried to make her take a bath, she climbed a tree and then Werner said she could come use the showers at the camp . . .'

'I'm sure it's fine. Nellie won't mind.'

'*Ja* – but, *oom*, I think the *tannie* is going to call the welfare, *oom*. She said . . .' Johann started crying and wiped away the snot and tears on his arm. 'She's going to tell my parents – and then when she talks to my father . . .'

'Calm down. Come inside.'

Johann nodded, but didn't stop crying.

'Stop being a baby,' Werner said.

'Werner, you shut your mouth,' Steyn said.

Johann sat on Steyn's bed and Werner sat in the corner of the room, glaring at Steyn and his friend. Steyn sat next to Johann, rubbed the top of his head and pulled the crying boy closer to him. Werner smirked.

'Listen here, *lightie* – are you listening?' Johann nodded. 'Sometimes *Tannie* Nellie has got a bit of a temper – okay? Nobody is going to the welfare about anything. You hear?'

'But . . . but . . . *oom* doesn't understand. My ma is sick, *oom*. I'm the one . . . that . . .'

'Johann, I know.'

Johann leant in against Steyn, so that his head rested against Steyn's chest while Steyn rubbed the boy's back.

Werner was seething. Steyn would steal whatever he could. He stared at the man's crotch, willing him to see what he was doing. He glanced up. Steyn had seen where he was looking. Johann's face was still buried in the man's chest and Werner smiled, before returning his gaze to the man's crotch.

'Werner,' Steyn said. His voice shook a little.

'What, *oom*?'

Steyn swallowed. 'Don't you think you should go and check on Johann's sister? And your mother? To see how they're getting on.'

Werner looked at his crotch again.

'Will *oom* take care of Johann?' he asked.

'Werner,' Steyn said. Werner slowly looked up from the man's crotch to meet his eyes. 'That's enough now, Johann,' Steyn said as he withdrew from the boy, taking his arm off his shoulder. 'You'll be fine.' But Johann, still upset, leant back into Steyn and Werner snorted.

'Werner, get out,' Steyn said.

Werner jumped up and slammed the door behind him.

Petronella wanted this girl clean. Perhaps if she sent her back the way a little girl should be, smelling of soap and talcum powder, she could drive out the infestation creeping into her life. Or maybe these people would get their act together. They'd look at their little girl and say, 'This is what a little girl should look like. This is the way a little girl should smell.' And they'd pull themselves together. She wanted to wash away the trash, she wanted to wash away the kaffir, so that everything was wholesome and normal. She grabbed Charlize's dress and lifted it over her head.

'Are you not wearing any panties?' she asked. Charlize shook her head. '*Sies*, man – what sort of girl are you? Lettie, Lettie, come here!'

Lerato opened the door. 'Yes, *missies*?'

'Take these clothes and give them a quick wash. And then get me the old bathrobe – it's in the cupboard.' Petronella opened the medicine cupboard and poured a capful of Dettol into the bath.

'Do you have any cuts?' Charlize nodded. 'Well, this will sting. But it will be good for you. Show me your hands.'

Charlize put her hands out, palm down.

'Look at your nails!' Embarrassed, the girl put her hands behind her back. 'No point in hiding them now. I've seen how dirty they are. Get in – get in.'

Charlize stepped into the bath and Petronella scrubbed. When the bath water turned brown, she took the girl out, ran a new bath and put her back in. She washed her hair three times and checked for nits. She clipped Charlize's nails and dug the dirt out from under them with such ferocity that some of the girl's fingers and toes bled. She brushed the knots out of her hair and ignored her wincing as she tugged a comb through her hair to get through a clump. Lerato came into the bathroom with clean towels and an old dressing gown.

'Have you washed her clothes?'

'Yes, *missies* – they're drying by the heater.'

'Good, give me the towel.' She took it from Lerato, pulled

out the plug and told the girl to stand. 'There, much better. You look almost like a normal girl now.' Charlize shivered as Petronella dried her from head to toe and wrapped her in a dressing gown. 'Lettie, take this girl to the kitchen and put her by the heater with the clothes, while they dry off. And give her a sandwich or something.'

Lerato led the girl out of the bathroom. Petronella's back ached from bending over. She put her hand on the small of her back and arched. She then proceeded to empty the remaining contents of the Dettol into the bath and poured bleach on the bathroom tiles.

Johann started crying again. For a few minutes Werner had made Steyn's stomach turn with fear. The way the boy had stared at him, with such knowingness, was like being stripped, flayed. People always said there wasn't a boy that Steyn couldn't break, but he wondered if, in Werner, he had not met his match.

Petronella had unwittingly lanced a lifetime of fear and hopelessness and chaos, so that all he could do was rock and say, 'It's all right.' And the boy, rather than relaxing, clung even tighter to him. His hair brushed Steyn's lips, and so he leant in and kissed him gently on the head. He kissed him again. 'It's all right. Everything is going to be fine.'

The boy did not release his grip and Steyn nuzzled his hair a little. The best thing to do would be to take Johann to the house now. He thought about putting his hand on the boy's thigh. Perhaps he and Johann could go somewhere? Into Barberton for a milkshake and a beer? And then? They could stay in a hotel. He needn't do anything. They could just lie together. He could give the boy some time away from his family. Was Johann not the person he'd choose to spend a night with? In the end – whatever happened – what this boy needed was love. Steyn knew he could love this boy better than anyone else. Johann relaxed completely as he caressed him. He could not smell the poison in Steyn's veins.

Perhaps he was man enough. Perhaps this was not so fucked up. Steyn held Johann tight; brown and beautiful and naïve and full of love and goodness and kindness – the antithesis of the dangerous boy skulking around the rondavel. He looked up. Werner was peering into the room, with his devil-eyes.

20

Werner knocks on the front door and Marleen opens it. She's wearing a nightgown.

'Hello, Werner,' she says.

'Hello – is Johann here?'

'It's late.'

He looks at his watch. 'Oh,' he says.

She sighs. He's had a lot to drink. 'Come in.'

Johann comes into the lounge wearing his pyjama bottoms and a white singlet.

'Werner, what's wrong?'

'I'm sorry – it's late. Should I go?'

'What's going on?'

Marleen says, 'I'm going to bed. I have to be up early.'

Johann sits next to Werner and rubs his eyes. 'So what is it?'

'I've just seen the most amazing thing. It's incredible.'

'What?'

'I was at Moedswill.'

'What were you doing there?'

'It's a long story. But I saw him. The son – his name is

Stefan. The one who nearly died. He's paralysed, of course, but he's brilliant He's a painter, Johann. The most brilliant painter. He does these huge canvases. They're all about the murders. I've never seen anything like it.'

'That's horrible.'

'They're so beautiful. Do you have anything to drink? I really need to drink something.'

Johann gets up and rummages in the kitchen for a bottle of brandy. He pours Werner a shot. He hands him the glass and sits next to him.

'Are you not going to have anything?' Johann shakes his head. Werner sips his drink. 'I don't like drinking alone, here in front of you. I wish you'd have a drink too.'

'I've got a delivery tomorrow morning.'

'I'm going back tomorrow. I'll ask Stefan if you can come along sometime and see for yourself. I really want you to see it, Johann. You've never seen anything like it in your life.'

'That's great, Werner.' His voice is flat.

Why is Johann not interested? Werner's words can't do the whole episode justice, of course. He cannot conjure up for his friend the sight of the paintings. 'You know how he does it? He has like . . . this chair, and these pulleys and ropes. And then he gets some bantus – oh, and I didn't tell you the first thing. The farm is like a squatter camp. I mean, he's sold most of the land or leased it, or something. Well, I know that because the lawyer told me – but then I understood when I was there.'

'What lawyer? Your father's lawyer?'

'Yes – but that doesn't matter now. The bantus all live in a squatter camp. It goes right up to the house. And in exchange for living on his land, they have to help Stefan paint.' Werner walks into the kitchen and helps himself to more brandy, which he gulps down. He pours himself another and feels his pockets. 'I've left my cigarettes in the car.'

Johann looks amongst the clutter on the coffee table and finds Marleen's cigarettes. He throws Werner the packet, which he tries to catch, but drops. He picks them up.

'Lighter?' Johann throws him a lighter, which again he drops. 'Ha-ha – butterfingers. But I'm shaking – look.' He extends his hand. He lights a cigarette, picks up his brandy and sits next to Johann, so close that they're almost touching. Johann moves away. 'Stefan has a chair that they lift up using ropes and pulleys. He has to, because the canvases are so big. And he just sort of . . . hangs there. For hours. Painting. It's incredible.' He leans back against the couch and blows out smoke. 'Oh, shit!' he says, noticing the ash that's about to fall. He cups his hand beneath the cigarette and catches it.

Johann takes an ashtray off the table and passes it to him. 'Here,' he says.

Is there a note of irritation in Johann's voice? He must be imagining it. How could Johann possibly be irritated after last night? How could he possibly be irritated with all that money – Werner's money – that he didn't even ask for? A door slams.

Johann says, 'I think we need to keep it down.'

Werner nods. 'Sure, sure.' He sips his drink. 'Maybe if I go tomorrow I can give you a call, once I've spoken to Stefan, and you can come over. I think he would let you come over in the afternoon.'

'I have to work tomorrow.'

'He's a bit touchy. He's very strange – I mean, you should hear the story he told me.' He leans forward and takes another of Marleen's cigarettes out of the packet.

'Werner, please don't smoke all of Marleen's cigarettes.'

'*Jissus* – sorry, man,' he says, putting the cigarette back. 'She is hard work, isn't she?' Johann shrugs. 'I mean, I can tell she doesn't like me.'

'She doesn't really know you.'

'No need to protect my feelings. I know she doesn't like me. I don't know what I did to her, though. I can imagine what she must have said when I left. She probably told you I just came for the money. You should have heard her carry on when you went out. She basically told me it would be best if I left you alone.'

'What?'

'*Ja* – you know. Let you get on with your own life. I didn't say anything, but you know I could have. I could have told her that we go way back. So what did she say?'

'About what?'

'When I left yesterday. Did she say I was bad news? Did she say I just came for the money?'

'No. No – she was in bed when I got home.'

Werner stands up and loses his balance. '*Jissus* – that last brandy went to my head.' Johann helps steady him so that he doesn't knock over anything on the table. 'I need some cigarettes. I have some in the car.' They walk to the battered Corolla parked in the driveway. Werner opens the passenger door and scratches around in the mess on the floor of the car. 'Fuck! I know I had a packet somewhere.' He opens the cubbyhole and finds a half-empty packet. He leans against the car and lights a cigarette, then offers one to Johann. Rather than give Johann the lighter, he cups his hand around the flame so that Johann has to lean into him. He can feel Johann's breath on his skin. He can smell the shampoo he must have used earlier in the evening. As they walk back to the *stoep*, Werner says, '*Jissus*, I'm drunk. I don't think I can drive.'

'I'll drive you,' Johann says. 'I can walk back.'

Werner thinks it would be simpler for him to stay over, but Johann does not offer this. He's probably afraid of what Marleen would make of it. They sit on the *stoep*.

'Don't worry, I'll walk back,' Werner eventually says. 'I'm sorry for barging in on you like this.'

'It's okay.'

'I was just really excited. I didn't know who else I could talk to.'

'I understand.'

'Where's your arm?' Werner asks.

'I don't wear it to bed.'

Werner throws the cigarette on the ground and crushes

it with the heel of his shoe. He clears his throat. 'Can I touch it?'

'What?' Johann asks.

Werner touches just below his own shoulder, where Johann's stump would be.

'Why?'

Werner shrugs. He can feel the set of his face. He can feel himself plead.

'I suppose,' Johann says and looks away.

Werner brings his hand towards the smooth stump. His hand shakes. There is still a purple scar that runs through the centre. How quickly Johann has conceded to this – to being touched. Werner runs his finger along the scar and it gives Johann goosebumps. He cups his hand around it; makes a socket for the stump and he thinks, like this, they fit together. His breath quickens and he is erect also. He leans forward and gently kisses the stump as he has fantasised, but Johann pulls away and says, 'What are you doing?'

'I was kissing you,' he says. 'I was kissing you – is that okay?'

'Well, don't.' Johann gets up. 'You're drunk. I think you need to go home.'

'I wasn't really doing anything. What do you care anyway? It was nothing.'

'Werner.'

'Such a small thing . . .' he says quietly. 'Why can no one do these small things for me?'

'I don't like you that way.'

Johann's voice is sharp. It is irritating to be spoken to

like this. Why is he being so narrow-minded? So provincial? So Afrikaans?

'I know! Okay? I know you don't – but what's it to you anyway? *Jissus*, Johann – we grew up together. You all thought I was so fucking stupid.'

'What are you talking about?'

They hear a door slam. Marleen is tying her dressing gown and walking towards the door that leads to the *stoep*.

'Marleen, go back to bed,' Johann says.

'I won't go back to bed. I heard you two talking about me – you think I'm deaf? What the hell is going on here?'

Werner turns to her. 'Nothing is going on – why don't you just fuck off!'

'You watch your mouth!' Johann says.

'You see!' Marleen shouts. 'I told you. I warned you about him.'

'You warned him?'

Johann does not answer. What was it they discussed? The money, or something else? Did Marleen sense something else about him?

'You're a piece of shit!' she shouts.

Werner turns to Johann. But his friend says nothing. 'Johann?' Can Johann not see that he is pleading with him? Why does he stand by, while this woman attacks him? Why is he being so cruel? 'You arsehole. You're supposed to be my friend. I have nothing! You took it all – you took my life. You have no idea what I've done – you don't know what I had to do.'

'What are you talking about, Werner?' Johann asks.

'Nothing. You're supposed to be my friend!' he shouts.

'I am your friend – but I'm not a faggot.'

'Yes, you are. I know. I know what happened!'

'What is he talking about, Johann? What did he do?'

'Nothing, Marleen – go back to bed.'

'What did he do, Johann?'

'I kissed him, okay – stupid bitch . . .'

'He's not a poof like you!' she shouts. 'You fat arsehole!'

'You miserable piece of worthless trash. You know nothing!'

Johann steps forward and punches Werner in the face. He falls to the ground and holds his head.

'You show him, Johann!' Marleen says.

Johann shoves her into the house. 'Go to bed!' Instead she sits on the settee and watches from inside. Johann rushes out and bends over to help Werner.

'Leave me alone! Get your hands off me.'

'I'm sorry,' he says. 'But you can't speak to Marleen that way.'

'Just give me my keys,' he says.

'You can't drive. I'll take you home.'

'Give me my fucking keys!' Werner goes into the house to get the keys. The pain is intense. The last time he was punched in the face was in high school. How strong Johann must be. Already he can feel his eye swelling shut.

'Come, let me take you back to your hotel.'

Werner wants him to. He wants Johann like this:

solicitous, tender, guilty. He wants to make up with him, but he can't. 'Just give me my keys.'

Reluctantly, Johann lets him have the keys. He follows Werner to his car. 'Werner, please wait.'

Before he gets into the car, Werner turns to Johann and says, 'You're going to throw your life away. Just like your father.'

With one eye swollen, and drunk, it is difficult to drive back to the hotel, but there isn't much traffic and it's not far. Werner goes to the bar and asks for some ice in a tea towel and a double whisky. He presses the ice against the side of his face. He drinks the whisky and orders another. He can't believe that Johann punched him. Johann let him touch him. He let Werner touch and caress him. How was that so different from a kiss? Everything was humiliating. He feels a surge of anger towards his father. He must remember to collect the ashes, so that he can do something thoroughly unholy with them – in front of his mother. He wants to shout at her: *This is what I think of that miserable, worthless prick!* And Marleen? What does he want to do with Marleen? He wants to put a shotgun between her legs and blow her cunt out the top of her head. He wants to watch dogs lick up her blood and remains on the floor and tear at her entrails. She takes his money and turns his friend against him. He thinks about Marleen using that money: a romantic dinner with Johann; new lingerie to excite Johann; a new bedspread on which to fuck Johann. The barman enquires about his eye, and Werner tells him to mind his own business and get him another drink. The rage, rather than subsiding, is building. He downs his drink and walks out of the bar, still pressing the tea towel with ice to his face. Aleksander and his parents pull into the hotel car park. The parents nod politely as they walk past, and Aleksander gives him a quizzical glance. He removes the ice pack to reveal his badly swollen face. The boy looks wide-eyed, turning around to take a second glance as he follows his parents to the hotel entrance. Werner thought it would be humiliating, but – drunk, dishevelled, beaten – he feels masculine. Was that admiration he saw in the boy's eyes?

The next morning Werner wakes up late with a headache. His face throbs. He inspects himself in the mirror. His face is less swollen, but a purple bruise extends beyond the eye socket, and he peers out of a slit. His hair is dirty and he smells. He throws up in the toilet, swallows the remainder of his painkillers and takes a shower. He is running out of clean clothes. He makes a mental note to enquire about a laundry service at the hotel. How much longer does he intend to stay?

He sits on the bed. There is little point really. He should simply pack his things and head back to Pretoria where, if he has any sense, he will redouble his efforts at his job and eventually be appointed manager. But should he set much store by this? How long did he wait for a position at the Bureau? And would they appoint a white man, a Boer, as manager? How has it come to this? Now even a more senior position in administration is, if he gives it any thought, unlikely. The sense that his life has been lived with an illusory future, which always seemed only fractionally out of reach, is paralysing. He should get up, do something, but he just sits. He touches his face. Johann punched him. After everything, Johann punched him. And yet he can feel, pressing up against the gloom, the darkness, little tumours of hope that threaten to burst through and set him again on a course of action to save his life. Johann's guilt. Stefan's paintings. He tries to push them away, but doing so is like needing them, feeling the growing solidness of magnificent, malignant *possibility*. What happened last night can be undone. Johann will ask for forgiveness. He will come pleading, if only to clean the money he took from his friend. And Stefan? That, he thinks, feeling a surge of energy, remains to be seen. He grabs his car keys and heads out.

When the maid opens the door, Stefan is waiting in the living room. 'You're late,' he says to Werner. He looks at Werner's face, but says nothing.

'Could I have some coffee?' Werner asks.

Stefan nods at the maid, who goes to the kitchen. Stefan does not intend to have Werner over for company. This time there are only two black men waiting in the dining room. Werner has been co-opted as free labour. No matter, he thinks. The maid brings a pot of coffee on a tray and sets it down on a small table. His hands shake as he spoons the sugar.

'I hope you will be a little more steady when I'm working,' Stefan says, looking at his hand. Werner nods.

They raise Stefan to the required height for the day's work. He is unsatisfied with the rendering of the ceiling. The reflections are not correct. There is a pile of photographs, which Stefan took at different times of day of the living-room ceiling. Werner is glad of the silence. He feels a certain kinship with this man who has the tact not to ask what has happened. He is concerned about the occasional waves of nausea, and has worked out what he will do if he cannot suppress the need to vomit. The important thing will be to move as far from the painting as possible. But it will not do to vomit. He cannot be dismissed, shunned, twice in twelve hours. He cannot have Stefan and his goons toss him out the house so that he's crawling around in the dust of a squatter camp, with nowhere to go but home, back to his devoured half-life, in a state of disgrace.

At one, they break for lunch. The black men are dismissed to eat their lunch outside and the maid brings in a plate of ham-and-cheese sandwiches for Werner and Stefan. The man has made some effort. Perhaps he was excited by the prospect of Werner joining him after all? Is it simply the fact of white company? The bantus, Werner thinks, are unlikely to have much time for a mad cripple painting scenes of violence. They will do what they must, for rent or money, but have little interest in this man or his work. Besides, they must wonder, is it really necessary for him to make so much of this minor tragedy? The bantus are so practised at the art of suffering; they are the masters of suffering: *I suffer therefore I am*. So perhaps this is what Werner is to Stefan; another white man who, as Afrikaners go, is cultured enough. He benefits then from Stefan's isolation. He must seem a veritable Renaissance man. Werner nibbles his sandwiches. It will be good to settle his stomach.

After lunch they set to work again. There are no interruptions this time and Stefan works without speaking much. Three times he asks to be taken down so that he can view the painting from the back of the room. When Werner is about to ask a question he is silenced by Stefan. Today there is more of a mania to his work than yesterday; an intensity that the two workers have evidently learnt to recognise. He is not belligerent and rude this time, but sharper and more impatient with their work. He expects an intuitive understanding of what is needed, and it is clear to Werner that the two black helpers are far more practised at this than he is. He is the awkward presence in the room; slower, sometimes confused about what's needed. The men step in to smooth things over, using few words. There is no music this time. Everyone conspires to maintain the silence. They break again at four and then work until eight. Finally Stefan says, 'I cannot manage another stroke.'

They lower him into the wheelchair. They are all exhausted. Stefan goes to the back of the room to survey the day's work. He flicks through the photographs and glances up at the painting. He makes a few notes in a book, the pages of which are covered in a dense black scrawl interrupted by a few sketches. In the book there are also newspaper clippings and other loose sheets of paper. The men leave and Werner is left alone with Stefan. Werner asks to use the bathroom. He walks down a passage that is filled with paintings: a bullet passing through a boy's skull, the dead body of the schoolgirl in the living room, like Ophelia floating in blood. There are portraits of all the brothers and sisters, bar Stefan. The bathroom is at the end of the passage, but he decides to go up the stairs to have a look at more paintings. On the landing is another large canvas: the house from afar, with the yellow police tape flickering in the breeze. In one of the bedrooms is another painting. It's a picture of a white man and a black woman in the cab of a *bakkie*. He looks at the picture more closely. The man is his father.

'What are you doing here?' It is a black woman, very thin, with severe features.

'I was looking for the bathroom,' he says.

'It's downstairs.'

'Lerato?' he asks. She nods. 'Do you remember me?'

'You have the same eyes as your father.'

'Is that him? With you?'

She nods. 'Stefan will not like it if you are here.'

He leaves the room and goes downstairs, but Lerato does not follow him. He takes a long piss in the bathroom. The sounds of his stream hitting the water echoes and he wonders whether Stefan can hear it. He could offer to become Stefan's carer. In his own way he could be a midwife to greatness.

Stefan has put on a CD. More Bach. He calls for Werner from the kitchen. He's opened a bottle of wine and has laid out cheese, crackers and grapes. He gestures to a chair and Werner takes a seat. He pours Werner and himself a glass of wine.

'If you want to snoop around my house you should at least ask,' he says.

'I'm sorry.'

'Did you meet Lerato?'

'I did.'

'Did you ask for your money?'

'No.'

'Did you recognise your father?' Werner is uncomfortable at having being caught out. 'I can hear every footstep from downstairs. And you're not a small man.' Werner blushes. 'Did you recognise him?'

'Yes.'

'How good is the resemblance?'

'Good.'

'Only good? Did you walk into the room and gasp with instant recognition? Or did you have to study the face? Is it just an approximation of the man? It's difficult, painting someone you don't know. I had a few photographs to work with – but Lerato gets very irritated with me. I make her study the pictures until she begs me to stop. I don't know whether I'm draining the venom or sucking her dry.' Stefan laughs. 'Probably the latter. She's a bit creepy, isn't she? The way she knocks about upstairs. All wan and wasted.' He laughs again. 'My little black spook. I call her my little kaffir muse – and when she tells me not to call her that, I say I only call her kaffir because she doesn't believe in my work.'

'Why do you paint these pictures?'

'*Jissus*,' he says, 'what else can I do? It is the defining event of my life. Nothing will eclipse it. Sometimes you choose what defines you and at other times it is thrust upon you. There is no point in pretending otherwise. There is no moving on. It is the only thing I think about. It will be the only thing I think about until the day I die.'

Werner wonders about defining moments. It is not the way he has thought about life. Does every life have one? Is so, has he had his? Was the murder of his father his defining moment? If so, it is rather feeble. Perhaps that should be his epitaph: *Werner Deyer – Undefined*.

'So what are you going to do?' Stefan asks.

'About what?'

'About your money. And the fact that you don't have it.'

Werner shrugs. 'I don't know. I will go back to Pretoria, I suppose.'

Stefan nods and refills their glasses.

'What are you going to do with the paintings?'

'Burn them,' he says, but when he sees Werner's expression, he quickly adds, 'Don't be ridiculous! I'm might be mad, but I am not stupid. When I am finished I will have an exhibition. I will sit there in my sad little wheelchair and watch the people walk from canvas to canvas in stunned silence. Occasionally they will glance over their shoulders to take a peek at the tragic artist who's stuffing his face with canapés and drinking red wine by the bottle. And when the room is packed to the rafters, I'll take out a gun and blow my brains out.' He takes a sip of wine. 'I don't know. Maybe I'll sell them all and spend the rest of my days fingering prostitutes. Maybe I'll take a job teaching at the university, and then you and I can have lunch everyday. Maybe I'll die in my sleep tonight. Then all you have to do is take a hammer to Lerato's head and bribe my bantus to help you get the paintings back to Pretoria. Then you can be a real curator, like you always dreamt. You can tell people how you discovered a mad artist living in a squatter camp. It would make a good story. It would be your making. I'd probably do better dead than alive. I think my being alive makes the whole thing a bit tabloid. There would always be the problem of the artist – and, really, what else can he do? He's a freak who can't escape a twenty-minute episode of his life.'

They eat the cheese and grapes.

'Can I ask you a personal question?'

'What is more personal than this?' he says, gesturing to the paintings.

'Is Lerato . . . your lover?'

He sips his wine. 'When I turned eighteen I moved back to the farm. Another farmer had leased the land. I brought a carer with me. She cooked for me and cleaned for me and wiped my arse. A jolly woman. I hated her. Very much. I didn't go looking for Lerato. I don't know if I even wanted to see her. I thought she would have left. It's what she should have done. But one day she turns up at the door. And she looks like me. Fucked. Fucked in the head. The first person I saw who looked like me. I needed her. So I told her she must come and live with me. She thought as a maid. That too, but I wanted her to sleep in my room.' He gestures towards his groin. 'I am quite incapable of *doing* anything. But she was a comfort to me. She's the only one who knows. She belongs to me. At first she refused. The bantus are very prudish.' He smiles. 'So I said, "If you don't sleep in my room every night until the day I die, I will drive all your family and all of your friends from my land." So she stayed.'

'Do you still need her?'

'We need each other.' He cuts a slice of cheese and eats it. 'I don't know if that counts as being lovers. I suppose it's as close as I am ever likely to get.'

Werner nods.

'And you?' he asks Werner.

'What?'

'I doubt you'll get the money. So what do you want?' Werner shrugs. 'Everybody wants something, Werner.'

'Would you ever consider a commission?' Werner asks.

'It depends. Do you have something in mind?'

It must be the wine that makes him think this way; it has taken away, for a short time, the hurt. 'I would like you to paint a man with a prosthetic arm.'

'Any man or a *particular* one?' There is something cruel about the way he says 'particular', but Werner chooses to ignore it.

'A particular one. Naked, with a hook.'

'Perhaps.'

The maid clears the dishes. Stefan invites Werner to spend the night. That way he can start working early tomorrow. The maid shows him to the room with the painting of his father. He is tired, but not sleepy. He can hear voices in the house: Lerato and Stefan.

He looks at the painting, bringing his face to within a few inches of his father. 'Hello, Pa. Was this your defining moment? With the bantu girl?'

21

Tonight, Petronella thought, was the night that her house returned to normal. Now she could clear that family out of the area. Social services must come and take those children away. She looked at the little girl sitting in the kitchen with a towel wrapped around her, drying by the heater; a pretty little girl really. Perhaps, if circumstances had been different, she might have turned out okay. The girl was frightened. Petronella thought about what she could say to make the girl feel better. She felt bad for the rough way in which she'd treated her. The girl stared at her with contempt and stuck her tongue out. Petronella took a deep breath, decided to ignore it and put the kettle on. Marius walked into the kitchen.

'Hello,' he said to Charlize. The girl squirmed with embarrassment, folded herself up in her towel and stared at the kitchen table.

'Where is your brother?' Petronella asked him. He shrugged. 'Don't just shrug. Why do you think God gave you a tongue?' With Petronella's back to her, Charlize stuck out her tongue and Marius started laughing. 'What are you laughing at?'

'Nothing, Ma.'

She turned to face Charlize. 'You had better watch yourself, young lady. I don't care what goes on at that *gom-gat* house of yours – but in my house you will behave like a civilised white.' The girl did not answer and stared at the table again.

Petronella checked on Charlize's clothes, but they were still wet. She wanted this child and her brother out of the house, but she would not send her home in wet clothes. Someone needed to set an example for these people. She looked at the girl. Her hair was still knotty and untidy at the ends. Her fringe was too long. The more transformed she was, the stronger the message. 'You need a haircut,' she said. She took out a pair of scissors and a comb from one of the kitchen drawers. 'Marius – go and fetch the broom.' She stood by Charlize, scissors in hand. 'Sit up straight and close your eyes.'

'*Tannie* mustn't cut my hair.'

'Sit up straight and close your eyes.'

The girl did as she was told and Petronella started cutting her fringe. Somewhere she had some ribbon. She thought about tying bows in the girl's ponytail and maybe putting a little perfume on her. Perhaps she should tidy up the boy too. Get him to take a proper bath and cut his fingernails. She would give him an old pair of Werner's jeans and a clean T-shirt. Then she would knock on their door and say, 'Excuse me. I have brought your children back.' And she wouldn't have to say anything else. They'd see for themselves and be ashamed.

The wet clumps of hair fell on the floor and Marius swept them into a pile. Petronella could hear the girls returning to camp. They were filing into the mess hall and she could make out the clatter of tin plates and cups as the girls formed lines at the serving counters. Hendrik would soon be home. If she dealt with these children, he'd have to deal with Maria. Unless, of course, that woman had already gone running to him. It would not be the first time. For years that woman had worked by her side, but still she went running to Hendrik with any grievance, any perceived slight. She needed Hendrik to understand that she was trying to put things right. It was good that this was all coming to a head. With Lettie she was making a fresh start. She blew some loose hairs off the girl's face, and Charlize wrinkled her nose in distaste at Petronella's smoky breath. 'Much better,' she said, inspecting the girl, and then turned her around to cut the back of her hair.

Johann had stopped crying, but he still clung to Steyn in the dark of the rondavel. Steyn wanted to get up to switch on the lights, but it was pleasant just sitting here like this. He looked out of the window. There was no sign of Werner. In the distance he could hear the beginnings of a fight in the bantu village. A man and a woman were shouting. The girls at the camp were busy washing their tin plates and mugs in the giant troughs that had been filled with lukewarm soapy water. Lately they'd been telling the children to rub their plates with sand after eating. There had been outbreaks of diarrhoea because the girls and boys never cleaned their plates properly. The girls giggled when rubbing their plates in the sand. Steyn could hear one of the teachers shouting, 'You didn't do it properly – I saw. Do you want to get diarrhoea in your sleeping bag?' This set off squeals of laughter. The fight in the bantu village was getting worse. Now another woman had joined in. All three were shouting at each other. He should get up and see what was going on, but it was good to let the world just wash over him. Shadows of the girls and their teachers crossed in front of his window. Someone could come in any minute.

'Come,' Steyn said, 'we can't sit here all night.'

Johann sat up, sniffed and wiped his face on his arm. 'My sister.'

'What?'

'I have to go and find my sister. She's with *Tannie* Nellie.'

'All right – let's go.'

It had turned cold and he slipped on a jersey. He tossed the boy one of his, which Johann put on. Steyn took the sleeves and folded them over. He enjoyed the pathetic listlessness of the boy.

Petronella was busy tying ribbons in a girl's hair. She was too young to be one of the camp girls. His wife had a stern expression on her face and she glared when Hendrik walked into the kitchen. Before she said a word he felt drained. It had been a long day, but that face – never satisfied, always bristling for a fight – was enough to make him turn around, walk out into the bush and never come back.

'And who is this?' he asked.

'This is Charlize,' Petronella said.

'Hello, *oom*,' she whispered.

Petronella jerked with her head towards the living room, but Hendrik decided for the moment to resist her. He opened the fridge and took out a can of beer. He pulled back the tab and dropped it into the open can. Petronella closed her eyes with irritation, but said nothing. He took a slug of beer, wiped his mouth with the back of his hand and set the can down on the kitchen table.

'What are we having for dinner?'

'That can wait. There are a few things we need to sort out.'

He lit a cigarette and blew the smoke into the lampshade. It pooled in the shade and then leaked out the top vents, revealing six beams of light normally too faint to see. Some of the smoke drifted down and then trickled out around the rim. He took a sip of beer, stifled a belch and blew more smoke into the shade.

'Don't do that,' Petronella said.

He took another drag of the cigarette and did it again. She clenched her teeth. He took another deep slug of beer and this time didn't supress his belch. The children laughed and Hendrik smiled at them. Petronella ran her hands down her dress.

'Marius, why don't you and Charlize go and play?'

'Ma,' he said, 'she's just a baby.'

'I'm not a baby,' Charlize said.

'Marius,' Petronella snapped, 'do as I say.' He rolled his eyes. 'And don't you roll your eyes at me.'

Hendrik was on the verge of saying 'Watch it, boy', but decided against it, instead just watching the scene unfold.

Petronella waited for the children to leave. 'Close the door,' she shouted. Marius closed the door with some force, but not loud enough that he could be accused of slamming it. Petronella jolted at the noise. Her hands balled into fists by her sides. She then crossed her arms and held her right fist by her mouth. Hendrik looked at his wife and wondered how it was that she managed to distil all the minor irritations and arguments and the general friction of life into a pure burning rage that was eating her from the inside out.

'Nellie?' he finally conceded. She'd puckered her lips with anger. This was all he would offer. He would not console her; would not coax the anger from her. She said nothing. So he said, 'What's for dinner?'

'Are you not going to ask what that girl is doing here?'

'What?'

'She's Johann's sister, and today I caught them using the camp showers.'

He shook his head while he exhaled. 'They shouldn't do that.'

'Hendrik, you should have seen the state of her. Never in my life have I seen a child that filthy. It looked like she was living in the bush.' Hendrik shrugged with a look of resignation. 'This is a problem,' she said.

'What do you want me to do, Nellie? Looks like the girl is all cleaned up now.'

'We need to talk to the parents. What have we come to? Children sneaking in to use the toilets because their parents can't take care of them. And the mouth on that girl! If those children hang around the camp, people are going to think I let my children hang around with that trash.' Hendrik shrugged. 'No, don't you shrug at me,' she said, wagging her finger. 'I need you to step up! What about your job! What will the inspector think?'

'Let me worry about the job.'

'But you don't!' She pulled out one of the chairs and sat at the table. 'I fired Maria today.'

'You did what?'

'That woman is out of control. So you need to get down there and make sure that she and her husband and the kids are off this property tonight. If you refuse to keep the bantus under control, I *blarry* well will. You hear me!'

'Who do you think you are, woman? You have no right interfering with my staff.'

'Maria is my maid! And I say I've had enough of her. Lettie will be fine. It's what you wanted, isn't it? Didn't you go all the way down to Moedswill to fetch the little *kaffirmeid* because you were so concerned for her? Well, she has a job now! So get Maria out of my sight.' Someone knocked on the door. 'Who is it?' she snapped.

'We're not finished talking about this,' Hendrik said.

Steyn opened the kitchen door and stepped inside. Johann stood a little behind him. Petronella looked at the jersey Johann was wearing. One of the sleeves had come loose and was hanging over his hand.

'It's like a *blarry* orphanage in here.'

'I need to take my sister home, *tannie*.'

'Don't worry, Johann – you will both be going home soon. But you tell me, Johann, when has Charlize last been in school?'

Johann looked at the floor and said nothing.

'Nellie,' Hendrik warned.

She ignored him and carried on addressing Johann.

'Johann, you tell me if I have this right, but I seem to remember that not so long ago you had problems with school. No one saw hide nor hair of you for over a year. It was only when social services came that you went back to school. And now we see the same thing happening again with your sister?'

'Nellie, that's enough!' Hendrik said.

'Nellie, the kid is upset – just give him a break.'

'Steyn, I am not interested in your opinion. Hendrik, you can't have a bunch of truants running around on property that belongs to the Department of Education! What is wrong with you two?'

How, Hendrik wonders, would he shoot this woman? From behind, so that she never knows? Would she feel a sharp pain in the back of her head for a fraction of a second? Perhaps longer. No one knew. But then again, if he came at her with the gun, there would be something more satisfying in that. He would point the gun between her eyes and she would start trembling and crying, like a dog, backing away into a corner. 'Have you gone mad?' she would say. 'Please, Hendrik, what are you doing? Have you gone mad?' For every step she took back, he would take a step towards her. Maybe she would trip over a chair and piss herself.

'Let me take these two home,' Steyn said.

'You can come with me – but we have to have a word with the parents,' Petronella said.

There was more shouting at the village.

'Something is going on down there, Hendrik,' Steyn said.

'I wonder, Nellie, what you think is going on down there?' He took another drag of the cigarette and blew smoke into the light.

'I don't care what the bantus are screaming about – maybe if you kept some control!'

Hendrik got up and walked out of the kitchen. How his wife chose to deal with these children and with Steyn was of little concern to him. In the bedroom he opened his bedside drawer and took out his gun. Sometimes it felt good to give in to these temptations. Radical possibility made him feel calmer. With a gun you could quell the screaming of kaffirs. You could quell the screaming of your wife. After you did these things there was silence. What did the metal taste like? He licked the tip of the gun and then put the barrel in his mouth. Was the gun even loaded? He checked and it was. He couldn't put the gun in a holster and then walk into the bantu village. He put on the safety, stuck the gun into the back of his trousers and untucked his shirt. In the kitchen Steyn and his wife were arguing. Marius, Charlize and Johann stood and watched in silence. The gun, he noticed, gave his voice authority. 'Shut up! I'm going to see what's going on,' he said and strode out of the kitchen.

It was impossible to dissuade Petronella. So all four of them walked through the bush to Charlize and Johann's house. Steyn wanted Petronella gone. She was such a meddling, difficult bitch. But did he want Charlize gone also? The bush was dark. Steyn and Petronella carried torches that they used to light the path, but this meant they missed the occasional branch that hung in the way. At one of the clearings Steyn said, 'Stop here for a second.' He took one of the ends of the ribbon in Charlize's hair and tugged it loose.

'I like the ribbons, *oom*,' she said.

'What are you doing, Steyn?' Petronella asked.

He took the other ribbon out of Charlize's hair, went down on his haunches and handed them to her. 'Here,' he said. 'You can put these in your hair yourself when you want. Okay? But not now.'

'Steyn – this is none of your business.'

'Johann, take you sister home.'

Petronella grabbed Charlize by the wrist. 'You're not going anywhere without me.'

Johann looked from Steyn to Petronella. '*Oom?*' he asked.

'You are coming with me, Johann,' Petronella said. 'For your own good.'

'*Tannie* is hurting me,' Charlize said.

'Shut up!'

Charlize bent over and bit Petronella on the wrist. She let go of the child. Charlize darted into the bush.

'Go straight home,' Steyn called. Petronella said nothing.

They all stood in silence and listened to the breaking of twigs and the swish of branches as Charlize made her way back to the path further along. Steyn expected a furious eruption from the woman, but she just stood in the clearing listening to the girl.

'Be careful, Charlize,' she finally said. 'Don't hurt yourself.' She took out a cigarette and started smoking. 'I'm trying to help you, you know that?' she said to Johann. 'Everyone thinks I am this interfering woman. But you are so young. You know nothing.'

'We know you're trying to help,' Steyn said.

'Then why do you and Hendrik always fight me?'

He sighed. 'Go home, Petronella.' She exhaled smoke, dropped the butt on the ground, shook her head and started walking home. Johann put the cigarette out with the heel of his foot. Steyn was alone with the boy again.

It was Maria's husband who was shouting both at Maria and at Lerato. He was struggling to understand how, in the course of an afternoon, his wife had lost both her job and the house they lived in. Lerato said little, but Maria argued with both of them, shouting at Lerato and then turning on her husband. Hendrik could see this from afar as he approached the village. When they saw him, they all fell silent.

'And now?' he asked.

Maria and her husband shook their heads.

'Maria – what happened today?'

'I don't know. Ask the *missies*. I was doing nothing. I was cleaning and then the children want to use the shower, so I wait for them to finish. Now she say I must go. She want this one to work in the house,' she said, pointing to Lerato. 'Fine. I go.'

'But where will you go?' he asked.

'I don't know where I must go. It's too hard to find a job.'

Maria's husband shook his head and said, 'This is not right, *baas*. Please, *baas*, the *baas* must talk to the *missies*. Where must we go?'

'Stop packing, Maria. You can stay here. Lerato – this can't go on. You must go back to Moedswill. Stefan, the *kleinbaas*, he is still alive.' She nodded. 'Pack your things. I'm taking you home.' Hendrik waited while Lerato gathered her few possessions. She handed him the two folded overalls.

'What's this?'

'The *missies* she give them to me for the job.'

'Keep them.'

Maria said something to her and Lerato shook her head.

She packed the overalls into the suitcase and followed Hendrik back to camp. His *bakkie* was parked just outside the kitchen door. 'What the *missies* going to say, *baas*?'

Hendrik ignored her and walked into the house to grab his keys. His wife was not in the kitchen. When he came out, Lerato was sitting in the back of the *bakkie*, holding on to her suitcase.

'It's cold,' he said. 'Get in the front.'

'*Baas?*'

'It's dark. No one will see.'

Lerato hopped out the back of the cab. Hendrik opened the door for her. Ridiculous, he thought. What would people think if they could see this? It's like I'm taking this *meid* out on a date. She was wearing the clothes she'd worn on the day he picked her up from Moedswill: the worn cotton dress that was indecently short. He thought about how in the cab he could reach over and put his hand on her thigh and then slip it between her legs. He closed the passenger door. If he did it right, if she gave in to him, she might writhe beneath his touch the way Nellie had once done, years ago, when he'd got her drunk.

'Hendrik?' Petronella pointed with the torch into the car to see who the passenger was. 'Who's that? Is that Lettie?' she asked.

'Did you take the children back?'

'Why is Lettie in the car? What's going on?'

'I'm taking her back to Moedswill, Nellie. This has gone on too long. Maria is staying here.'

Nellie walked round the front of the *bakkie* and yanked the passenger door open. 'Out!' she shouted at Lettie. She grabbed the suitcase from the back and threw it on the ground. The old buckles sprang loose with the force, strewing the clothes. 'And who said you could take these overalls? Huh? I bought these for you to work in the house! You can't just take them! You're a thief!'

Hendrik started picking up Lettie's clothes while she sat in the cab with her arms folded across her chest. He picked up an old bra and panties and stuffed them into the suitcase. He walked over to the left front wheel of the car to pick up one of the overalls, but Nellie grabbed it from him and put it behind her back.

'No!' she shouted. 'I won't let you!'

'Give it here, Nellie!'

'Make me, you useless prick!' As he walked towards her she stepped backwards, facing him. 'You spineless waste of space . . . you pathetic joke. Look at this place! The children and the bantus walking all over you. What would your father think? He would die of shame.'

'Give it to me, Nellie.'

'I stopped listening to you a long time ago. Now tell that bitch to get out of the car and go back to the house.'

Hendrik reached round and took the gun out of the back of his trousers. Nellie stood rooted to the spot and started shaking.

'Hendrik? Are you mad?' She dropped the overall behind her.

'Give it to me,' he said. Nellie didn't move. He cocked the gun. 'Give it to me!' Petronella did not move. He fired a shot.

Werner pushed the bed to the side of the room and took out a stack of A4 sheets. With sticky tape he created a new canvas for his picture and laid it on the floor. He called Marius.

'What?' his brother asked.

'Where's Ma and Pa?' Marius shrugged. 'Come, I need your help.'

'Are you making a new picture of Jesus?'

'*Ja,*' Werner said. 'But this time I want you to trace me.'

Marius nodded. Werner stripped off his clothes and lay on the sheet of paper with his arms outstretched and his chin resting forward. Marius took a pencil and started tracing around Werner's head, down his neck and shoulders and along his arm. Werner had placed his one foot over the other, like Jesus's feet when they crucified him. Marius traced his sides and his legs. He brushed against his brother's body. Werner closed his eyes and thought about Jesus. Outside they could hear their parents arguing. There was a gunshot and a scream. Werner jumped up.

'Ma!' Marius shouted. 'Ma! Ma! Pa!'

'Shut up,' Werner said. He was struggling to get dressed.

'Ma! Ma! Ma!' he shouted.

Werner slipped on a pair of jeans. Someone was still screaming in the bush, but his mother was silent.

'Pa!' Marius shouted.

'Calm down.' Werner grabbed his shirt and put it on. 'Come,' he said, grabbing his brother by the wrist. As they ran to the kitchen, they heard a car door slam. By the time they opened the back door, the car was speeding down the driveway towards the main road.

'Ma!' Werner shouted. 'Ma! Where are you? Pa?'

Steyn sat alone in the bush. He stared at the spot where Johann had turned to look at him with a strange expression on his face. When he held the boy and nuzzled him, he did not sense Johann tense under his touch. The boy rested his face against Steyn's neck. The boy loved him. He'd stroked the boy's back. Johann was drawing the poison to the surface. He was drawing the poison into his hands and into his cock. He wanted to take the boy and rape him. He'd thought about holding the boy by the wrists, face down, with his knees on either side of his arse, and then in a single thrust relieving himself of the lust, of fucking the boy and then drowning himself in the dam. 'Get off me, Johann,' he'd said. The boy did not listen and clung to him. 'Get off me!' he'd said and flung the boy to the ground.

'*Oom?*'

'Don't touch me like that!'

'*Oom?*'

'Fuck off! Before I do something you'll never forget.'

The boy had scrambled to his feet, taken a last look and run away into the bush.

Steyn was filled with lust. It made him heavy. He lay down on the ground. It was completely dark and the skies were cloudless. He lit a cigarette and stared at the stars. He thought about lying there all night. He would apologise to the boy tomorrow. He'd fallen into a light doze when he was woken by the gunshot.

Hendrik dropped the gun and ran back to the car. He slammed the passenger door shut and ran round to the driver's side. 'Hendrik!' Petronella shouted. He started the car and sped down the driveway. Somewhere in the bush she could hear screaming. 'Marius! Werner!' she called. At the dormitories she could hear doors being slammed and teachers speaking to students. 'Everybody stay where you are,' they shouted. 'Stay where you are!'

Marius and Werner came running out of the house. 'Ma!' Marius shouted.

When she saw her sons the panic drained away. She embraced them and kissed them. 'It's all right,' she said. 'Just a little accident. Wait here.'

One of the teachers came running towards her. 'What's going on?'

'Nothing. Please go back to the dormitory and wait with the children. Keep them inside.' The teacher nodded and ran off. Petronella looked for the gun. With the torch she criss-crossed the spot where her husband had been standing. She picked up the pistol and emptied the cartridges into her apron. She listened for the moaning, but the bush was silent. 'Steyn!' she shouted. 'Steyn!'

'Ma, what's going on?' Marius asked.

'Nothing, darling. There's just been a little accident. Everything's fine.' She needed to go into the bush. He's shot one of the bantu children, she thought. Somewhere in the bush is a dead bantu child. 'Steyn!' she shouted again.

From some distance away she heard Steyn shout in reply. 'Petronella? What's going on?'

'Steyn, I need your help. Come now!' She ran into the house and opened a kitchen drawer, into which she flung the gun. 'Werner,' she said, 'take your brother and go and sit in your room and wait until I call you, okay?'

Steyn opened the door and came into the kitchen. 'Petronella? What's going on?'

'Boys – to your room.'

'Ma,' Werner said, 'let me help.'

'I heard screaming,' Steyn said.

Petronella tried to bite back the tears. 'I think someone has been shot.'

'Where? Where are they?'

'I don't know. Someone was in the bush when the gun went off.'

'Come on then,' Steyn said.

Petronella followed him out of the kitchen. She turned to see that her children had closed the door, but Werner was following with his own torch. 'Werner,' she shouted, 'go home!'

'No, Ma, I need to help.'

'Petronella, don't argue. Where do we need to look?'

'I don't know. I don't know. I think it's one of the bantu children!'

'Where's Hendrik?'

'We had a fight. He's gone.'

'*Jissus!*'

'Werner,' Steyn said, 'I want you to take the path towards the dam. Walk slowly, checking on your left and your right.'

'Okay, *oom*.'

'Nellie, you take the car track – can you do that? Nellie, listen to me! Are you all right? Can you do this?' She nodded. 'Where's the gun, Nellie?'

'The house. In the drawer.'

'Is it loaded?' She shook her head. 'Who fired the gun?'

Petronella opened her mouth, but she couldn't speak.

22

Werner awakes in the middle of the night. There is a commotion outside; people fighting. He gets up and looks out of the window. One of the shacks is on fire and a large group of men and woman are pushing and shoving. Someone starts banging on the door. '*Baas* Stefan!' she shouts, '*Baas*! Stefan! You must come – there is big trouble. *Baas* Stefan, they are burning down our house! They are burning the shebeen. Come quick – please, *Baas* Stefan!'

'Stefan,' Werner shouts, 'Stefan!'

'Go back to bed, Werner.'

Werner peers out of the window. Outside a man looks up at him and drags his finger across his throat, grins.

'Stefan!'

'For fuck's sake, Werner – leave it!'

The woman outside is still screaming. '*Baas* Stefan, please!' she shouts. 'They are going to kill us! Please, *Baas* Stefan! Please!'

'Will someone tell that woman to shut the fuck up,' Stefan says.

Werner goes downstairs.

Hearing him, Stefan calls after, 'Do not open the door to that woman! Oh, for fuck's sake. Help me get up,' he says to someone. Werner stands at the bottom of the stairs, wide-eyed. From the top of the stairs, Stefan calls, 'Werner, come here. There's nothing to worry about.'

Werner turns around and goes back up the stairs, and stops on the first landing. Stefan, wrapped in a dressing gown, is waiting for him at the top of the stairs in his wheelchair. Werner glances out of the window. There are a few fires in the distance, but nothing out of control, nothing that seems to be threatening the house. Lerato stands behind Stefan and puts her hands on his shoulders.

'It's the company,' she says. 'It's the people from the company.'

Stefan shakes his head. 'We don't know that.'

'What do you mean?' Werner asks.

'People think the company is trying to clear the squatters. They say the people steal fruit – which they probably do. Someone is bribing a bunch of thugs to cause trouble.'

'It's the same people that came that other time,' Lerato says.

'No.'

'This happens every few weeks. Just go back to bed. We need to get up early.'

Werner turns around and goes back to bed. It is true that things have died down. There is still noise and he can smell smoke, but the worst seems to be over. He goes back to bed and lies awake for an hour before falling asleep.

The next morning he is woken by Lerato knocking at his door. She tells him to come and get breakfast; Stefan wants to start work. There is no interest in discussing the events of the previous night. Stefan seems unperturbed. In the time Werner's been here, Lerato has not come downstairs. The maid carries a breakfast tray with toast and porridge to the room. He does not ask about this.

They wait in the dining room – Stefan calls it his studio – for the two helpers. Stefan looks at his watch, irritated. Thirty minutes late, the two men arrive. One has a cut above his right eye. Stefan says nothing and they begin work. Werner admires his devotion, his absolute and singular focus. Everything in the household is put in service of this. As they did yesterday, they break for lunch, tea and finish a little before eight. There is an expectation that Werner will spend the night. He wonders whether Stefan has dismissed the third man. Perhaps his free labour is what allows the money to go further. At dinner, Werner asks Stefan what he expects of him. Stefan says he expects nothing, but if he would like to be his assistant, he should move in. It will be more efficient. He should not, however, expect pay. In return for his services Werner will receive board and lodging. Werner says that he will mull it over. In any event, he needs to return to the hotel to collect his things and settle the bill.

He drives back to Barberton and considers the improbable offer that has been made. He could abandon his life in Pretoria entirely and apprentice himself to Stefan. Apprentice? Is that what he would be doing? Not exactly, but then again it is not merely a question of free labour, either. Stefan is drawing him into his work. Stefan is becoming his friend. It would be a shame not to be a part of it when this work is finally revealed to the world. The work today has been exhausting and by the time he gets into bed, Werner falls into a deep dreamless sleep.

He wakes early the next morning, packs his things and settles his hotel bill. He puts his bag in his car and walks towards Johann's house. He sits in the bush and waits. After ten minutes Johann comes out. Werner has to suppress the effort not to break into the clearing and fix things. For now, it is enough to look at Johann.

In Barberton town centre he withdraws money from his savings account and purchases a cellphone: a ridiculous extravagance, but after last night he feels too unsafe in the house without it. The first call he makes is to his mother. A what? A cellphone, Ma. I bought a cellphone. Ridiculous, she says. From where do you get the money for that?

He buys a new pair of jeans, clean underwear and a few T-shirts before driving back to Moedswill. He unpacks his things in the room he'd stayed in previously and asks the maid about a washing machine. She tells him to put his dirty clothes in the laundry. The *baas* has instructed her to take care of it. Also, he must hurry. *Baas* Stefan is waiting.

For the next week he does not leave the farm. They work from early in the morning until late at night. And then, as before, Stefan and Werner sit in the kitchen and eat dinner before going to bed. There is no further trouble with the people on the farm. Occasionally the shebeen closest to the house gets rowdy. At first Werner woke up in a panic, thinking that things were kicking off again, thinking this time they'd burn the house down, but by the third night he was used to the noise and managed to sleep through it. He is due to return to work in two days' time. He calls his manager at the university. Reluctant to play the part of a grieving son who still cannot face work, he says there are a number of complications with the estate. This explanation, he thinks, has the merit of being truthful, from a certain perspective. His manager agrees to a further week's leave. Werner tells Stefan that he will stay for at least another week. If he expects gratitude, it is not forthcoming. Stefan simply nods and says that would be acceptable. Werner is irritated. 'You know,' he says to Stefan, 'I could do with a little time off.'

'Of course you can have time off,' Stefan snaps. Werner just needs to say when. Unless Werner asks, the assumption is that they will be working.

Werner says he needs to run an errand in Barberton the next morning.

That night he writes a note:

Dear Johann,
I'm sorry about what happened the other night.

He crumples up the paper and throws it away. He is not sorry. Johann punched him in the face.

Dear Johann,

    I do not have any hard feelings about what happened the other night.

Again Werner throws it away. He does have hard feelings, but he also thinks it would do to be gracious.

Dear Johann,

    I am sorry about what happened the other night. I was shocked and hurt by what you did, but I suppose even the best of friends must have their disagreements. I do not have any hard feelings about what happened. I am living on Moedswill farm at the moment. I am helping Stefan with the paintings for an exhibition he hopes to hold soon. The work is brilliant and I think it will be a big success.

    I'm writing to invite you to visit me on the farm. It will be good to see you again so that we can talk things through. Also, I would very much like for you to meet Stefan. I have a proposal for both of you, though it is not something I feel I can put in this letter and would prefer to talk to you about it in person, after you have seen Stefan's work. You may not understand it now, but you are also a part of this story. I have bought a cellphone, so it should be easy for you to get in touch.

He adds his cellphone number and directions to the farm. After debating how best to close the letter, he simply signs it:

Your friend,
Werner
PS I don't think you should bring Marleen.

He reads through the letter a few times: not eloquent, but simple.

The next morning he drives to Barberton. He considers putting the letter under the front door, but then opts to put it in the postbox instead. He drives straight back to Moedswill to begin work. He knows that Stefan is irritated because he took the morning off. If he returns early he can begin winning him round again. There is a silent setting on the phone, which means it will vibrate if someone calls. He puts the phone in his pocket and goes straight to the dining room.

Despite the fact that Werner returned early, Stefan is in a bad mood. He snaps at Werner and the other two assistants. Today it is impossible to do right, but Werner does not care. He is simply waiting for the phone to ring. Soon Johann will call and they will talk and be friends again. And then Johann will arrange to come round. And when Stefan sees him, he will know that Johann is a worthy subject for his next painting. Werner will no longer just be the white helper. Stefan will recognise in Werner a talent. Werner will win back his friendship with Johann and it will be the beginning of his career. It is perhaps a late start, but the story will be a good one.

By six o'clock Johann has still not phoned. It's disappointing, but Johann has probably not read the letter yet.

Stefan declares the day a complete waste and spends the rest of the night in his bedroom. Werner, bored and impatient, decides to have a drink in the shebeen. The woman behind the counter eyes him with suspicion, but serves him anyway. The people keep their distance and he drinks his beer without talking to anyone. He takes out his phone and stares at it. Why has Johann not called? If Johann had called and for whatever reason he'd missed it, there should be a message on the screen that reads: *1 missed call*. Did he give Johann the right number? Perhaps, after what he'd done, Johann was too embarrassed to call? Werner decides to leave it for the night and goes to bed.

The next day Stefan's mood has not improved. They begin work early. Just before lunch Werner feels the phone in his pocket vibrate. He excuses himself and goes into the kitchen.

'Hello,' he says breathlessly.

'Werner?'

'*Ja*, Ma.'

'Thank God you're alive.'

'What are you talking about?'

'You were supposed to pick me up from the airport.'

'But Ma knows I went on holiday.'

'I thought you'd be back. When you weren't at the airport, I thought something terrible had happened to you. I had to take a taxi home. Do you know how much that cost? Fifty rand.'

'Sorry, Ma.'

'When are you coming home?'

'I don't know, Ma. Maybe a week?'

'A week? Are you mad? What about your job?'

'I took more time off.'

'Now, you listen to me. Now is not the time for you to be taking time off. You need that job, Werner. What will happen if you lose your job? It will be over for us. How long do you think I can carry on working for? I'm an old woman. And there is something I need to talk about.'

'What?'

'Your brother is moving to Australia.'

'I know.'

'Why didn't you tell me?'

'I didn't want to upset you.'

'I suppose it's for the best. This country is going to the dogs. That *blarry* ANC is destroying the place. You see what that Mandela has done – he's driving my son out of the country.'

'Ma – I am actually in the middle of something. Let's talk later, okay?'

'When are you coming home, Werner?'

'I don't know.'

'I'm scared to be here alone. It's not safe.'

'Ma, I'll call you tonight – okay?'

'It's just you and me, Werner. When your brother's gone, you're all I have left.' She puts down the phone.

He goes back to finish the day's work. There are no further calls.

That night he writes another letter:

Dear Johann,

I'm not sure why you haven't called me yet. I really need to speak to you soon. Maybe I gave you the wrong number by mistake, or maybe you're too embarrassed to talk to me. I'm sorry about what I did. I'm sorry if it made you uncomfortable. I can't quite explain why I did it, but I promise not to do it again. I haven't been myself since my father died – there is more to that than you'd believe – and one day I would like to tell you about it. But that is another story. Are you waiting for me to call? I thought it would be easier this way. Please don't make me beg. You just need to understand that it's really important that you come here. I think you will understand for yourself when you see what's going on.

Again he includes the telephone number and the directions to Moedswill. Perhaps Johann will just turn up. Before folding the letter, he adds the following:

PS I know you think I love you. And I do, as a friend. And even if I did love you in that way, I would never expect anything from you other than friendship.

The last part is a mistake, so he crosses it out. But to ensure it can't be read he has to scratch over each of the words in a way that makes him look pathological. He writes the letter again. He decides not to call his mother and goes straight to bed.

The next day Stefan is irritated. Werner apologises and says that it is a pressing matter. He will return as soon as he can. This time he parks at the hotel and walks to Johann's. There are no cars parked in the driveway. He goes up to the house and slips the note under the door that opens onto the *stoep*. He considers waiting in the bush to see if anyone picks up the letter, but decides that it's more important to get back to Moedswill.

Werner becomes increasingly irritated as the hours wear on into the evening. They finish at seven-thirty. He goes upstairs to his bedroom and calls Johann's number. Marleen answers and he puts the phone down. Five minutes later he calls again. Marleen answers.

'I need to speak to Johann,' he says.

'Was that you before?'

'Can I speak to Johann?'

'He's not in.'

Werner slams down the phone and writes another note:

Marleen, I know you are reading these letters and not giving them to Johann. It is a terrible invasion of privacy. If you are reading this now, I insist you tell Johann to call me. I don't really think you understand what I am capable of. I am not threatening you, but I am running out of time.

He cannot afford to start work late again, so he gets up at five the next morning and leaves a note for Stefan explaining that he will be back before they are due to begin. He parks on the dirt road that leads to Johann's house and walks down the drive that leads to the back of the house with the *stoep*. It's just before six. He slips the note under the door and hides in the bush. Ten minutes later he sees Marleen in the living room. She bends down to pick up the note. She reads it and immediately goes outside on the *stoep*.

'Werner!' she calls out. 'You crazy son of a bitch!'

She crumples up the note and throws it into the bush. Johann comes out of the house and Marleen throws her arms around him. He kisses her on her head and leads her back into the house. Then he comes outside and calls out, 'Werner! Are you here, Werner? I think it's time we had a little talk.' He starts walking in Werner's direction. 'You crazy fuck!' he calls out. 'This has to stop. You're scaring Marleen – you understand. This is not on.'

'Shit!' Werner mutters under his breath. If Johann comes further down, he will see him. He starts walking down the path and then breaks into a jog.

'You little fucker!' Johann calls out. 'I can hear you!'

Werner leaves the path and hacks his way through the dense bush towards the camp. Johann is still calling for him from the path. Marleen shouts, 'Johann – don't leave me alone here. Come home!'

Eventually Werner finds another trail that leads him to the obstacle course. He sits down on the rotten log that he'd cleared and looks at his watch. He's going to be very late. *Fuck him!* he thinks. What a complete fuck-up! If Johann wasn't involved with that crazy bitch, he wouldn't be in this position. He walks back up to the main road and then down the dirt track that leads to Johann's house. His car is not there.

At first he thinks he's made a mistake and that he must have parked somewhere else, but after hunting around, he's sure that his car is gone. His car is not stolen. He doesn't have to walk far to confirm his suspicion. It is parked in front of Johann's house. What an idiot he's been. Why did he write that stupid letter? And why didn't he just leave? He walks down the path. Johann is sitting on the *stoep*. From here, Werner can see that the small front window has been smashed.

'Come for your car?' Johann asks.

Werner ignores him and walks to the Corolla. He gets in the car and puts his keys in the ignition. There is a tangle of wires hanging from the steering shaft. He rests his head against the steering wheel. He no longer has the energy to do anything. He just wants to lie like this all day. He even feels safe, with Johann watching over him. He sits like this, resting his head for a long time. Johann walks down the stairs that lead from the *stoep* to the back garden. He opens the passenger door and gets in.

'What's going on, *boet*? Have you gone mad or something?'

'Will you come with me to Moedswill? When Stefan sees you, he will paint you. I know he will. It will be wonderful. You will be my new Jesus.'

'Huh? I think maybe you're not *lekker* any more. I think you need to talk to someone. Marleen is scared, Werner. You really scared her.'

'You won't come with me then?'

322

'No.'

Werner nods. 'Maybe I can bring Stefan here?'

'No. I don't want you coming back here. Do you understand?'

'Can we still be friends?'

'No. No, Werner, we can't be friends any more. You must go. I never want to see you here again. Get some help, Werner, I think you're sick.'

Johann shows him how to start the car and he drives back to Moedswill. *I think you're sick.* How humiliating! How sordid the whole thing is turning out to be. Johann telling him he is mentally ill. He is not mentally ill. What he is, is trapped. Hovering just out of reach is a magnificent possibility that no one else can see, and there is no way to forge towards it. It would all be so simple, but for the stupidity, the stubbornness, the blindness of everyone around him. Stefan is blinded by his own arrogance and his own obsession. Johann is blinded by Marleen.

His phone rings. It must be Johann. He's phoning to say he's changed his mind and he will come to Moedswill after all. He will meet Stefan. Werner struggles to get the phone out of his pocket. His thighs are so fat that it's pressed tight against the fabric of his trousers. Perhaps Johann feels guilty about the money or he's decided that he was being unfair after all; that it was ridiculous to take the side of Marleen over that of his best friend.

'Hello,' he says.

'Werner – someone was going through my cupboards. Someone was digging around in my stuff. Was it you?'

He puts the phone down on his mother. Let her think what she wants. He doesn't care.

He does not have the energy for Stefan. How can he explain that he was trying to do something to help Stefan? The man will not believe him. Werner sits in the car for a while, looking at the damage to the steering. This will cost a fortune. He goes inside and greets the maid. She mutters a shy 'hello' and disappears into the kitchen. She's not in the mood for fireworks. In the studio Stefan has found himself a third helper for the day. It is not the man who was helping before.

'I'm sorry,' Werner says, 'let me take over.'

Stefan, suspended above the floor with his back to Werner, says, 'Get out!'

'What?'

'Get out of my house. You're no good to me. I don't want you here any more. So pack your things and get out.'

'Stefan, please, you don't understand. I was working on your next exhibition. It will be magnificent – I swear, I was doing it for you.'

'I'm not interested in you or your ideas. Now get out, before these men throw you out.'

'Fuck you!' he shouts.

Stefan says something to one of the men. Two of them approach Werner and grab him by the shoulders. 'All right – I'm going. Get your hands off me. I'm getting my stuff, okay?'

He walks up the stairs. Lerato is standing in the passage staring out of the window. He sits on the bed.

'Lerato,' he says.

She turns to him and stands in the doorway. 'Yes.'

'Do you really remember me?' She nods. 'Why is my father in this painting?' She looks at him, but says nothing. 'Did you love my father?'

'No, he was a bad man.'

'Maybe. Did he love you?' She shrugs. 'I think he did.' Werner stares at his feet. 'I have nothing left.'

'What do you want?'

'Do you love Stefan?'

'Maybe. I don't know. Me and Stefan. We must be together.'

'Is it true? That you saved his life?'

'We are not living. It is better that we died.'

'What are you going to do with the money?'

'Stefan. He must decide this thing.'

'Will you talk to him? Will you tell him that I am sorry. He can keep the money. I want to help him. I have nothing left.'

'Get a job.'

'But will you talk to him?'

'No. I don't want you here. You are like your father. I don't trust. It is better that you leave.' She walks out and he packs his things.

He wants to take something. The painting of his father?

It's too big. He couldn't carry it on his own. He peers into Stefan's room. There are no paintings in the room. Perhaps on this point Lerato got her way. There is a pistol on the bedside cabinet. A distant shape in the recesses of imaginative possibility compels him to take at least that.

23

Hendrik turned onto the main road to Moedswill. He was sweaty and shaking. The scream in the bush was not human. Most likely it was a baboon. What would someone be doing in the bush anyway? He turned to Lerato, 'It was a baboon. I saw it was just a baboon.' Lerato nodded. 'Don't worry,' he said, 'everything is going to be fine. It's going to be fine.' He worried that he'd shot one of the students. Sometimes even the little girls snuck out to smoke cigarettes in the dense parts of the bush. Where were Werner and Marius when the shot was fired? Inside the house – he was certain they were inside the house. He dismissed the thought of Werner always skulking, of Werner always close when he and Nellie fought, spying, feeding off their misery. 'Idiot!' he screamed and slammed his hands down on the steering wheel. 'Fucking bitch! Ruining my fucking life!' he shouted and again slammed his hands down on the steering wheel. Lerato folded her arms across her chest and stared at him. 'Don't worry, Lerato. I'm taking you home. To your family. Everything is going to be fine.'

The road was empty and Hendrik drove fast. He put his foot flat on the accelerator to gain as much speed as he could on the downhill. The speedometer jerked around the 140 mark. Perhaps it was not wise to speed. He did not need to be pulled over by the police now. Would the police be looking for him? What would Nellie be doing now? His chest felt tight when he thought about his wife. She knew, surely she knew, that he'd missed on purpose. It was frustration. Rage. That's all. He wanted to frighten her. Pulling the trigger was just like throwing something. Would she tell people he tried to murder her? 'I was just trying to frighten her,' he said aloud. 'I didn't mean any harm.' On the steep uphill before the turn-off, the little Datsun started losing speed. 'Piece of shit! I hate this piece of shit.' The car started juddering and Hendrik geared down to third. The engine whined loudly and he had to slow down. He wanted to get off the main road. He wanted to be driving down the dark farm road, where if necessary he could turn off his lights and hide in the dark. He did not want to be in a speeding *bakkie*, with two headlamps lighting his intended direction of travel, for God and sundry. When they turned off onto the farm road he dimmed his lights. It was so dark that he nearly crashed into the farm gates. Lerato shouted out just in time. 'It's fine. It's fine. I saw it,' he said. 'Calm down, okay? Just be calm.' He opened the door and hopped out to open the gate. Someone had tried to secure it with a lock, but it had since been broken. Still, it took some time to untangle the rusted chain that had been looped several times over it.

He turned round to ask Lerato to turn up the car lights. The passenger door was open. 'Lerato!' he shouted. 'Please!' He could just about see her running away and chased after her. 'Lerato! Come back!' The girl was crying and stumbling. She tripped over something and Hendrik sprinted towards her. She tried to get up, but he grabbed her with such force that she fell again. He went to help her up, but she kicked his knee and he collapsed next to her. Lerato screamed and beat her fists against him. 'Calm down, please!' he said. 'Don't leave me alone! Don't leave me alone! Calm down, calm down.' He wrapped his arms around her and hugged her small frame against his body. With her arms pinned down, she tried to kick him, but he wrapped his legs around her until she was completely enveloped in his large Boer frame. 'Don't leave me,' he whispered. 'I promise, I am going to take you home. But don't leave me like this. I'm not like him. I swear. That's why I wanted you. That's why I came for you. I'm not like him.' He nuzzled the back of her neck and she arched to get away from him. 'I'm going to show you. I'm not like him. I love you. I really love you.' He kissed the back of her neck, as gently as he could manage, and rubbed her thin arms. They lay like that, in the grass, for a long time. He could take her now, he thought. She was the thing he wanted. His life was quite possibly over. He could have her now. He ran his hands over her small breasts and squeezed them gently. She was so beautiful.

He rubbed her thighs and buttocks. 'You make me so hard,' he said. 'When I picked you up that day, I wanted to take you into the bush and fuck you. But I didn't, because I am not like that.' He closed his eyes and the thought of the dead children came back to him. They formed a circle around him and Lerato lying in the long grass. He lost his erection. As the blood drained from his cock, he could feel Lerato relax. He could no longer hear her crying, but he could feel some tears that ran down her face drip onto his arm. 'Come,' he said. 'Let's go back to the car.' He stood up and held her wrist firmly.

'Please,' she said, 'I want to go home.'

'I can't be alone. Just come with me.'

He led her like a child back to the car. In the back of the *bakkie* he took out an abseiling rope, which he tied tightly around her right wrist. He gave a metre's slack and then tied the rope around his wrist. Both doors were still open and the car was still idling. They walked round to the driver's side. Lerato got in and scooted over to the passenger seat. Hendrik followed. 'Close the door,' he instructed. She did so. They drove through the gates towards the farmhouse. The headlights caught ribbons of yellow police tape that fluttered in the breeze.

'Stefan,' Lerato said.

'He's alive,' Hendrik said. 'He's alive. Everything is going to be fine. And anyway, it was just a baboon.'

When they reached the house, Hendrik turned off the

car. The headlights were still on. They lit the *stoep* and the front door from which Labuschagne was said to have emerged, shotgun in hand, chasing his youngest son down like a dog, after having blown the head off the sister. The door was firmly shut.

'I was thinking,' Hendrik said, 'about going somewhere. You can come with me. I will care for you like a white woman.' He put his hand on her thigh and she pulled away. He removed his hand. 'You've probably never even seen the sea.'

Werner walked down the path leading to the dam. It was difficult checking both sides of the path on his own. He wanted to make the important discovery. He grabbed a stick and hacked at the undergrowth. He could hear his mother and Steyn calling. He did the same. 'Hello! Is there anyone here? Hello!' Ahead he could make out the old overgrown obstacle course. On the ground was a folded body. He ran towards it. The bullet had hit Johann in the arm. The blood had soaked his shirt and the surrounding earth. 'Johann?' he said quietly. 'Johann?' Werner saw the rise and fall of his chest. He was taking quick, shallow breaths, but was unconscious. 'Ma!' he shouted. 'I found him! Ma! Ma! Steyn! Come quick! I found him! I found him!'

'We're coming!' Steyn shouted.

He leant over his friend. 'Johann. My ma is coming now. She's a nurse. She'll fix you, okay? Then we'll take you to hospital. Okay, Johann?' He held up his torch into the sky to help his mother and Steyn see where he was. 'Come quick, Ma,' he shouted. 'He's hurt bad. He's hurt really bad.'

'We're coming, Werner!' she called. 'We're coming. Just stay where you are!'

Johann was pale and cold. There was blood everywhere. Werner took off his jersey and put it over his friend. He could hear his mother and Steyn running down the footpath.

'Werner!' Steyn called.

'I'm here, *oom*,' he said, holding up the torch. 'Here.'

His mother and Steyn came crashing through the thicket. 'Move!' she commanded Werner. 'Oh God,' she said. She pulled the jersey off and looked at the arm. 'Oh God!' Her hands were shaking. She checked the boy's mouth for vomit and then handed Steyn the jersey. 'Tear off the sleeve,' she said. Steyn stood on the jersey and tugged at the sleeve until it tore at the seam. 'Help me,' she said. She took the sleeve, threaded it under Johann's arm and, with Steyn's help, made a tourniquet. Steyn lifted the boy in both arms and ran as quickly as he could back to the camp. Werner followed Steyn and his mother. Johann was leaving a trail of blood on the path. From behind, Werner could see that his friend's arm was not right. It hung, like a twisted piece of meat, from his body.

Petronella opened the passenger door of Steyn's *bakkie* so that Steyn could put the boy in the car. 'The keys,' she shouted. 'Where are the keys?'

Steyn checked his pockets, then ran into his rondavel. Werner could hear him throwing things around in the frantic search. 'I can't find my fucking keys!'

'Hot-wire it!' Petronella shouted. Steyn came running back to the car.

'Is he going to die, Ma?'

'Not if we hurry,' she said. 'Werner, go back to the house and stay with your brother.'

'Where's Pa?'

'I don't know.'

Steyn got into the driver's seat, ready to pull the wires out of the steering column. 'The keys are in the ignition,' he said. 'Get in.'

Petronella got in the car and put her arm around Johann. 'Drive!' she shouted.

The car sped off down the driveway. Werner stood in his friend's pool of blood and watched the red tail-lights disappear into the bush. In the house Marius was hiding underneath the kitchen table. Werner went down on his haunches.

'What's going on?' Marius asked.

'Someone shot Johann,' he said.

'Is he going to die?'

'I don't know.'

'Who shot him?'

After a long time Werner said, 'I think maybe it was Pa.' He shuffled in next to his brother and put his arm around him. They sat under the kitchen table and waited.

* * *

When Hendrik woke up the next morning the sun was rising. It reflected on one of the house windows and made him squint. Lerato was gone. The rope was still tied around his wrist. He undid the rope, got out of the car and looked around. The place was deserted. He was stiff and had a crick in his neck. He felt giddy. He leant against the car, undid his fly and urinated. The morning was cool and his piss steamed. It smelt sharp. The earth was hard and it made a little puddle by his feet. Hendrik felt indifferent about being caught here now. He felt as if he were dead, or just about to be. He strode up to the house and knocked loudly on the door. 'Anyone here?' He tried to open the door, but couldn't break the lock. He pressed his face against the glass of one of the windows, with his hands on either side, to block out the sun. Some of the furniture had been knocked over. He pressed his forehead against the glass. It was warm. He wanted to press his face against something cool. He was thirsty. He walked round the house and found an outside tap. A thin stream of tepid water trickled out. He lapped it up, but then the water stopped running. The borehole had not been pumped, or the services had been cut off. He leant against the wall and closed his eyes. He could carry on driving, to Mozambique perhaps. Even without a passport there would be a way to cross the border. But there was civil war there. And civil war in Rhodesia too. Anarchy had its appeal. In an anarchic state, nobody would care about a stray bullet. These things happened.

He held his head in his hands. 'Oh God,' he said.

'What am I going to do?' If he had his gun, he would have shot himself. Why had he not taken his gun? He walked back to the *bakkie* and searched amongst the pile of rubbish in the back. He found a short length of hose-pipe. He jutted it into the exhaust pipe, but it was too short to reach the front of the cab. He started the car, then climbed into the back of the *bakkie* and covered himself with a tarpaulin. The hosepipe slipped out of the exhaust. He looked for something with which to secure it. He tried to use some old electrical tape, but the exhaust was too hot, so he shoved the pipe as deep into the exhaust as it would go. Again he climbed under the tarpaulin with the hosepipe. A trickle of fumes from the pipe made him cough. He felt a little light-headed. Was it really possible to kill himself this way? He thought about the rope lying on the car seat. There were many difficulties to hanging oneself. It was easy to get it wrong. He wasn't sure he wanted to die, but he had enough time to think about it a bit before ripping off the tarpaulin. The gas was giving him a headache and making him dizzy. The car engine cut. He flung the tarpaulin off. 'Fuck!' He sat up. Standing on the *stoep* were the dead Labuschagne children. They were watching him trying to commit suicide. Was this God's doing? Did God cut the engine? Did God send the children? He waved at them and the children waved back. The children were smiling. He felt peaceful with them here. They waved at him again and walked back into the house. In the window he could make out the face of the father, staring at him. He got up. 'Come back!' he called. 'Don't go inside! He's there. He's inside . . .' His voice trailed away. He was still unsteady on his feet. A pain in his head brought with it a thought: hallucination. He sat down again.

He saw someone walking towards the car. Another hallucination: the old bantu with the yellow teeth; the one with the Bible name. The man stood and stared at him. Hendrik picked up a small screwdriver and threw it. It hit the man's chest, but he barely flinched. The man picked up his *knobkierrie* and brought it down with force on Hendrik's arm. He jumped up and screamed. 'Fuck!' The man raised his *knobkierrie* above Hendrik's head. He jumped out of the way. The pain cleared his mind. He got into the cab, but the man pulled the door open before he could lock it. He tried to start the *bakkie*. The engine wouldn't take. He didn't want to die. He didn't want to be beaten to death by an old bantu. The man grabbed his arm and pulled him out of the car. He was stronger than Hendrik had anticipated. The man kicked his knee and Hendrik fell to the floor. 'What the fuck!' he shouted. 'Leave me alone!' The old bantu kicked him in the stomach and he doubled over. 'Please, leave me alone!' The man raised the *knobkierrie*. Hendrik could see Lerato running towards them, screaming at the man. He brought the heavy knob down on Hendrik's head with some force. He felt a moment of searing pain and lost consciousness.

Werner woke when someone opened the kitchen door. He sat up, forgetting that he was under the kitchen table.

'Ma?' he said.

'Hello,' Petronella said.

'Is Johann dead?'

'No. Have you seen Pa?'

Werner shook his head.

'It's still very early. Why don't you two go to bed for a bit and I'll make us some breakfast.'

The boys went back to their rooms. Werner lay in bed listening to his mother in the kitchen. He could hear her washing dishes. She filled a pot of water and put it on the stove. In the distance he could hear buses arriving. Today was Saturday. The girls were only due to leave tomorrow. He thought about Johann in the hospital. Did they put tubes in his nose and his mouth? Did they have to attach him to a breathing machine? Did his mother tell Johann's parents? Where was Charlize? Were they at the hospital now? His mother was taking something out of the bottom cupboard. The toaster. If he walked down the path now, would he still see Johann's blood everywhere? There would be ants in the blood. He could hear Steyn and the teachers barking instructions to the girls. All of this must have been decided while he slept. It was the first time that a camp had ended early. It was nearly cancelled when all the children got sick, but his father said they would 'soldier on'. Was it his father? Was his father in jail? Johann looked very beautiful when he was so pale. If he – Werner – had been shot instead of Johann, then Steyn would have cradled him like that too. Steyn would have run through the bushes to his car. Werner could hear a car outside. He sat up on his bed and looked out of the window. It was his mother. He ran out of the house to stop her.

'Ma!' he shouted. 'Ma! Where are you going?'

She stopped the car and wound down the window. 'I'm going to look for your father. Go back to bed,' she said and drove off.

24

Werner parks the car at the hotel. He knows he cannot go back to Pretoria. He sits there for a long time. There is a knock at the passenger window. It's Aleksander. Werner smiles and opens the passenger door. The boy places both hands against the roof of the car and peers in.

'Hello,' he says.

'Hello.'

'What are you doing?' he asks.

'Oh, nothing much. Just thinking. What about you?'

'I've just been for a swim. It's our last day here.'

'Oh, where are you going next?'

'Australia, I think.'

Werner nods. 'Well, say hello to my brother when you're there.'

'How will I know who your brother is?'

'Well, when you see someone who looks a bit like me, you say, "Hi, Marius."'

'Okay, I will give it a try. Bye, Werner.'

'Bye, Aleksander.'

He walks towards Johann's house. The bushveld smells

good and the sky is clear. He feels light; not happy, but carefree. The route he takes is along the banks of the dam. At the boathouse he stops to watch the children. A group of boys are carrying canoes to the water and several teachers are checking their life jackets. The children are of different races: black, white, Indian, coloured. They all speak with the moneyed accent of Johannesburg's northern suburbs. They're all laughing and smiling. They are carefree too, but also happy. It is tragic, he thinks, that he will never know the pleasures of childhood again; a life full of promise, unblemished, ripe to bursting with possibility. He waves at the children, but they – warned about the dangers of strange males – do not wave back. No matter, he thinks. No matter. He hesitates for a moment before stepping out into the clearing. He has to act with absolute clarity of purpose. He is certain they will both be there. For a moment he thinks that maybe they have left, but then he sees Marleen bent over on the *stoep*, busy with the washing. She stands up, sees Werner and shouts, 'Johann!' He removes the gun he took from Stefan's house and fires three times. He does not know whether he hit her, but she falls to the ground. Johann comes running out of the house and bends down over Marleen. Werner puts the gun in his mouth. He watches Johann. He waits for Johann to stop him, to give him some signal. Johann does not. His finger is tight on the trigger. A few millimetres to infinity. His last thought is: Am I really going to do this?

25

He walked down the main street with the thirty rand in his pocket that he had taken from his parents' cupboard. He counted on the fact that nobody would care what he did with the money.

'Hello, *tannie*,' Werner said as he walked into the shop.

'Hello, Werner,' Miss Hammond said. 'We're not a museum, you know.'

'I've come to buy the picture, *tannie*.'

'Really?'

'Yes, *tannie*.'

'Very well, sir,' she said.

Werner liked this. He had never been called 'sir' before. Miss Hammond fetched the painting from the back of the shop.

'Would you like to take it just like this?' she asked. Werner blushed. 'Of course, this is rather a small-minded town. If you'd prefer, I could wrap it in brown paper for you.' He nodded. Miss Hammond wrapped the picture and handed it to Werner. 'I'm so glad you bought it. I don't know what I would have said to you if it had been sold.'

'Thanks, *tannie*,' he said.

He carried the large painting back to his mother's car. She was still busy in the building society. When she got back, she said, 'What's that?'

'It's a picture. I've been saving up.'

'Of what?'

'Jesus.'

'Oh.'

They drove back to the camp. He waited until his mother went to the hospital to visit his father and then hammered a nail into the wall opposite his bed. It would only be for two nights, but he wanted to hang the painting up anyway. He lay down on his bed. When he squinted, it looked like Jesus was ascending towards him. He lay there for a very long time. He thought about Johann and what had happened. He thought about how Johann would now have a hook for an arm. It made him want to cry, because Johann had been so beautiful. By the time it was dark he was still lying on his bed. Jesus sucked up all the noise: the sound of Maria washing the dishes in the kitchen, the creak of the bed and the little black children playing in the village. Calm down, Jesus said. Calm down. Calm down.

Acknowledgements

I'd like to thank:

Ben Mason, my agent, who is not only great, but great fun to work with.

Beth Coates, my editor, who makes everything I write so much better.

Richard Pitschmann, always my first reader.

www.vintage-books.co.uk